UTOPIA, TEXAS

A NOVEL

MICHAEL E. GLASSCOCK III

GREENLEAF
BOOK GROUP PRESS

Published by Greenleaf Book Group Press
Austin, Texas
www.gbgpress.com

Distributed by Greenleaf Book Group LLC

For ordering information or special discounts for bulk purchases, please contact Greenleaf Book Group LLC at PO Box 91869, Austin, TX 78709, 512.891.6100.

Design and composition by Greenleaf Book Group LLC
Cover design by Greenleaf Book Group LLC

Cover images
©iStockphoto.com/THEPALMER-Roberto A Sanchez
©iStockphoto.com/101PHOTO-Eduard Titov
©iStockphoto.com/mammuth-Peter Zelei
©iStockphoto.com/brainmaster-Hayri Er
Image Copyright Smailhodzic, 2012. Used under license from Shutterstock.com

Publisher's Cataloging-In-Publication Data
(Prepared by The Donohue Group, Inc.)
Glasscock, Michael E., 1933-

    Utopia, Texas : a novel / Michael E. Glasscock III. -- 1st ed.
    p. ; cm.
    Issued also as an ebook.
    ISBN: 978-1-60832-416-3
    1. Game wardens—Texas—Utopia—Fiction. 2. Drug traffic—Texas—Utopia—Fiction. 3. Drug dealers—Mexico—Fiction. 4. Utopia (Tex.)—Fiction. I. Title.
PS3607.L27 U86 2013
813/.6   2012945270

Part of the Tree Neutral® program, which offsets the number of trees consumed in the production and printing of this book by taking proactive steps, such as planting trees in direct proportion to the number of trees used: www.treeneutral.com

Printed in the United States of America on acid-free paper

13 14 15 16   10 9 8 7 6 5 4 3 2 1

First Edition

To my seven children:

Mike IV, Tina, Angie, Bill, Ann, Heather, and Julia.

And to my good friends, Julie A. Daugherty and Christi Walker.

The problem with death is that it lasts forever.

—Gabriel García Márquez

PROLOGUE

He came down from the Sierra Madre, like so many before him, and headed north toward the Rio Grande. He traveled only at night, unseen, ghostlike, never heard. By sunup each day he'd found a safe and secure hiding place where he stored energy for the next evening's journey.

He stopped occasionally by a roaring mountain stream to drink the cold water and refresh himself. Within minutes he would again push toward the north. From time to time he passed a quiet village, its inhabitants oblivious to his presence as they slept peacefully in hammocks or on straw pallets. A stolen chicken, a lamb, or an occasional rabbit quelled the pangs of hunger that gripped his stomach.

On the sixth day, just as the eastern sky turned red, he reached the river. He settled into a stand of tall grass near the bank and immediately fell into a deep sleep. It was a cloudless April day, and the ground was covered by light dew. The temperature hovered in the high sixties and his muscular body shivered as he slept.

By nightfall a group of day laborers had gathered on the riverbank close to where he lay. He watched them as they huddled together, talking softly and smoking, the glow of their cigarettes intensifying each time they inhaled. Later, the men shoved their small wooden boat away from the riverbank and drifted silently across to the opposite side.

He waited as they hid their boat from the prying eyes of the Border Patrol and watched them climb the bank and recede into the darkness. Then he arose and stretched his cramped muscles. He hadn't eaten in twenty-four hours, and his stomach rumbled as he took his first steps toward the river. The bank was steep where he'd decided to cross, and he stumbled once, descending to the edge of the river. He lowered himself slowly into the cold, rapidly moving water. He didn't fight the current but let it carry him to the other side where he climbed the sandy bank, his long claws and powerful legs lifting him effortlessly toward the grassy field above.

He'd crossed the Rio Grande midway between Del Rio and Eagle Pass and had entered Texas in a desolate area of Maverick County about 150 miles west of San Antonio. That night's journey took him north to the edge of the small town of Uvalde, where he spent the day hidden in a mesquite thicket. All he'd eaten since crossing the border was one hapless jackrabbit he'd ravaged around midnight.

Sundown saw him across U.S. Highway 90, headed north toward Utopia, a community of some three hundred inhabitants lying at the head of the Sabinal Canyon in the lower range of the Texas Hill Country. Through the night he traveled, walking tirelessly across the fertile farmland. Around 3:00 a.m., he arrived at a cattle ranch seven miles east of Utopia. He settled into a cedar brake on the side of a rock-strewn hill and fell into a bone-weary sleep.

CHAPTER 1

UTOPIA, TEXAS
APRIL 1997

Monty Kilpatrick, the Utopia-based game warden, sat on the hood of his state-owned pickup cradling an AR-15 assault rifle fitted with a powerful night scope. The early morning sun crept over the mountain range to the east, washing out the soft glow of the full moon he'd been counting on. Bluebonnets dotted the field in front of him, their bell-shaped buds glistening with dew. A gentle southeasterly breeze rustled the leaves of a large live oak tree a few feet from the truck.

The six-foot-two-inch policeman was 190 pounds of pure muscle. He had robin's-egg blue eyes and sandy hair worn longish. He was an even-tempered man of good cheer, unless someone crossed him. Then all hell could bust loose.

He'd seen the puma's tracks the afternoon before and had taken a plaster cast of the paw prints. The right rear one had a broken toe. The depth and stride of the prints indicated that the big cat was most likely a male weighing at least 600 pounds.

The game warden had been waiting all night for a chance to bag the mountain lion. The local ranchers were up in arms at the loss of some prize calves. He slid off the hood and placed the rifle in the rear window rack of the pickup. With the sun up, there was no need to continue the vigil. The puma was most likely sleeping in a cedar brake somewhere in the vicinity.

Monty lit a Camel cigarette and inhaled deeply. He'd never smoked until the accident. The memory haunted Monty and he often remembered it during his long nightly vigils. Monty, his wife, and their son, Monty Jr., had been vacationing in Garner State Park in the Texas Hill Country a few miles north of Uvalde. Monty had arranged a long weekend. They arrived on Friday around noon and the boy was yearning for a chance to canoe the Frio River. He'd been pestering his father from the time they left Utopia. After lunch Monty rented a canoe and two life jackets.

They pushed off from the bank around two o'clock that afternoon, with Monty Jr. sitting in the front of the boat. Halfway across the river, the boy untied his life jacket for a brief moment so he could get a pack of chewing gum out of his shirt pocket. Noticing a large bass jump out of the water and flip its tail, an excited Monty Jr. stood and pointed at the fish. In his excitement he lost his footing and fell overboard. The life jacket slipped off and the boy went down. He knew how to swim, but his clothing made it difficult for him to move.

Monty threw off his vest and went over the side. Normally the Frio River is crystal clear, but on this occasion, there'd been recent rains and the water was murky. Monty dove for his son so many times he'd come close to drowning. After fifteen minutes of fruitless searching Monty gave up.

Exhausted, tears streaming down his cheeks, Monty climbed back in the canoe and paddled to shore where Martha Jo, his wife, waited with a horrified expression. The sheriff's deputies dragged the river and located the boy's body the following morning.

Losing his ten-year-old son had changed Monty's life in numerous ways. The first year he'd dropped twenty-five pounds. And after the accident he threw himself into his work. If he kept busy, he had less time to think about his loss.

Shaking his head as if that would wash away the memory of that terrible day, he poured coffee from his thermos into a chipped mug and sipped the hot liquid. Then he turned the key in the pickup's ignition and followed a deer trail around a small hill on his way back to the gravel road he'd used to enter the premises of the Double K Ranch.

As he drove past a small pond, he noticed what looked like a pile of rags next to the water. Stopping the pickup, he got out and walked to the area. There, instead of rags, he found the body of a young man who appeared to be in his early thirties. A single bullet hole had been placed neatly in the center of the man's forehead. His hands were cuffed behind him with large cable ties, and duct tape covered his mouth. Monty didn't touch the body, but kneeling beside the man he could tell there were no signs of livor mortis, indicating the murder was recent. *It could have occurred*, Monty thought, *while I was sitting not more than a hundred yards away*.

Back in the truck, he picked up his radio microphone and dialed the Uvalde County sheriff's frequency. "Uvalde dispatcher, pick up. This is Monty Kilpatrick," he said.

"Uvalde."

"Sheriff there?"

"Just walked in. Hold on."

"What's up, Monty?" Sheriff Tim Boswell asked.

"Looks like a homicide over here on the Double K. Young guy in his early thirties."

"Hang around. I'll grab the coroner and be there in about twenty minutes."

Monty continued to sip from his mug as he studied the body. The guy was dressed in jeans and black cowboy boots. A heart-shaped tattoo with "MOM" written across it had been inked on his right upper arm. A pack of Marlboros was rolled up under the sleeve of his

T-shirt. Monty hadn't seen anyone do that in years. A ball cap lay on the ground about three feet from the man's head.

It took closer to forty-five minutes for the sheriff to arrive at the crime scene. The big man parked his patrol car next to Monty's truck and stepped out onto the grass. The sheriff in many southern states is an elected official and often the job requires no formal police training, but Uvalde was fortunate to have a crackerjack sheriff in Tim Boswell. He'd been on the San Antonio police force for twenty years before retiring and moving to Uvalde. He had a sharp, analytical mind and a no-nonsense attitude toward police work. He was as honest a cop as ever took the job.

The coroner, a family physician from Uvalde, exited the passenger side and followed the sheriff to where Monty waited.

"This is Dr. Baker, our new coroner," Boswell said, introducing a sandy-haired young man in his early thirties.

"Nice to meet you, Doc," Monty said, shaking the man's hand.

"Likewise," the doctor said.

He slipped on some latex gloves, knelt next to the body, and felt the man's skin with the back of his fingers. Then he turned the man on his side and examined his back. "No rigor mortis or livor mortis, and the body's still warm, so this must have happened a few hours ago. No powder marks on the forehead, either. I guess he was shot from a few feet away."

"Looks like a .22 caliber wound. I was here all night so the shooter probably used a silenced pistol," Monty said. "They must have walked in from the road because I didn't hear a vehicle."

Boswell nodded. "Twenty-two's the most popular gun for hit men. Only caliber you can silence effectively."

"I called for an ambulance. We'll have to send him to San Antonio for an autopsy. The Bexar County coroner is a forensic pathologist. All I do is pronounce them dead," Dr. Baker said as he stood.

"I suspect this has something to do with drugs," Monty said.

"You can be sure of it," Tim Boswell replied.

The Uvalde EMS ambulance pulled up and the driver and his assistant stepped out. They placed the victim in a black body bag and zipped it closed. Then they slid the stretcher into the big truck and left.

"What were you doing out here all night, Monty? Looking for poachers?" Boswell asked as he headed for his automobile.

"Trying to bag a puma that's been taking out some calves."

"Next time you come to town, drop by the office and I'll give you a cup of coffee," Boswell said as he slid behind the wheel of the patrol car.

Monty got back in his truck and headed for Utopia. He planned to eat breakfast at the Lost Maples Café with his friend Arthur Jepson, as he did every morning, then go home to sleep for a few hours.

Thirty minutes later he turned into the Circle M Quick Stop parking lot. He jumped out, leaving the engine running. Inside, he stopped at the glass-topped counter. Not seeing anyone, he pounded on the counter and yelled, "Cindy, you in the back?"

Cindy Moffitt came out of the storeroom carrying a case of Bud Light. She was wearing jeans, Roper boots, and a man's white button-down oxford shirt. Her blonde hair was pulled back with a red bow at the nape of her neck. Cindy was in her mid-twenties, had a figure that drove the cowboys crazy, and had eyes the color of a clear Texas sky at dawn. She set the case on the floor with a thud, the bottles rattling.

"Hi, Monty. What's up?"

"Give me a quick pick, will you? I heard it's up to twenty million."

"Just want one?"

"One is all it takes. If I only spend a dollar a week, I don't feel guilty for gambling. The odds are at least twenty million to one, so it doesn't make much sense to buy more anyway."

Cindy handed the ticket to Monty.

"Do you play this thing?" Monty asked.

"I barely make ends meet as it is. When you're a single mom, it's tough."

Monty handed Cindy his dollar bill and she opened the cash register, never taking her eyes off him. She smiled and asked, "Anything else?"

Shaking his head, he said, "See you, Cindy."

"Monty?"

"Yeah?"

"You seem to be limping this morning. Old football injury?"

"Sort of. It just bothers me when it's going to rain. Better get out your umbrella."

The intermittent limp was not Monty's only unpleasant memory of Vietnam. He'd volunteered for the Marines early in the war and gone to Southeast Asia with the appropriate military zeal. After two months in the rice paddies, he realized he'd made a terrible mistake.

Cindy had hoped Monty would stay and talk to her as he sometimes did when he wasn't in a hurry. He was the one man in town she felt comfortable to be alone with. Even though he was twice her age, she found him attractive and wished he wasn't married.

Monty stuffed the lottery ticket in his breast pocket and got back into his truck, then drove up the street to the Lost Maples. When he walked in, Arthur Jepson, the justice of the peace, was waiting for him in a corner booth.

"You up all night?" Arthur asked. "You look like hell."

"What else is new? I'm trying to bag that mountain lion everyone's complaining about."

Gertrude, the morning waitress, strolled over to the booth. As she poured coffee into his cup, she asked, "What you want, Monty?"

"You ask me the same question every morning and I give you the same answer. Why don't you just bring me what I usually have?"

"Don't you wise off at me, Monty Kilpatrick. I've been known to pour hot coffee over a smart-ass's head."

Monty raised his hands in mock surrender and said, "Sorry, Gertrude. I'm a little spaced out. I found a body out on the Double K this morning."

"No shit," Arthur said. "Anyone we know?"

"No. Looks like a drug-related hit."

Gertrude wrinkled her nose and left.

After breakfast, Monty drove home. When he walked into the kitchen, Martha Jo was having a cup of coffee and reading the morning paper. Two years younger than her husband, she was tall and slender with dark brown hair worn to her shoulders. Her hazel eyes reflected a keen intellect. She'd been an English major in college when she met Monty. She looked up at her husband and asked, "How was your night? Did you get the puma?"

"No. I'll try again tonight."

"Don't you get sleepy out there?"

"Sure, but it's my job."

"I barely see you these days. You're gone all night and you sleep most of the day."

"We've been over this a thousand times. I have a lot of responsibilities."

"You have a responsibility to your wife as well, Monty. We need some time together."

Monty shook his head and headed for their bedroom. Looking over his shoulder he said, "Don't wake me unless it's an emergency. I'm really tired."

JIMMY RHEA MOFFITT AWOKE WITH A pounding headache and a queasy stomach. Two six-packs of Budweiser were more than he usually put away in one evening, but he'd been out of the Bexar County jail for less than twenty-four hours. Six months previously he'd met up with a prostitute in a San Antonio bar, and when the girl asked for her money, he had beaten her. Jimmy Rhea enjoyed slapping women around, particularly if he'd been drinking, and Jimmy Rhea loved to drink. No one who knew him thought six months in the slammer for assault and battery would change his outlook on life.

He'd been released on a Monday morning, and by that evening, he'd driven his small Toyota pickup as far as Hondo, where he'd rented a room at the Whitetail Lodge. He'd bought the two six-packs at the Exxon Gas 'n' Go next to the motel and then sequestered himself in his room, where he'd watched ESPN drag races and monster trucks until finishing the twelfth bottle of Bud and passing out.

He climbed into the shower and let the cold water cascade over his head, but it didn't help. After five minutes he gave up. He didn't have a razor because someone had stolen it along with his toothbrush. He groped around in his small toiletry case and found a bottle of Old Spice aftershave, which he sprinkled on his hair and under both arms. He'd had no need for deodorant in jail. He squeezed some toothpaste on his index finger and ran it over his teeth.

Back in the room, he searched through his small canvas bag. Like the character in the Kris Kristofferson song "Sunday Morning Coming Down," he was looking for his cleanest dirty shirt.

He'd checked into the motel with a stolen credit card, so he left without the formality of picking up his bill. When he started the Toyota, he noticed the gas gauge needle sitting on E. Cursing under his breath, he reached into his jeans pocket and pulled out two rumpled five-dollar bills, his entire bankroll.

"Now what the fuck am I supposed to do?" His head pounded and his eyes felt as if someone had rubbed sand in them. He lowered his head to the steering wheel and tried to think how he was going to get out of his predicament.

He drove to the Exxon station next door. Inside, a pretty young woman of about thirty sat behind the counter reading the *National Enquirer.* A mop of kinky, bright red hair worn long and held back in a ponytail highlighted her chalk-like complexion. Her green eyes reminded Jimmy Rhea of a cat, but what he liked most about her was the way her bosom pushed her blouse out. She looked up but didn't say anything as he walked in.

Jimmy Rhea turned on his boyish charm, added a big smile, and said, "Morning, ma'am. It's a fine day, don't you think?"

"I guess."

"Look, I'm right embarrassed to admit this, but I got robbed last night. Yes, ma'am, at gunpoint. Old boy had me cold before I knew what was coming down. He took my wallet, a hundred dollars, and all my credit cards. Happened over in Castroville about eleven o'clock last night at the Texaco station. You know the one?"

The woman nodded. She set the *Enquirer* on the countertop and followed his tale with rapt attention.

"I ain't got enough cash to get home on. My poor momma's sick and gonna be awful worried about me 'cause I was due home about noon today."

"Where you live?" she said.

"Uvalde."

"What you want from me? I ain't got no money."

"Thought you might let a fellow do a little work around here for enough gas to get home on. Sweep the floor, stack boxes, something like that. What you think? I'm a damn good worker."

The girl frowned and said, "I ain't allowed to hire anybody on. Don't know how I'd pay for the gas. The boss checks the register real careful every day."

Jimmy Rhea wandered over to the counter and said, "You got a cigarette, darlin'?"

"Winston okay?"

"Beggars can't be choosy now, can they?"

"I guess not," she said as she reached into her purse and retrieved a flip-top box of Winstons. She pulled one out and passed it to Jimmy Rhea.

"Thanks, darlin'. Got a light?"

She dragged out a Bic lighter and ignited it. Jimmy Rhea leaned over and pulled her hand toward him and lit the cigarette, all the time staring intently into her beautiful eyes.

"I thought you might want me to smoke it for you too," she said with a crooked smile.

"No, darlin', all I want is enough gas to get to Uvalde. Tell you what. I'll show you how to do this, okay?"

"Do what?"

"Get me some gas money."

"But I ain't got it."

"I don't want your money, darlin', just the gas. Now listen, I'm going to hang around here all morning and help you. I'll take out the trash, sweep the floor, and carry stuff out of the storeroom for you. All you got to do is adjust the credit cards a little bit till we get enough gas set aside for me."

"I don't understand."

"It's easy. How many people actually look at their receipt when you give it to them?"

"Not many."

"There you go. All you got to do is add a few cents here and there and by noon we've got a good ten dollars' worth of gas left in the pump. That's plenty to get me to Uvalde. It's only a few pennies off each customer, they'll never miss it, and you'll have the pleasure of my company all morning."

Jimmy Rhea had a smile that melted women's hearts. It made him seem vulnerable, a quality most women simply couldn't resist. The young woman bit her lower lip. After a few moments of indecision, she nodded and said, "Okay."

"Thank you, darlin'. Bless your soul. Now where's the broom?"

By noon Jimmy Rhea had enough credit for a tank full of gasoline. He'd swept about half the floor and then spent the rest of the time telling jokes to the young woman, Darlene. They chain-smoked and laughed so hard, Darlene had to wipe tears from her eyes.

"You ever come this way, Jimmy Rhea? I mean from Uvalde?"

"Sure, darlin'. You want me to look you up when I pass through?"

"You like to dance?"

"Sure do."

"I love to line dance. There's a couple of places up at Bandera where I go. I like the Silver Dollar Saloon the best. You ever been there?"

"Lots of times. You want to go, I'll take you next time I come around."

After Jimmy Rhea filled the Toyota he went back into the market to tell Darlene good-bye. Next time he spent the night in the Whitetail Lodge he sure as hell didn't plan on sleeping alone.

He walked behind the counter, put his arm around Darlene's waist, drew her to him, and kissed her softly on the lips, letting his tongue slide over hers. She blushed like a schoolgirl. "Bye, Jimmy Rhea. Here's my number," she said as she slipped him a small piece of paper.

He stuck it in his shirt pocket and swaggered to the door like a marine second lieutenant on parade. As he passed a newspaper box next to the front door, he glanced in and read the big headline on the front page of the *San Antonio Express-News*. What he saw made his heart race. With trembling hands he slipped two quarters into the slot and pulled out a paper.

The lead article described the murder of one Bobby Littlejohn. The thirty-two-year-old man had been shot in the forehead in what the police were calling a professional hit. They assumed the murder to be drug related.

Perspiration dripped from Jimmy Rhea's forehead and his palms were so wet they soaked the newsprint and made it run down the page like black tears. Bobby and Jimmy Rhea had made a terrible mistake just before Jimmy Rhea had been sentenced to his six months in jail. They'd ripped off a Gurya cartel mule from Chihuahua, Mexico. In all, they'd taken a kilo of cocaine and $20,000 in cash. Jimmy Rhea had lost his half in a poker game.

Standing there in the early morning heat, sweat soaking his shirt, Jimmy Rhea tried to figure out how the Mexicans had found Bobby. How did they know Bobby was involved in the theft? "Jesus, I'm next," Jimmy Rhea said to himself in a hoarse whisper.

CHAPTER 2

T he next evening, again sitting on the hood of his pickup, Monty
Kilpatrick smoked a cigarette, the tip glowing slightly as he
inhaled. He'd still seen no sign of the puma. A full moon lit the
landscape in front of him, a soft, southeasterly breeze rustled his
hair, and the smell of wildflowers filled the air.

Glancing to the west, he saw a flash of light and heard the crack of
a rifle. Images of rice paddies and explosions gripped his mind as he
turned the key in the ignition, released the parking brake, and drove
slowly in the direction of the sound without turning on his headlights.

Monty passed the gate of the Double K Ranch and was almost to
the far end of the front pasture when he saw the two men. One was
holding the fence open, and the other was passing the carcass of a
buck through the gap in the wire. Monty was still a good fifty yards
away. He sat in the truck with the engine idling and watched them for
a few minutes, trying to determine if there were just the two of them.
He placed the truck in neutral, turned off the ignition, and let the

pickup roll silently down the incline. He hoped against hope that they might be the Greeley brothers, Mack and Jerry. He'd been trying to catch those poachers for years.

The brothers had become an obsession with him because they openly bragged about their road kills all over southwest Texas. They indiscriminately slaughtered wildlife in or out of season and were so brazen that they always left a little hint that they'd been responsible for a kill. On more than one occasion Monty had found a matchbook from a restaurant in Leakey, where they lived.

He planned to roll onto the scene quietly and then restart the engine and turn on his headlights. When he exited the pickup, he'd have his Glock in hand.

He slipped the pistol out of its holster and placed it in his waistband. When he was about twenty yards away, one of the men looked up at the sound of Monty's tires on the gravel road.

"Run, Jerry!" the man shouted as he dropped the carcass. Monty pulled on the lights and started the truck. The two men were blinded by the headlights but kept running toward their truck.

Monty picked up the microphone of his radio and switched to the loudspeaker that was hidden behind the grille of his truck. "Game warden! You're under arrest!" Monty said as he opened the driver's door of his truck.

Sliding off the seat, Monty pulled the Glock from his waistband as his feet touched gravel. He aimed for the Greeleys' left rear tire and squeezed off two rounds, both of which missed, throwing gravel in a cloud of yellow dust. At that moment, the Greeley brothers' pickup roared to life and jumped forward like a scalded jackrabbit.

The Greeley brothers were thirty to forty yards away before Monty could get off another round. "Shit," he growled and jumped back in his pickup. He jammed the gearshift into drive and pushed the accelerator to the floor. The truck fishtailed across the gravel road, but he kept it under control. The poachers now had a hundred-yard lead.

Monty flipped on his blue and red lights but not the siren. No need waking the ranchers along County Road 354. Monty couldn't decide what kind of pickup the Greeleys were driving, but whatever it was, the damn thing was new and fast.

The gravel road went up and down hills and had numerous curves. He saw only glimpses of the Greeleys' taillights. They were having as much trouble staying on the road as he was. Each time he hit a curve he went into a four-wheel slide to get out. The driving schools he'd attended early in his career had paid off. Monty didn't like high-speed chases, but sometimes he had no choice. Asphalt highways were one thing. Country roads were something else.

Just as Monty slid through a sharp curve in front of the Triple Bar Ranch, his headlights fell on a big buck with three does crossing the road. He slammed his hand down on the horn and kept going. The buck and two does cleared the fence on the far side, but the third doe lost her footing and Monty's brush guard hit her in the flank, sending her flying over the hood and into his windshield. She bounced off and fell to the ground. *Jesus, Kilpatrick, you're supposed to protect the wildlife, not kill it.* The impact threw the truck off course, and he skidded into the ditch on the right side of the road. He ran the ditch for a few yards and then slowly pulled the truck back into the center of the road. The accident cost him ten to fifteen seconds.

Up ahead, Mack Greeley was fighting to keep his new Dodge Ram pickup on the gravel road. Jerry looked at the speedometer and shouted, "Jesus, Mack, you're going to kill us!"

"Shut up! I think that's Monty Kilpatrick back there and I don't want to mess with him. He's the toughest game warden in the state of Texas. He damn near killed old Willie Parsons last year. Beat the shit out of him. Poor fellow couldn't eat nothin for two damn weeks. Hold on. We ain't that far from the Sabinal-Utopia highway."

"The way you're driving we ain't never gonna to get to the goddamn blacktop! Shit, slow down. Hell, we've got a damn mile lead on him now."

"Put your fucking seat belt on and shut up."

There'd been heavy rains in late March, so Little Creek was high and the concrete ford was flooded. Seeing the high-water mark, Mack slammed on the brakes and all four wheels locked, sending the Dodge Ram into a sideways slide. The poacher fought the wheel, trying to get the vehicle under control. The truck hit the water broadside and rolled over one complete turn, landing once again on its wheels. The engine still ran, but the jostling inside the cab had left both brothers dazed.

When he recovered, Mack spun the wheel and jammed the accelerator to the floor. The truck fishtailed, then leaped out of the water, and up the hill. Monty was within fifty yards of them.

The Greeley brothers' truck was covered with mud, and the top was pushed in from the rollover. Monty still didn't know what kind of pickup it was, but he knew he would recognize it if he ever saw it again.

Mack flew through the stop sign at the junction of 187 and 354 and headed toward Utopia. Once on the blacktop, he took the pickup out of four-wheel drive and pushed the truck to the limit. The poachers sped through Utopia at 110 miles per hour with Monty thirty yards behind them.

At three in the morning, the streets were deserted. Where the highway split, Mack veered to the left toward Vanderpool. The Sabinal River was also swollen, so when the Dodge Ram hit the first ford, it was engulfed in water. The ignition system survived, and the big truck shot up the hill effortlessly with Monty a scant ten yards behind the poachers.

They drove like that all the way to Vanderpool, Mack with the accelerator to the floorboard on the straightaways and in four-wheel slides through the curves. Monty had to admit, the bastard could drive like a stock car racer.

At the bridge in Vanderpool, Mack turned toward Medina. The Dodge went up on its outside two wheels for a split second and Monty thought the pickup would flip, but it didn't.

Just as Monty's truck topped the first hill after the bridge, the alternator light lit on the dash. Monty groaned as he hit the steering wheel with his fist and pulled to the side of the road. A fan belt had broken, leaving the alternator without power.

Up ahead, Mack saw Monty's disabled truck in his rearview mirror and shouted, "He's down, Jerry! We've outrun him!"

"Then for Christ's sake take your foot off the accelerator. You've already ruined our new truck."

Mack laughed. "Hell, we've got to get through Medina and back to Leakey before sunrise. I ain't got time to slow down."

"I'm driving next time," Jerry said.

"If you was driving, we'd be in the damn Uvalde jail by now."

Monty watched the Greeley brothers' taillights fade into the distance and sighed. The bastards were damn lucky, and one of them could drive the hell out of a pickup.

He picked up his microphone and tuned his radio to the Bandera sheriff's frequency.

"Bandera, this is Kilpatrick."

"Go ahead, Monty."

"I'm on the road between Vanderpool and Medina with a busted fan belt. Can you send a tow truck?"

"Jesus, it's three thirty, Monty."

"I think there's an Exxon station on 16 that stays open all night."

"I'll do my best."

Monty lowered the windows, slumped in the seat, and turned off his lights and radio. A gentle southeasterly breeze drifted through the cab, and the aroma of freshly cut hay settled over him.

Lighting a cigarette, he looked through the windshield and studied the heavens. Monty enjoyed solitude. It was one of the main things he liked about his job. Over the years he'd learned a lot about the eighty-eight groups of stars that made up the constellations. He knew where each could be found at any given time of the year. He'd gone to a bookstore in San Antonio early in his career and bought a book on astronomy. After twenty years on the job, the stars were a diversion and a constant pleasure to study.

With the windows down, night sounds drifted across the open fields like a symphony. The leaves of the oak trees rustled in the gentle breeze, frogs croaked around the water tanks, owls hooted, bobcats growled, and raccoons, armadillos, and possums rummaged through the undergrowth. Monty's trained ear could sort them all out.

Monty closed his eyes and within a few seconds was sound asleep.

"MR. KILPATRICK."

Monty sat up. There was a faint glow in the eastern sky.

"You got a tow truck?"

"Sorry I couldn't get out here sooner, but we're real shorthanded right now."

"That's okay. Let's get going."

After his truck was repaired, Monty drove back to Utopia and met Arthur at the Lost Maples for their regular breakfast.

When he walked in, Gertrude was just serving Arthur his first cup of coffee and a plate of fried eggs and sausage. Looking up, Arthur asked, "You get the cougar?"

"No. I wasted an hour chasing those damn Greeley brothers. If I hadn't thrown a fan belt, I'd have gotten the bastards for sure."

Monty lit a Camel and exhaled through his nostrils; a thin blue stream of smoke engulfed Arthur.

"Damn it, Monty, why don't you stop smoking? You smell like an ashtray."

"Mind your own business for a change."

Gertrude set a cup of coffee and a plate of scrambled eggs and bacon in front of Monty. Smiling, she asked, "Well, your highness, did I get it right?"

"Don't be a smart-ass, Gertrude. It's not becoming," Monty said, laughing.

She saluted him with her middle finger and stalked away.

Arthur said, "One of these days she's going to dump a pot of coffee over your head."

WHEN MONTY PULLED INTO HIS DRIVEWAY, Martha Jo walked through the kitchen door on her way to her car. She looked up as he stepped out of the pickup and said, "There's a murder mystery playing in Uvalde with Wesley Snipes and Diane Lane. I'd sure like to see it."

Looking at his watch, Monty said, "If I get some sleep I'll think about it."

"We need to get out of the house. We don't go anywhere these days," Martha Jo said.

"That's hard with my schedule, you know that."

"You make your schedule, Monty. No other game warden in the state works your hours."

"Where're you headed?" Monty asked.

"Walmart in Uvalde. You need anything?"

"When you get back we'll talk about the movie," Monty said, heading for the kitchen door.

CHAPTER 3

Jimmy Rhea sat in his truck at the Exxon station grasping the steering wheel with white knuckles. Every time he let go his hands shook violently. He kept trying to reassure himself that the Mexicans didn't know who he was. But they'd found Bobby. He and Bobby had ripped off the mule in East Texas. How did they find Bobby in Southwest Texas? Should he go east or lie low around Hondo? He had a goal he desperately wanted to accomplish in Utopia. He decided it was worth the risk. He would wait it out.

He knew he needed a couple of days to figure out his next move so he went back into the convenience store and approached Darlene. She looked up and said, "I thought you'd gone to Uvalde."

"I got to thinking about that kiss I gave you and decided to come back for another one. You okay with that?"

She blushed again but nodded. He went around the counter, pulled her up, and wrapped his arms around her waist. Then he kissed her firmly on the lips, once again letting his tongue enter her mouth. This time she reciprocated and gave a soft groan.

He looked into her eyes and said, "My momma can wait a couple of days to see her baby boy. What time do you get off, darlin'?"

"In about ten minutes."

"What say you and me go to your place and finish this kissing business?"

A big smile crept across her face. "I'd like that a lot."

Darlene lived in a small apartment in Castroville just off Highway 90. Jimmy Rhea followed her to the building and parked his truck in back so it couldn't be seen from the street. The one-bedroom dwelling was stark. The furniture was worn and threadbare. The small kitchen had a table and two chairs, a stove, refrigerator, and microwave. Darlene had bought two six-packs of Budweiser before turning the store over to the clerk who followed her shift. She took two bottles out of the cardboard pack and placed the rest in the fridge.

Jimmy Rhea popped the tops off, handed one bottle to Darlene, clicked his bottle against hers, and said, "To us, darlin'. Let the loving begin."

They dropped their clothes on the floor as they headed for the small bedroom. Darlene was naked by the time they reached the bed. She threw the covers back and plopped herself on the double bed. Jimmy Rhea peeled off his Jockey shorts and slid in beside her.

Darlene was much better in bed than Jimmy Rhea had expected. In fact, she wore him down after an hour. They slept and then did it three more times before dinner. She fixed steaks on a small charcoal grill outside her kitchen door. Jimmy Rhea went to a video store and rented three porno movies and after dinner they watched the movies and drank the rest of the Bud.

Sexually, they were a perfect match. Darlene loved it as much as Jimmy Rhea. The next two days, Darlene skipped work and they screwed off and on until Jimmy Rhea complained about his dick being sore. Darlene rode him like a bucking bronco until he begged for mercy.

"Darlene, darlin', I got to get me some rest," he said on the third day. "I love to fuck, but you're wearing me down, girl. I got some business over in Utopia I need to take care of. I'll be gone this afternoon but I'll be back around dinnertime. If you want, I'll move in with you," Jimmy Rhea said with a smile on his face.

"I was hoping you'd say that, Jimmy Rhea. You're the best lover I ever had. I might even be in love with you," Darlene said.

"Well, now. Ain't that just something to write home about. My dear momma's gonna be real excited."

Jimmy Rhea dressed and grabbed a beer out of the refrigerator on his way out the door. "I'll see you in a few hours, darlin'. Keep that pussy warm for me," he said with a grin.

As soon as he was out of sight of Darlene's apartment building, he pulled to the side of the road and took out his Texas map. Jimmy Rhea spread the map out on the steering wheel and found Hondo. He traced his finger along U.S. Highway 90 until he found D'Hanis and then Sabinal. From Sabinal north to Utopia appeared to be about 22 miles on FM 187. He looked at his watch and saw it was one forty-five. Calculating the miles, he figured he could be in Utopia by two thirty or two forty-five. He'd never been there before, but he had no doubt he could find what he was looking for.

JIMMY RHEA REACHED THE CITY LIMITS of Utopia at two thirty-five and was flabbergasted at how small the town was. The Circle M looked like a place where he might get some information, so he parked the Toyota and walked through the front door. Jimmy Rhea didn't see a clerk anywhere. Dying for a smoke, he decided to spend part of his last ten dollars on a pack of Camels.

He picked up a flip-top box from a shelf just as Cindy walked out of the storeroom. She couldn't see him, but he could see her. "Bull's-eye, got you, girl," he whispered under his breath.

Cindy was restocking the glass counter with candy bars when Jimmy Rhea walked over. She could see his legs through the glass. "May I help you?" she asked.

"You know, darlin', if it weren't for that blonde hair and them pretty blue eyes, I'd say you were a dead ringer for a girl I once knew."

Cindy felt the breath escape her lungs and her heart race. She stood and faced her tormentor with tears in her eyes.

"My little wife's missed me so much, she's crying with joy. Now ain't that sweet?"

"How'd you find me?" she asked in a whisper.

"It was easy, darlin'."

"What do you want, Jimmy Rhea?" she asked, her voice stronger now.

"Why, you, darlin'. That's all I've ever wanted—my sweet, loving wife."

"I'm not your wife. I haven't been for a year and a half. Why can't you get that straight?"

Jimmy Rhea shook a cigarette out of the box of Camels and picked up a Bic lighter from the countertop and lit the cigarette. Letting the blue smoke out of his nostrils slowly, he leaned against the wall and said, "But I love you, baby. You'll always be my wife. I don't care what some dumb piece of paper says. Let no man put aside what the Lord grants, or however the saying goes. Know what I mean, darlin'?"

Just then the door opened and Monty Kilpatrick walked in. Jimmy Rhea instinctively stepped back, and Cindy managed a smile despite her tearstained cheeks. Monty wasn't sure what was going on, but he was distressed to see Cindy crying. *Who is this piece of shit?* he thought. *"Love-Hate" tattooed on his knuckles and he won't look me in the eye. Bastard has to be an ex-con.* He placed himself between Jimmy Rhea and Cindy and said, "You okay, Cindy?"

Cindy shot a drop-dead look at Jimmy Rhea and tried to decide what to do. She didn't want to cause trouble for Monty. All she wanted was to get rid of her worthless ex-husband.

Wiping her eyes, she said, "This is my brother. He's just passing through town and stopped to tell me our uncle Zeke died last week. He was a favorite of mine, helped raise me. He was a sweet old man."

Monty questioned Cindy's story but decided to let it ride. He had an idea she was shielding the guy for some reason. Maybe he really was her brother.

"Give me a quick pick, please," he said in an even voice.

"Is this your one for the week?"

"One a week, remember?"

"Avoid the guilt. Yes, I remember."

Cindy handed Monty his ticket. He dropped a dollar bill on the counter, picked up the ticket, and placed it in his shirt pocket. Turning to Jimmy Rhea, he said, "Sorry to hear about your uncle. Cindy's a good friend. I sure don't like seeing her upset. Know what I mean?"

Jimmy Rhea nodded. He suspected the game warden hadn't bought Cindy's story. That wasn't a good sign. He didn't want any more run-ins with the law, but he wanted Cindy back. He'd have to play this one really cool.

Cindy didn't want Monty to go, but knew no way to keep him in the store without telling the truth. Maybe if she played along with Jimmy Rhea, gave him some money or something, he'd go away.

"Bye, Monty. Hope you win the lottery. It's up to twenty-five million this time," she said.

"Tell you what, Cindy. If I win, I'll give you a million. How's that?"

"I could use it."

"You need anything, you call my house. Martha Jo always knows how to find me."

Monty gave Jimmy Rhea a hard look as he walked out the front door. He had the feeling he hadn't seen the last of that one.

As Monty walked through the door, a tall skinny fellow with long black hair tied in a ponytail stepped inside the store. His dark complexion, hook nose, and beady, close-set eyes sent a shiver down Cindy's spine. The man walked to where Jimmy Rhea and Cindy stood talking and asked, "You got a pack of Marlboros?"

Cindy picked one up from behind the counter and handed it to the man. He took it and asked, "How much?"

"Five twenty."

Turning to Jimmy Rhea, he said, "Fellow has to be nuts to smoke these days."

Jimmy Rhea nodded. There was something about the man that made a chill run down his spine as well.

The man paid Cindy and stuck out his hand to Jimmy Rhea. "My name's Vic. What's yours?"

"Jimmy Rhea Moffitt. This here's my wife, Cindy."

"Pleased to meet you both. See you around, Jimmy Rhea," Vic said as he walked through the door.

BACK IN HIS TRUCK, MONTY HEADED for Bandera. When the meter on his mobile phone indicated a strong signal, he speed-dialed his home number.

Martha Jo answered and Monty said, "Do me a favor, sweetheart. Cindy Moffitt may call. I think she might be in trouble. Hunt me down if she does."

"What's up?"

"There was a skinny red-haired man with a ponytail in the store talking to her when I went in. Said he was her brother, but I think she was lying. I've got him pegged as an ex-con. He could be an ex-husband as well. She was crying."

"Where're you headed?"

"I've got a meeting with the sheriff in Bandera at four thirty."

"If I can't get you on the phone, I'll call the sheriff's office and have them call you on the radio."

"Thanks. I'll be home for supper."

THE NEXT MORNING WHEN MONTY WALKED into the kitchen, he found Martha Jo sitting at the kitchen table having her usual cup of coffee. He poured himself one and sat down across from her. "Do me a favor, will you? Check on Cindy Moffitt today. I'm worried about her."

"I'll be happy to. She seems like a nice young woman and the little girl is a doll. I love the way Cindy dresses her for church, frills and all."

"She's a cutie."

After taking a quick nap, Monty slipped behind the wheel of his pickup and headed for FM 187 and Uvalde. He saw a big whitetail buck jump the fence as he drove by the bed and breakfast—Utopia on the River. The nine-pointer sailed over the barbed wire as if it were a mere two inches off the ground. The deer was in a cedar brake within seconds and totally hidden from view.

It was an overcast day, and Monty hoped it wouldn't rain. They'd had more precipitation than usual in the last few months. The stock tanks were full and the Sabinal River was higher than normal. A gentle breeze drifted in from the southeast, and he rolled the windows down.

Monty loved most aspects of his job. He was proud of the fact he protected wildlife. He'd grown up hunting and fishing and had shared the experience with his son. But after years of dealing with poachers and greedy hunters, he'd been turned off by the thought of killing anything with big brown eyes.

What most people didn't understand were the other duties Monty had. Texas game wardens have all the powers of a state trooper and, on occasion, Monty would be the only police officer in the county. That aspect of his job meant he might be forced to shoot a perpetrator.

And then there was Nam. Killing had taken on a new meaning for him after those first two months in the rice paddies. By that time, he hated the war, the president, and most of all the demonstrators. He still had the occasional nightmare in which he was wounded, half submerged in water, and being dragged by a comrade to a hovering Huey.

LATER THAT MORNING, MARTHA JO KILPATRICK drove to the Circle M to check on Cindy Moffitt. When she pulled into the parking area, she didn't see Cindy's old faded-blue Pinto. Once inside the building, she saw a new person behind the counter, a woman in her mid-fifties. "Where's Cindy?" Martha Jo asked.

"She called in sick yesterday. I'm the owner's wife. We live in Uvalde and I'm just filling in until she's able to come back to work."

"Do you know what's wrong with her?"

"She sounded real bad on the phone."

"I guess I'd better check on her."

"Are you a friend?"

"Just an acquaintance."

"I hope she's all right. It'd sure be hard to replace her."

When Martha Jo knocked on the door of Cindy's trailer a few minutes later, there was no answer. She waited and then knocked again, this time with more force. Several moments passed before she heard footsteps on the other side of the door.

"Who is it?" a weak voice asked.

"Martha Jo Kilpatrick. That you, Cindy?"

"Yes, ma'am."

"Are you okay?"

Cindy was racked with indecision. Should she or shouldn't she acknowledge her plight? There was a certain safety in anonymity, but she was frightened and perhaps Mrs. Kilpatrick or her husband could help.

"Cindy, answer me. Are you all right?" Martha Jo said with an edge to her voice.

Cindy unlatched the chain on the trailer door and opened it. When Martha Jo saw the younger woman's face, she gasped. Cindy's upper lip and her left eye were swollen. Her arms were covered with bruises, and she grimaced with pain each time she took a breath.

"My God, child, who did this to you?" Martha Jo asked.

"I'd rather not say."

"Do you mean you're afraid to say?"

Cindy was indeed afraid. Jimmy Rhea had been very specific in his threat: "Say a word to anyone and the next time it'll be worse." Cindy knew she needed help. She couldn't deal with her ex-husband by herself. Somehow she had to get him out of her life for good.

Screwing up her courage, she said, "I'm scared to death, Mrs. Kilpatrick. I think he's going to kill me."

"Who did this to you?"

"My ex-husband, Jimmy Rhea."

"So, Monty was right," Martha Jo whispered. She'd always known Monty had good instincts.

"Where's Jody?"

"She's asleep in the back."

"Does she know what happened?"

"She was here."

"That's terrible! She saw everything?"

"Not everything. We were in the bedroom when he raped me."

Martha Jo felt woozy. She steadied herself on the doorjamb and said, "May I come in, Cindy? I want you to tell me exactly what happened."

The two women walked to the couch and sat side by side. Martha Jo stroked the side of Cindy's swollen face and asked, "Did you put ice on this right away?"

"Yes, ma'am, it helped a lot."

Cindy took a gasping breath, grimacing in pain at a broken rib, and said, "I got divorced a little over a year and a half ago in Houston. I had a peace warrant sworn out on my husband. When the divorce was final, I got in my Pinto, hooked up a U-Haul trailer, and drove Jody and me directly here. I'd seen one of the Utopia water bottles on a shelf at HEB and thought the name was just wonderful. Utopia meant something perfect. I didn't know how tiny the town was or I probably wouldn't have come. I sure didn't realize jobs and a place to stay were so hard to come by. I was really lucky to rent this trailer and get work at the Circle M.

"I didn't tell anyone where I was going, not even my best friend. I just got in the car and drove. I thought a year and a half was long enough that Jimmy Rhea would give up. He didn't want the divorce; it was me. I was scared to death of him because he beat me up all the time. Some men beat women when they're drunk. Jimmy Rhea does it when he's cold sober.

"He didn't find me until two days ago. I did something really stupid. About seven months ago I wrote my friend Gilda and, like a fool, used my return address. Jimmy Rhea broke into her house when she wasn't home, found the letter, and traced me here after he got out of jail. Your husband came into the store only minutes after Jimmy Rhea. I begged Jimmy Rhea to leave, but he wanted to see Jody. Said if I'd let him see Jody, he'd go back to Houston. He's a terrible liar, I should have known better. Soon as I got off work he followed me here and made me fix him dinner. Didn't pay any attention to Jody, bless her heart. After dinner I asked him real nice to leave, but he just laughed. I said I was going to call the sheriff over in Uvalde, and that's when he slapped me."

Tears welled in Cindy's eyes. "I ran back there to the bedroom so Jody wouldn't see what was happening. He followed me, kicked the door open, and threw me down on the bed. I fought him off as best I could, but he started beating me with his fist and I just gave up. I didn't have a chance. He pulled my jeans down, ripped off my panties, and forced himself into me. It hurt so bad.

"I begged him to go away and leave us alone, but he just laughed and said as far as he was going was Castroville. He went into the kitchen and took a hundred dollars out of the freezer. He knew that was where I keep my emergency money. I've always kept one or two hundred dollars in an ice-cream carton in the freezer. I figure burglars wouldn't think to look there. But Jimmy Rhea knew and he cleaned me out.

"Before he left, he told me if I said anything about what he'd done, he'd beat me up so bad I'd wish I was dead. Said he was going to find a job and get me and Jody back whether I liked it or not."

Cindy sank back into the soft cushions of the couch, tears streaming down her cheeks. "I don't know what to do. What if he hurts Jody? He just acts crazy sometimes."

Martha Jo asked, "May I get a glass of water?"

"The glasses are up there over the sink."

"Would you like some?" Martha Jo asked.

"Yes, ma'am, I would."

Martha Jo took two glasses out of the cabinet and filled them with water. When she handed Cindy's to her, she said, "You don't have to call me ma'am, dear. I wish you wouldn't. It makes me feel old. Call me Martha Jo, like everyone else does."

"I'm sorry. Yes, ma'am. I mean, I will, Martha Jo."

Martha Jo said, "The first thing that needs to be done is to swear out a warrant for this man. I'll call Arthur Jepson, the justice of the peace, and he'll take care of that. Then the sheriff or Monty or some police officer will arrest Jimmy Rhea and put him in jail. We'll have the bail set so high he can't possibly get out, and then you'll have to press charges. He'll be put away for a long time. You and Jody will be safe. You won't have to worry anymore."

Cindy gave a wan smile. "I'd love to believe you, but I don't think it'll play out like that. He'll get free somehow and he'll kill me."

CHAPTER 4

Pepe Diaz knocked on his brother's office door, still hungover from a night on the town. His head throbbed, his eyes were bloodshot, and he wobbled when he walked. Pepe, like most Mexicans, was a man of small stature. He'd been slender in his youth but at thirty-three had developed a small beer belly that hung over his belt. His close-set dark eyes had redundant bags under them and his teeth were yellow and crooked.

"Come in," Juan said.

"Good morning, brother. You sent for Pepe?"

"I have a job for you."

Juan Diaz was the chief of operations for the Gurya cartel. He was the opposite of his younger brother in every way. Six feet tall, he stood ramrod straight with military bearing. His close-cropped hair was as black as coal and bushy eyebrows hung over his dark brown eyes. Juan rarely smiled.

His office was in a large second-story room looking out on an irrigated garden of palm trees and flowers. His massive antique desk had once belonged to General Huerta, the previous owner of the nineteenth-century hacienda. Two straight-backed chairs stood like sentinels in front of the desk, and in the corner of the room an old oak coffee table sat between a large leather couch and two leather wing-back chairs. The atmosphere was austere and unfriendly. The rock walls were bare. A large chandelier of wood and wrought iron hung from the center of the ceiling, and one lone lamp sat on Juan's desk.

Focusing on the two straight-backed chairs, Pepe walked carefully to one of them. He looked sheepishly at his brother and said, "Pepe was a bad fellow last night, brother. He took too much of the wine with his supper."

Juan was used to Pepe referring to himself in the third person, but this particular morning it irritated him more than usual. He glared at Pepe and said, "You drink too much. In this business that'll get you killed. Your life depends on a clear head. You know I allow no drug use in our organization. You don't set a good example for the men, and it makes me very angry."

Pepe was used to these tongue-lashings. He'd come to expect them and had long ago decided to let them slide off his back like so much rainwater. "Pepe will do better," he said.

Juan walked around the desk and sat in the second chair. He pulled out a thin Cuban cigar, offered one to Pepe, and then lit his own. Inhaling deeply, he blew the blue smoke out his nostrils. In Pepe's fuzzy mind, Juan resembled a dragon.

"Miguel Garcia is in the hospital with a broken leg," Juan said. "He's to be in traction for six weeks. This leaves me without a supervisor for my border drivers. I want you to fill in for him."

"But of course, brother. Pepe would look forward to such an assignment. You know Pepe is eager to become more involved in the business."

"I don't want you directly involved. Under no circumstances are you to drive across the border. Your job is to assign drivers, make sure the cars are properly outfitted, and grease the palms of the Mexican border police. Do you understand?"

"Of course."

"I don't intend for a member of this family to rot in some gringo jail. Once you reach Ojinaga, I forbid you to drink while you're on duty. If you fail me in this, I will cut your funds off for six months. Do you understand?"

"Pepe understands very well."

Juan gave Pepe a cold stare and wondered if his lecture had made any impact. Time would tell. He stood and said, "You should leave for the border immediately. Two days from now I want a massive shipment to pass through Presidio for San Antonio."

The older man extended his hand, and they sealed the assignment. Pepe said in an even voice, "Don't worry, brother. Pepe won't let you down."

Pepe arranged for one of Juan's men to drive him to Ojinaga. Their distribution center was located in a large warehouse on the outskirts of town. There was a small one-bedroom apartment in the warehouse where Miguel Garcia stayed during the shipments. Drivers were sent across at random times of the day and at different times in the week to avoid establishing a pattern the Border Patrol would recognize. The apartment was simply furnished but had a forty-two-inch flat-screen Sony television hooked up to a DirecTV satellite dish.

Pepe arrived at the warehouse late in the afternoon just as a load of cocaine was being delivered in a panel truck. The drugs were flown from Colombia to Mexico where the planes landed at secret airfields. Panel trucks that met the aircraft were then loaded with the merchandise, and driven to the Ojinaga warehouse.

Pepe stood in one corner of the large room and watched the beehive of activity. Workers wrapped packets of cocaine in plastic, then in aluminum foil. A second layer of plastic was applied and sealed with duct tape. Each packet was dipped in a rubberized liquid, forming an airtight seal. All workers used latex gloves, changing them at each stage of the operation, thereby reducing the chance of contamination with the white powder. The final product was a four-by-six brick that was almost impossible for the Border Patrol dogs to detect.

Car fenders were removed, filled with bricks, and replaced. False bottoms in the trunks were lined with bricks. By the time each car was outfitted, it carried in excess of a million dollars' worth of cocaine.

The target date of two days hence seemed reasonable and safe to Pepe. He was sure he'd be able to accomplish the job for his brother. There'd be one more day of preparation, and then at eight o'clock on the following morning, he'd send ten drivers to the border all at once.

The following day went without incident, and by five in the afternoon all ten automobiles were ready. Pepe instructed each driver to be at the warehouse no later than seven thirty the following morning. True to his word, Pepe had abstained from alcohol since meeting with his brother.

With all the cars loaded and ready to roll across the border, he was in the mood to celebrate. His car and driver from Chihuahua were still available, so he showered, changed clothes, and went out on the town.

His first stop was a bar where he downed three Jack Daniel's on the rocks. Next, he went to a fine restaurant and consumed a bottle of Robert Mondavi Cabernet Sauvignon along with a big steak. By the time Pepe left the restaurant he was fully inebriated and intent on going to the local whorehouse.

Stepping into his limousine, Pepe told the driver, "Take me to Boys' Town."

Twenty minutes later they pulled up to a small bar on a side street. A neon sign flashed *Juanita's Hideaway*. Turning to the driver, Pepe asked, "Is this the best whorehouse in Ojinaga?"

"The very best. My sister-in-law runs it. I called ahead and alerted her to your visit."

Pepe stepped out of the car and on unsteady legs approached the door and then swung it open. Inside a bar lined one wall and six tables with chairs surrounded a small dance floor. The ceiling opened to the stars and soft music filled the room. A dumpy woman in a flowing dress walked up to Pepe and said, "We are honored to have such an important man visit our establishment. My brother-in-law speaks very highly of you, Señor Diaz."

"I want the most beautiful and talented girl here. Money is no object," Pepe said.

"Please come with me."

Pepe followed the woman across the dance floor to a back hallway. They climbed a set of stairs and on the second level she led him to a spacious room with a king-sized bed and a large Jacuzzi. Sitting in the tub was a gorgeous woman in her early twenties. When Pepe walked into the room she stood and stepped out of the water. Her tall, slim body dripped water as she walked naked across the tile floor. Her pale skin glistened in the soft light and she raked her long, wet, raven hair back from her forehead with her slender fingers as she walked toward Pepe.

He stood transfixed. Never in his life had he seen such a beautiful woman. His heart raced as she came closer. When she did reach him, she unbuttoned his shirt and loosened his belt. Pulling his pants to his ankles, she helped him step out of them. Then silently she led him to the bed. Throwing the covers back, she lay on the black sheets and waited for him to finish undressing.

Pepe had been with many beautiful prostitutes in his life but none like this woman. She smiled and crooked her index finger, coaxing him to hurry and join her. He fumbled with his underpants and fell to the floor trying to get them off. Finally, he crawled beside her and wrapped his arms around her slim waist.

They made love for a long time and Pepe experienced the most intense sexual climax he'd ever imagined. Then he fell into a relaxed sleep. The woman slid out of bed and threw on a robe. She had other clients to service.

When he awoke two hours later, Pepe took a shower in the

luxurious bathroom, dressed, and sought out the madam. He handed her five hundred American dollars on his way out the door, never bothering to ask the remarkable girl's name.

MONTY KILPATRICK HAD BEEN OUT ALL night looking for the cougar. He was sleepy when he drove into Utopia, so he decided to stop at the Lost Maples Café for a cup of coffee. As he parked the pickup in front, someone said, "Hold up, Monty. I want to talk to you."

Monty turned to see a local rancher approaching, the owner of the Double K, Wally Hampton.

"Come in, Wally, and I'll buy you a cup of coffee," Monty said.

Wally was a second-generation rancher following in the footsteps of his father. He was in his late seventies and still had a full head of silver hair. His face was furrowed from years of sun exposure but his blue eyes still sparkled.

The two men took a booth at the front of the restaurant and the afternoon waitress, Jasmine, took their order. As she walked away, Monty said, "Bring me a scoop of vanilla ice cream, too." Turning to his companion, he asked, "What's on your mind, Wally?"

"That damned cougar. I've lost two calves this last week. He's a hungry bastard. Why can't you kill him?"

"Why can't you? You know how to use a damn rifle. I've got more things on my plate than babysitting a bunch of cattle. I've spent almost every night this week trying to bag the damn cat," Monty said. "Killing hungry cougars isn't in my job description."

"What's eating you, Monty? It's not like you to fly off like that."

Monty took a deep breath. He felt a tinge of guilt for complaining. It was his job to protect the wildlife and assist the ranchers when he could. "Sorry, Wally. Things have just been a little crazy the past few days."

"I heard you were having trouble catching the Greeley brothers. That what's bothering you?"

Monty smiled. "I wish. It's more complicated than that. Look, I'll keep trying to take the lion off your hands. It's just that you'll have to be patient."

"Fair enough. I'll start doing my share, too," Wally said.

Jasmine placed their orders on the table and Monty said, "If you run into Arthur Jepson, tell him I'm looking for him. He's not answering his mobile."

THE NEXT MORNING PEPE AWOKE TO the sound of men milling around the warehouse. He forced himself out of bed and into a cold shower. By the time he got to the staging area it was eight fifteen. The drivers were waiting to see if there were any final instructions or changes in the plan.

Through bloodshot eyes, Pepe counted the drivers. He was one short. Motioning to the lead driver, he said, "Come here, Manuel." When the man approached, Pepe placed his arm around his shoulder and said, "Pepe counts ten cars and nine drivers. Is he mistaken?"

"One is missing."

"And who might that be?"

"Luis. I've called his house, but he didn't come home last night and his wife has no idea where he is."

"Do we have a backup?"

"Not today."

Pepe tried to clear his head. He shrugged his shoulders and said, "Which car has no driver?"

"The 1955 Buick station wagon."

"Pepe will drive it," Pepe said.

Manuel said, "Your brother would not approve, Pepe. We should leave the Buick for tomorrow or the next day. I don't think you should drive. It's much too dangerous and puts you and your brother at great risk."

Pepe shook his head. "No," he said, "Pepe will drive the Buick and take full responsibility. Have no fear; you won't get into trouble with my brother."

Pepe asked if the drivers had any final questions about their mission. All were veteran smugglers who had made many crossings. As he told them he'd be in the Buick, a murmur floated across the large room. He waved them on and got behind the steering wheel of the station wagon.

THE CARS MADE IT THROUGH THE Mexican checkpoint without difficulty. On the American side of the Rio Grande, a Border Patrol officer motioned for Pepe to park the Buick. "Please step out of the car," he said.

Pepe complied and as he stood next to the automobile, he said with a smile, "The Texas sun seems hotter than our Mexican one."

The officer nodded and led a German shepherd around the car. The dog stopped at the trunk but didn't bark. Pepe held his breath, his pulse racing. His head pounded and he questioned why he'd been so foolish as to drive across the border. The dog circled the automobile several times but didn't detect the cocaine that had been so cleverly processed and hidden.

"May I see your driver's license?" the officer asked.

Pepe handed it to the man but didn't say a word.

The officer examined the license and asked, "How long will you be in the U.S.?"

Pepe shrugged. "Not long. I have an aunt in San Antonio who is ill. I will return to my home in Chihuahua in three or four days."

Handing the license back to Pepe, the man said, "I hope your aunt recovers."

Behind the wheel of the Buick once again, Pepe held his breath until he'd cleared the area. Perspiration soaked his shirt and it stuck to his back. He couldn't wait to get through Presidio and reach the open road.

CHAPTER 5

Pepe headed up Highway 67 toward Marfa. It was a clear, cloudless day but a blistering Texas sun beat down on the asphalt.
At nine o'clock the temperature hovered in the mid-eighties.
Pepe's forehead was wet with perspiration as was his shirt and
his head pounded. His palms were so wet he could barely control the
steering wheel.

Once in Texas, the drivers were to divide into pairs and take different routes to San Antonio. Some would use Interstate 10, some 20,
and the others Highway 90 East. Pepe and Manuel took Highway
90 at Marfa and were in Alpine by eleven. They pulled into a Dairy
Queen for a hamburger and were back on the road by eleven thirty.
They drove 65 miles an hour, 5 miles below the legal limit, and carefully observed the local traffic laws.

Pepe's 1955 Buick passed in front of Monty Kilpatrick's truck as
Monty stopped for the red light at the intersection of Highways 1023
and 90. He'd been discussing the cougar with John Payne, the game

warden stationed in Carrizo Springs. Something about the old station wagon with Mexican plates caught Monty's attention. He couldn't put his finger on why he was suspicious, but he decided to follow the Buick.

He slipped into the right-hand lane and trailed the car by fifty yards. The driver was doing exactly 40 miles an hour. When they got to the city limits, the car sped to 65.

Monty scrutinized the car. It appeared to be in good mechanical condition for a fifty-year-old automobile. There were a few dents and the green paint was sun-faded, but it seemed to run smoothly. A fine trail of thin blue smoke arose from the tailpipe.

Eight miles out of Uvalde, just before Knippa, Monty flipped the toggle switch that controlled his blue and red lights and hit the siren for one short blast.

Pepe had almost gone to sleep two or three times and was in the process of dozing off when the siren blared. It startled him and he jerked the steering wheel, causing the Buick to swerve to the shoulder of the road.

Juan's instructions were to surrender immediately if challenged by the authorities in the United States. The one exception was at the border. If detected, they were to run for their lives and melt into the Hispanic population. On the open road, they'd been told to stop because there was no way for them to escape.

Pepe cursed under his breath. He knew what his instructions were, but he was Juan Diaz's brother. For him to be captured was unthinkable. For an instant he considered flooring the accelerator and trying to outrun the pickup behind him. Even in his muddled mental state he realized this was a ridiculous thought. A roadblock would be awaiting him at the next town.

There was only one way out. He must kill the policeman quickly and be on his way. Pepe's youth had equipped him well for such an assignment. He was a practiced and accomplished master of the switchblade knife. His had a six-inch, razor-sharp edge, and he kept it

in the waistband of his pants at the center of his back. He leaned back
in the seat to reassure himself that it was there. Feeling the hard steel
gave him reassurance and bolstered his spirits.

Seventy-five yards behind Monty's truck, a frightened Manuel
tried to decide what to do. Juan Diaz's instructions were clear. Should
one driver be apprehended, the other was to keep moving. But Pepe
was no ordinary driver. He was Juan's only brother.

Manuel's hands shook on the steering wheel and he felt hot bile
enter his mouth. He slowed to 35 miles an hour to give himself time
to think.

Pepe pulled the Buick onto the shoulder and placed the gearshift
in park, leaving the engine running. He rolled down the window and
waited.

Monty swung his truck in behind the Buick and turned off the
ignition. Glancing in his rearview mirror, he saw a 1965 Chevrolet
four-door sedan moving slowly about a hundred yards behind him.

Monty stepped out of the pickup and undid the safety catch on
his holster. He walked cautiously to the open window of the Buick.
Standing back about three feet, he said, "Please step out of the car."

Pepe, pretending not to understand, said, "No hablo inglés, señor."

"Bajate del coche, por favor, señor."

"Sí, jefe."

As Pepe swung the car door open, Monty watched every move like
a hawk. The Mexican left the door open and stood in a relaxed manner as if two old friends were passing the time of day.

"Su licencia, por favor," Monty said evenly.

"Sí, señor." Pepe's right hand went toward his back pocket.

His fingers wrapped around the handle of his knife, and as he
slowly lifted it out of his waistband, his thumb found the button that
released the blade. In one flowing and lightning-fast motion, Pepe
opened the blade. Monty caught a glimpse of the sun's reflection on
the knife and twisted his body away from the Mexican. Pepe's knife

missed its mark and slashed across Monty's chest, cutting through his shirt. The blade incised the skin and chest muscles and the outer third of his abdominal muscle.

Excruciating pain sucked the air from Monty's lungs. He grabbed Pepe's arm, stepped behind the Mexican, and brought the knife up into the man's chest, imbedding the blade into Pepe's right lung. There was a hissing sound as the Mexican gasped for air.

Shocked and breathless, Pepe dropped to his knees with the knife still protruding from his chest. Monty was bleeding badly from his wound, but he took a pair of handcuffs off his belt, pulled Pepe's hands behind him, and cuffed him. The Mexican, groaning and short of breath, rolled over in the dirt and lay on his side.

Monty pressed his handkerchief into his wound. He staggered back to his truck just as the car he'd seen behind him sped by. He grabbed his microphone and switched to the Uvalde sheriff's frequency. "Uvalde dispatcher, come in please. It's Monty Kilpatrick."

"What's up, Monty?"

"I'm on Highway 90, about 2 miles west of Knippa. I'm wounded and have a wounded Mexican national. I need an ambulance and assistance immediately."

"Ten-four. We'll be there in a minute."

Monty slumped back in his seat and looked over at the Mexican. There was a trickle of blood seeping around the knife handle but no massive hemorrhage. He was cuffed and immobilized, so Monty examined his own wound. What he saw didn't please him. Now that the rush of adrenaline was abating, the pain intensified. Each time he tried to remove his handkerchief, bright red blood gushed.

It took eight minutes for the ambulance to get to the scene. A squad car with the sheriff at the wheel led the way.

Sheriff Boswell lunged from his car and dashed to Monty's truck.

"You okay, Monty?"

"Yeah."

"Let me see your wound," Boswell said as he opened Monty's shirt. "Jesus, he filleted you like a fish."

"I think it looks worse than it actually is. There's only one spot that's actually bleeding now. Check on the Mexican, would you?"

"We'll get you in the ambulance."

"Put the Mexican in the ambulance. I'll ride with you. And get his car impounded. I'm sure it's loaded with cocaine."

The EMS technicians placed Pepe on a stretcher and carried him back to the ambulance. Two additional squad cars arrived on the scene, and Sheriff Boswell instructed his deputies to tow the car to Uvalde.

Monty and the sheriff reached the emergency room just moments after the ambulance delivered Pepe, now unconscious, to the care of one exhausted and very nervous Dr. Jim Baker, the coroner and family practitioner whose office was across the street from the hospital. Most hospital ERs are staffed by trained emergency room physicians, but in many small towns, the doctors take turns. In Uvalde, each doctor took one full day of rotation.

The EMS technicians transferred Pepe to a hospital gurney, as Dr. Baker placed his stethoscope on Pepe's chest. The Mexican's heart rate was rapid and weak. When a nurse appeared, Dr. Baker said, "Put in a stat call for Dr. Maxwell, then get me a bottle of Ringer's lactate and send for two units of red tag blood. You better call the nursing supervisor and get some help down here quick."

Dr. Baker unbuttoned Pepe's shirt and studied the wound. He found a 20-cc syringe and an 18-gauge spinal needle. After wiping the skin with an alcohol sponge, he plunged the needle deep in Pepe's chest and pulled back on the plunger, filling the syringe with blood. He drew off a total of 200 cubic centimeters, and Pepe began to breathe more easily.

The nurse informed Dr. Baker that Monty Kilpatrick had been wounded and was in room 1. Jim Baker pushed his glasses up on his nose and wiped the back of his hand across his perspiring forehead.

"Jesus," he said, "you'd think we were at Ben Taub Hospital in Houston. Have you heard from Dr. Maxwell?"

"He's on his way."

"Call the OR and tell them to get set up for an emergency chest case. Then start a unit of blood. If Dr. Maxwell isn't here in a few minutes, I'm going to have to put a chest tube in this man. Let me check on the game warden."

Dr. Baker went to the exam room where Monty sat talking with the sheriff, holding his handkerchief to his chest.

"You need to lie down. Let me help you up to the examination table," Dr. Baker said as he pulled Monty's shirt open so he could look at the wound.

"Thanks but I can move okay," Monty said. "The bleeding's stopped except for the mammary artery. I've got it under control with compression."

Dr. Baker asked, "How do you know it's the mammary artery?"

"I'm a veterinarian."

Monty lay back on the table, and Dr. Baker pulled out the leg rest. He said, "I didn't know game wardens were veterinarians."

"After I graduated from A&M, I went to school at Ohio State in Columbus. I tried a small animal practice in San Antonio, but that lasted only about six months. I couldn't deal with the overprotective pet owners."

"I've often wondered how vets deal with pet owners. Some treat their dogs and cats better than their children. What prompted you to become a game warden?"

"It was my wife's idea."

The doctor always made a point of engaging people in conversation while he worked on them. He knew if he could coax them to talk about themselves, they'd become distracted and less anxious.

Dr. Baker inspected Monty's wound meticulously and thought how lucky the man had been.

"I think you're right," he said. "This doesn't seem as bad as it looks."

He removed a large sterile pad from a cabinet and said, "Pull your handkerchief out now and let's put this in the wound instead."

Monty followed instructions, and immediately there was a rush of bright-red blood. Dr. Baker quickly stopped the hemorrhage with the pad and said, "Now hold this in place until I get back. I've got to check on the Mexican."

"How is he, Doc?"

"I'm not sure he's going to make it. He's got a collapsed lung, a lot of blood in his chest cavity, and I suspect he's bleeding from one of his intercostal arteries. I've called for a general surgeon and alerted the OR."

"Go and take care of him. I'm okay. I would like a little something for pain, though."

"I'll send the nurse with some Demerol."

When Dr. Baker got back to Pepe, Dr. Jason Maxwell was examining the Mexican.

"Damn, I'm glad to see you. I was just on the verge of putting in a chest tube. I drew off about 200 cc of blood. I'm sure he's still hemorrhaging."

"Thanks for leaving the knife in place. If we take him directly to surgery, he won't need a chest tube until I get the bleeding stopped. How did this happen?"

"He had a run-in with the game warden. Kilpatrick's pretty badly cut up himself. I can take care of him. This guy is the one I'm worried about."

"How much blood has he had?"

"This is the first unit of red tag. He's got another ready."

"I'm going to wheel him to the OR. Is there any family here?"

"I get the impression this guy might be a Mexican national, possibly a criminal."

"We've got to operate now, consent or no consent."

"Keep me posted."

As Dr. Maxwell hustled Pepe's gurney toward the operating room, Dr. Baker went back to check on Monty. The nurse had just given him a shot of Demerol.

Sheriff Boswell looked a little pale. He said, "Monty, looks like you're in good hands. I'm going down to the jail and check out that car."

"Do me a favor, will you?" Monty asked. "Call Martha Jo and tell her I won't be home on time."

"You don't want me to tell her you're hurt?"

"I don't want to scare her. Just tell her that I'm detained and that I'll be home later."

Dr. Baker pulled Monty's shirt off and said, "I think you need to spend the night."

"Sorry, Doc, but I can't. Just stitch me up and I'll be on my way."

"We'll talk about it later."

The knife had cut through Monty's leather belt but not the nylon one that held his holster and Glock pistol. The doctor undid the buckle and pulled the holster and gun off. "I don't think you'll need this for the next hour or so."

The nurse opened a suture set and arranged all the instruments on a Mayo tray. After washing his hands and pulling on rubber gloves, Dr. Baker asked the nurse to take the abdomen pad out of Monty's chest wound. Using two hemostats, he clamped the mammary artery. Monty grimaced in pain.

"Sorry. I wanted to get the bleeding under control first. I'll deaden the skin edges and it won't hurt again."

"It didn't hurt all that much. Besides, I'm beginning to feel the Demerol."

Dr. Baker injected the wound, scrubbed it, and sutured the muscle and skin edges. As the last skin suture was applied, Monty awoke.

"Did I sleep through the whole thing?" Monty asked.

"I really must insist that you spend the night, Dr. Kilpatrick. I want to check your blood pressure and pulse. You'll need a tetanus booster,

IV antibiotics, and more pain medication. This thing is going to hurt like hell when the novocaine wears off."

"You talked me into it, Doc," Monty said. "Besides, I want to know what happens with the Mexican. Please call my wife and tell her what happened, that I'm okay and not to worry. I'll be home in the morning. I'll write the number down for you. Tell her there's absolutely no need for her to come over here."

"Just relax while I write some admission orders."

Dr. Baker applied a large bandage to Monty's wound and asked the nurse to admit the game warden to the hospital.

Meanwhile, upstairs in the operating room, Dr. Maxwell was scrubbing Pepe's chest with an antiseptic solution. Dr. Jennifer Campbell, the anesthesiologist, was taking Pepe's blood pressure.

"Better hurry, Jason," she said, "his pressure's dropping and I've got a dopamine drip running as fast as it'll go. I've called for a third unit of blood, but things don't look good."

"I'm working as fast as I can." Turning to the circulating nurse, he said, "Drape this off while I get gowned."

Dr. Maxwell was gowned and gloved by the scrub nurse. Perspiration beaded on his forehead.

"Call maintenance and ask them to cool it down in here, will you?"

He returned to his patient and made an incision in Pepe's chest wall. The Mexican's blood pressure was so low, the wound barely bled. When the doctor opened the chest cavity, it was full of blood. He found the injured artery and clamped both ends. He used 2-0 silk suture on a round needle to tie off the artery. He lifted Pepe's knife out of the chest wall and handed it to the circulating nurse, saying, "I guess the sheriff will want this for evidence."

The surgeon inserted a chest tube and asked the circulator to put the other end in a bedside bottle. After closing the incision he looked over the anesthesia drape and asked the anesthesiologist about the blood pressure.

"Systolic is seventy," Dr. Campbell said. Now that you've got the bleeding stopped, I believe it'll stabilize. I need to figure out how much blood he's lost and replace it. I hate like hell giving him all this O negative blood."

"You had to do it. Keep checking his hematocrit, and when it gets to forty, ease off on the blood and fluids."

"I'm going to stay with him in the recovery room until he's awake. I'm concerned about him."

"I'm going down to check on the game warden. Jim Baker said he thought he could handle it. I just want to make sure everything's okay."

Dr. Maxwell left the operating room in a blue scrub suit and took the elevator to the first floor. An orderly was just rolling Monty's stretcher onto the elevator as the doctor was about to step off.

"How do you feel?" he asked.

Monty was still groggy and had no idea who Dr. Maxwell was. He opened one eye and said, "Who're you?"

"I'm Dr. Maxwell, the general surgeon. I just got out of the OR and wanted to see if Jim Baker needed any help with you."

"How's the Mexican?"

"Touch and go. He's lost a lot of blood. Pressure's low now. We're giving him a transfusion."

"When can I see him?"

"He's unconscious and I'm not sure when he'll wake up. You don't look like you're in great shape yourself."

"I'll be out of here in the morning."

The nurse gave Monty a shot of Demerol every four hours, and he slept soundly through the night. The following morning, his chest felt as if someone was holding a hot poker to his ribs. He groaned with every movement.

Across the room, in an overstuffed chair, Martha Jo slept. When she heard Monty's groans, she awoke.

"I guess you thought I'd let you lie over here and die without checking on you. And why did you have all those people call me to relay your messages? Have you forgotten how to use a phone?"

"I couldn't get to a phone. Besides, I'm not hurt that badly."

"It sounds like you're hurt. I've never heard such pitiful groans in all my life. What kind of fight did you get into?"

"I think you'd call it a knife fight."

"What happened to the other guy?"

"I don't know. I've got to talk to his doctor this morning. I need to see Sheriff Boswell and check on the car the Mexican was driving. I'm sure it's loaded with cocaine."

"I don't think you should leave the hospital. Dr. Baker seemed to think you'd be here for a few days."

"I'm sore as hell, but I'm okay. I want to get to the bottom of this."

"Do you really think your job is more important than your health?" Martha Jo asked with a frown.

"My health's fine. I have a job to do."

"Monty, it's always about the job. I know what you're doing. You don't fool me for a minute. This all started with the accident. You won't give yourself time to think about it. You've got to let it go. It wasn't your fault."

Looking past her, he asked, "Did you bring me a change of clothes?"

"A clean shirt, underwear, and one of your belts. Dr. Baker said the one you were wearing was sliced in two."

"Thanks. I don't know when I'll be home."

"Do you ever?"

CHAPTER 6

Monty got to the sheriff's office at nine and parked his truck beside the sheriff's squad car. It was a clear day with a few scattered clouds. The temperature hung in the low nineties and the humidity was higher than usual for that time of year. Forgetting his wound, he took a deep breath and the pain was so intense it shocked him.

The county jail was in an old rock building that had been erected by the WPA around 1933 and sat on the corner of Scott Avenue and Columbus Street, two blocks from the courthouse. Monty had never understood why some enterprising inmate hadn't figured out how to chip out two or three of the stones and escape. Perhaps it was just too much work. Convicts were mostly a lazy lot, in his opinion, which was what got the majority of them in trouble.

As Monty entered the sheriff's office, Tim was just hanging up the telephone. The older man smiled when he saw Monty and said, "I didn't think they'd keep you down very long. Knives are hell. I'd rather be shot than cut any day. You don't expect them. That's the problem. We're all trained to look for guns but we forget about knives. Damn things are deadly."

"I've learned my lesson. I'll never be caught off guard again. Where's the car?"

"Mark Freeman, the DEA guy, is going over it now."

"Cocaine?"

"And cash. Seems the big deal now is transporting cash across the border. Evidently, the Colombians are cutting back on the amount of cocaine they sell to the Mexicans, so the Mexicans have to buy cocaine in the States to resell."

"That's an interesting twist. When did this start?"

"Early nineties. Seems the DEA guys caught three Suburbans with a million bucks in each gas tank. They seal the money so it's waterproof and slip it in the tanks. They get by the Border Patrol every time. There's so much money being shipped now, they don't even count it anymore. They weigh it. One million dollars' worth of uncirculated hundred-dollar bills weighs 22 pounds, or 24 pounds for circulated ones."

"You know, Tim, I'd never have said this five years ago, but I think they'll have to legalize drugs. There's so damn much money floating around, it's a temptation some people just can't resist. It's ruining Mexico and it's tearing up our law enforcement agencies. I hate the damn drug lords as much as anyone, but if there wasn't a demand for drugs, they couldn't stay in business. Unless the dopers kick the habit or the government legalizes, we'll never win this war."

Tim took a sip of coffee from the mug that always sat filled and hot on the corner of his desk. He frowned and said, "I guess you're right, but think of all the police officers it'd put out of work. The DEA would go back to chasing doctors and nurses who can't keep out of the Demerol bottle. Plus, the politicians and preachers would never let it happen." The sheriff set his cup on the desk and said, "Let's go out back and see what Mark has come up with."

Monty eased out of his chair and followed his friend through the door. "I don't know this guy. Is he clean?"

"I don't know him either. He's new to this section. I think he was over in East Texas for a while, just north of Houston."

"Rumor has it that the largest cartel in the U.S. is run by some renegade DEA agents," Monty said.

"There's so damn much money at stake, it tempts a lot of guys. What's the average DEA guy make a year, thirty, forty thousand bucks? On an average day he'll pick up some punk kid with that much rolled up with a rubber band around it and stuck in his shirt pocket."

They found Mark Freeman in the garage behind the sheriff's office. He was in his mid-thirties, tall, muscular, and with an easy smile. Monty didn't trust him from the moment he laid eyes on the man. Monty never trusted anyone who had a chronic smile on his face. It was one of the reasons he'd never liked President Carter.

Tim introduced the two men and then asked, "What've you found?"

The DEA agent raised the back door of the station wagon and said, "There's a false bottom and no spare. On the other side I've taken off the front fender and it's packed full as well. Damn car's carrying a million bucks' worth of cocaine."

Monty peered into the trunk and said, "Most of the cocaine I've confiscated was in plastic bags. These look like bricks."

"It's some new way they've come up with to throw the dogs off. The bricks are coated with rubber. They've only been doing it a few months," Mark explained.

Tim picked one up and turned it over in his hand. "Where'd this come from?" he asked.

"Chihuahua. I'd guess this shipment is from the Gurya cartel. Most likely came up through Presidio. That's why you picked him up on Highway 90. They control the border from Eagle Pass to El Paso. What made you suspicious? This thing's well camouflaged."

"A hunch. For one thing he was driving too cautiously, like a guy who knows he's had too much to drink."

"Their modus operandi is to blitz the border, so I suspect this was only one of several cars that went through that day. We figure 70 percent of the Colombian cocaine entering the U.S. comes across our border with Mexico. There're probably five active cartels transporting drugs, including Gurya's operation. The Ricardo Lopez family is responsible for the east coast of Mexico, while Tijuana is thought to be under the influence of Juan Sanchez and his brothers. We're not sure who the other two are. Laredo has been experiencing a lot of gang warfare in the last few years. How's the Mexican? I understand you laid him up pretty badly."

The sheriff answered, "I checked with Dr. Baker this morning and he said the fellow was awake and alert, but he had a high fever, probably pneumonia or a lung abscess." He added, "I'll send one of my deputies out to help you inventory this stash."

"That won't be necessary. I can handle it," Mark replied, his smile widening.

"Well, it's in my custody, and I'd feel better having one of my men inventory the thing. No offense, but if I'm responsible, then I take responsibility."

"Suit yourself. If I wanted to lift some dope, I could do it a lot easier and under better circumstances."

Monty asked, "Are you going to interview the Mexican?"

"This afternoon."

"Mind if I talk to him? I have a personal interest in this one."

Mark dropped his smile for a moment and said, "This has nothing to do with wildlife management. And if you think it's personal, that's a damn good reason not to get involved. I do mind if you talk to him. Don't."

Monty was used to offhand slights by the DEA. They seemed to have no qualms about asking for his help in undercover operations, but they never wanted to give him recognition for his service.

"All I want is a chance to ask him a few questions."

"I can't allow it."

Monty left Tim Boswell and Mark Freeman counting cocaine bricks and got back in his pickup. He clamped his jaw and swore under his breath. He was pissed. Who did that jerk think he was talking to? It was a ten-minute drive to the hospital. Monty was determined to interview the Mexican whether Mark Freeman liked it or not.

Pepe Diaz was still in the surgical intensive care unit when Monty inquired at the information desk. He took the elevator to the second floor and went directly to the nurses' station. A ward clerk was typing on the computer when he walked in.

The young woman looked up from her work. "May I help you?"

"I'd like to talk with the nurse who's looking after the Mexican with the collapsed lung," Monty said.

"That's Ann Crawford. She's in his cubicle now, last one on the right."

Monty had an aversion to hospitals. It had nothing to do with the doctors or nurses, because he respected their dedication. It was more personal. His injury in Vietnam had required several weeks of orthopedic traction and two skin grafts. The inactivity and boredom had been devastating for him. He could never walk into a hospital without feeling pain in his leg and a sense of captivity, a closing in on his soul. His most recent hospitalization had only increased his distaste for confinement of any sort.

He was surprised to find that Tim Boswell hadn't assigned a guard outside the Mexican's room. Tim must've figured the man was too sick to escape. There wasn't much risk of a rescue attempt. Mules were considered dispensable by the cartels. Just the same, Monty thought a deputy should be stationed there, and he planned to mention it to the sheriff.

He found Ann Crawford in the Mexican's cubicle emptying the bag of urine attached to the injured man's Foley catheter. She was a young woman of about twenty-five, just out of nursing school, and gave the impression that she was competent and self-assured.

When Monty entered the small glassed-in room, she looked up and asked, "May I help you?"

"My name is Monty Kilpatrick," he said, showing her his identification. "I'd like to ask him a few questions if you think he's up to it."

"He won't talk to us. He just looks at me with a blank expression."

"Do you speak Spanish?" Monty asked.

"I've tried formal Spanish and Tex-Mex. He just looks through me like I'm not here."

"He's conscious, isn't he?"

"No question about that."

"How sick is he?"

"He's got pneumonia and a possible lung abscess. Fever is still really high, 103 when it spikes. Dr. Baker is going to transfer him to the University Hospital in San Antonio or ask a specialist to come out here."

As he and the young woman conversed, Monty casually observed the Mexican out of the corner of his eye. The man appeared to comprehend everything that was being said, yet Monty remembered him saying he didn't understand English.

"If you don't mind, I'd like to talk to him alone."

"Let me empty this bag and I'll get out of your way."

Monty waited until the nurse left the cubicle, then he said, "I know you understand English, so let's cut the crap. The feds are going to talk to you later today and they won't be as nice to you as me. You almost killed me and I almost killed you, so we have a bond of sorts. I realize you're just a mule, you're not one of the bosses of this shit business you're in, but you can save yourself some serious grief by telling me who you work for. I can help you if you cooperate with me."

The Mexican's expression didn't change. Monty had the distinct impression that the man was in considerable pain. His face had a sickly pallor, and his dark eyes appeared dull and listless. Monty suspected the man was much more seriously ill than Nurse Crawford realized. *Don't die on me, you sorry bastard*, he thought. *We've got a score to settle.*

MANUEL ORTEGA HAD BEEN SITTING OUTSIDE Juan Diaz's office for an hour, perspiration dripping from his forehead and armpits. The palms of his hands were so wet, the cigarette he held was limp. He'd been saying Hail Marys and Our Fathers for the past two days, and each time he heard the slightest noise he crossed himself.

The massive wooden door to Juan's office swung open and a wedge of light pierced the darkened hallway where Manuel sat. Juan's housekeeper, Maria, shuffled out with a silver tray in her hands and said, "The captain will see you now."

Manuel snuffed his cigarette between his boot and the wooden floor, and then slid the butt into his pants cuff. He crossed himself once more and said, "Thank you, Maria. How is his mood?"

"Be careful."

Manuel arose as if he were lifting a heavy weight with his shoulders and entered the room, closing the door quietly behind him. Juan stood by the window, looking out at his garden. He had a thin Cuban cigar clenched tightly between his teeth. Without looking at Manuel, he said in an even voice, "Sit in one of the chairs facing the desk."

"Thank you, Captain." Manuel walked slowly, cautiously, toward the center of the large room. He sat in one of the straight-backed chairs and placed his hands in his lap. He desperately wanted a cigarette but would never consider lighting one in Juan Diaz's presence without permission.

Several moments passed in silence. Juan continued to look out at his moonlit flower garden, and Manuel sat whispering Hail Marys. Finally, Juan walked swiftly to his desk. Manuel noticed the captain wore his military-issue Colt .45 automatic pistol in a highly polished leather holster.

Juan sat in his leather chair and snuffed out his cigar in a sterling silver ashtray. Fixing Manuel with a cold stare, he said, "Tell me in your own words everything that's happened since I last saw my brother. Talk slowly and don't leave out anything. If I'm satisfied with your story, you will walk out the door you just entered. If not . . ." Juan raised his eyebrows very slightly, and Manuel sucked air like a drowning man.

Trying to compose himself, Manuel glanced at his boss and asked in a weak voice, "Would the captain permit me a cigarette?"

"Of course. But use the ashtray. Maria doesn't allow ashes on her floor," Juan said as he passed the silver ashtray to the frightened man.

Manuel fumbled in his pocket and took out a pack of unfiltered Camel cigarettes, removed one, and with a palsied hand lit it with a small gold lighter. Inhaling the smoke deeply, he leaned back against the chair and in a slow, determined tone began the story that would seal his fate. He explained in detail everything that had transpired the morning of the delivery.

"I pleaded with Pepe, Captain, not to drive to the border." Manuel stopped here to allow this information to register with Juan before going on.

"I told him you'd be very unhappy if he were to be captured by the gringo police. He refused to listen to me and insisted he drive the car. I'm not sure, Captain, that Pepe was thinking clearly at the time." As he said this, Manuel took a long drag on his cigarette and wondered if the captain had picked up on his suggestion that Pepe had been hungover, possibly still drunk, when he decided to drive across the border.

Relaxing slightly, Manuel said, "We made it through the checkpoint easily. The new method of rubberizing the bricks fooled the dogs completely. We split up as usual and I took Highway 90 out of Alpine as ordered. Pepe drove ahead and I followed about one hundred yards behind." Manuel explained how Pepe had pulled a knife on the policeman and in turn had been stabbed in the chest.

He snuffed out the cigarette and considered pulling out another, but this was the most critical part of his story, so he decided against it. Juan continued to stare dispassionately at him.

"My mind was racing, Captain. I knew our instructions, but your brother was injured. I had no weapon, you forbid them, of course, and the policeman was armed. He'd handcuffed Pepe by this time, even though he himself was bleeding heavily. I made a quick decision, Captain. I thought it was best to make the rendezvous, send word back to you, and then try to find Pepe. I assumed they would take him to the closest hospital."

Manuel wanted a cigarette desperately now and automatically reached into his pocket without thinking to ask permission. His life hung in the balance and would be determined by what he said in the next few minutes. Once the cigarette was lit, he went on. "When the cars were unloaded at the warehouse in east San Antonio, I instructed Jose, my oldest and most trusted driver, to deliver the unfortunate news to you. Instead of returning with the others as usual, I stopped in Uvalde to locate Pepe.

"I found him in their hospital. He was unconscious when I saw him, but he'd only been out of surgery for a few hours. I located an orderly of Mexican descent and gave him $5,000 in cash to keep an eye on Pepe. I told the man I would call him at home for details of your brother's progress. I explained to this man very carefully the importance of your brother and emphasized to him that his life depended upon complete secrecy. When last I checked, two hours ago, Pepe was awake, in great pain, and had a very high fever. As God is my witness, Captain, I tried to do what I thought was best for your brother."

Manuel slumped in his chair with an exhausted sigh. He'd done his best. He'd told the truth. He could do no more. When he'd arrived in east San Antonio, after Pepe had been wounded and captured, he'd been frantic with worry. He'd considered taking the car and cocaine and running away. But his wife and two daughters were still in Mexico, and he'd never see them again. He couldn't return home if he abandoned the captain's brother and stole the captain's money. On the other hand, if he returned, the captain might kill him. In the final analysis he'd done his best to please the captain.

Juan Diaz nodded, shifting his eyes away from Manuel for the first time, and said, "You did well, Manuel. Pepe had his instructions. You're free to go. I must have time to think. Contact the orderly in Uvalde. I want to know everything about this gringo policeman. When you have his name, I'll contact our attorney in Dallas. Please stay close. I may need you on short notice."

Manuel smiled, his two gold-capped incisors glistening in the light of the desk lamp. He could have kissed the captain's feet, he was so happy. Instead, he arose from his chair with dignity, a vindicated man, and said sincerely, "I am always at your service, Captain. I'll be staying at my sister's house and will give Maria her phone number should you need me."

He turned and walked slowly to the door, like a bullfighter walking away unafraid from an angry and dangerous bull. He was halfway to the door when Juan said sharply, "Manuel!"

Manuel's heart skipped a beat. Without looking back he said, "Yes, Captain."

"You will be rewarded handsomely for your bravery."

"Thank you, Captain. If you need me just pick up the telephone."

Juan walked back to the open window as Manuel gently closed the door. He was exhausted, for he hadn't slept since learning of his brother's arrest and injury. He was furious with his brother, yet worried sick about him. Juan knew the American doctors and their hospitals were excellent. Pepe was in good hands, but if he survived, he could spend the rest of his life in a gringo jail. He could, under certain circumstances, jeopardize the entire Gurya operation.

There was a soft knock on Juan's door and Maria stuck her head into the room. "Vic is here to see you, Señor Diaz."

She stepped back and a tall, thin American entered the room. He went directly to one of the chairs in front of Juan's desk and took a seat. Casually, he removed a cigarette from a silver case and lit it with a gold lighter. Blowing smoke out of the side of his mouth, he fixed on Juan with his dark, close-set eyes.

"The one known as Bobby has been dealt with as you wished. I've located the second one, Jimmy Rhea Moffitt, in the town of Castroville near San Antonio. He's living with a woman who works in a convenience store. As per our agreement, I'm here for the first $10,000. As soon as I dispatch Jimmy Rhea, I'll be back for the second payment."

Vic tensed as Juan opened the middle drawer of his desk. Smiling, Juan removed a stack of hundred-dollar bills held together with a large rubber band and tossed it to the hit man, who caught it with his left hand.

Juan laughed. "Had I wanted to renege on our agreement, Vic, I'd simply have shot you."

CHAPTER 7

Pepe Diaz's chest hurt each time he took a breath. He'd been drifting in and out of consciousness for two days. Most of the time he didn't know where he was and could barely remember what had happened to him. The visit from the gringo policeman had caused a rush of recollection concerning the incident on Highway 90.

Each time he tried to move or get out of the hospital bed he realized he was tethered by a number of tubes, none of which he understood. He had one coming out of his penis, one emerging from his chest wall, and one stuck in his right arm. He was surprised that there was no policeman in his room, but then it dawned on him that he couldn't escape if he wanted to. From time to time he had a chill that caused his teeth to chatter, and then he lapsed into an unconscious state for an hour or two.

He hadn't said a word to anyone. The nurse who took care of him during the day had tried to talk to him in Spanish, but he hadn't responded because he was afraid he would betray himself or his brother. The visit from the policeman had shocked him, for he thought he'd killed the man. He was baffled by how he had ended up in the hospital. He vaguely recalled seeing his knife buried in his chest, but he had no idea how it got there.

There was a noise at his door and when he looked in that direction, a man in a starched white uniform walked into the room. At Pepe's bed, the man said, "Señor Diaz, my name is Carlos. Manuel, who works for your brother, asked me to keep an eye on you. I came in two days ago, but I was not sure you would remember. Off and on you have been out of your head."

"Is there word from my brother?"

"I report to him every day by fax. He's most concerned about you. I must go now, but I wanted you to know you have a friend here. I'll try to see you at least once a day. Hasta la vista."

"Hasta mañana, amigo. Gracias."

Pepe knew that his brother must be worried about him and angry. Pepe'd done a foolish thing, driving across the border. He might pay for his folly with his life. Even if he survived, he faced the possibility of years in a Yankee prison.

Until he was in better physical condition there was no hope of escape, and if he did survive, the gringos would assign a policeman immediately. No, his options were very limited. His only hope lay in his brother. Juan was a smart man. Somehow he'd get Pepe out of this predicament.

JUAN HAD BEEN WORKING ON A plan for the past thirty-six hours. Dr. Gomez had responded immediately to Juan's message and was admitted to the hacienda by Maria at 11:00 p.m. on the third day of Pepe's confinement. Juan stood by his garden window, smoking a Cuban cigar, as Maria escorted Dr. Gomez into his office.

"Thank you for coming, Roberto. I apologize for the lateness of the hour. Please express my regrets to your lovely wife. I wouldn't impose upon you if it were not a matter of some urgency."

"What's the problem?"

"My brother, Pepe, lies near death in a hospital on the other side of the border. In a town known as Uvalde."

"What happened to him?"

"Sit down, and I'll explain." Juan walked to his desk and sat in his leather chair.

"Pepe had a little trouble across the border and is in the custody of the police. He's suffered a rather severe knife wound. The doctors took him to surgery and stopped the bleeding. I have a Mexican orderly observing everything that is going on. Pepe evidently has a high fever and may have a lung abscess. I need to extract him from that hospital and, at the same time, take care of his medical needs. The extraction part I can take care of. The other is why I need your help."

Roberto sat quietly, absorbing everything his friend said. How did Juan think he could get his sick brother out of that hospital? He swallowed hard and said, "If Pepe is that sick, Juan, perhaps he is in the best place. The American hospitals and doctors are excellent. He couldn't be in better hands. How would you get him back?"

Juan had no choice. He had to get his brother across the border before Emilio Gurya got wind of the fiasco. His boss would not be happy about the breach of security Pepe posed.

"Getting him back is not the problem, Roberto. My main concern is for his life."

Juan took a thin cigar out of a silver box and lit it with his gold lighter. Blowing a thin blue smoke ring, he leaned back in his leather chair and said, "Under cover of darkness I plan to fly across the border to the hospital. I'll take a small contingent of well-armed men, and we'll find Pepe, place him in my helicopter, and bring him here to my hacienda."

Juan opened the center drawer of his massive desk, pulled out a piece of paper, and handed it to the doctor. "This was faxed to Manuel from the orderly, just an hour ago. It's a hand-drawn but detailed floor plan of the hospital showing exactly where Pepe is being held. For some reason known only to the U.S. authorities, he's not under armed guard. I believe we can find him quickly."

"But you're talking of invading the United States! It's incredible to even think of such a thing," said Roberto.

"That's not your concern, Roberto. I want you to go with us to look after Pepe and to take care of his medical problems."

Roberto felt as if someone had kicked him in the stomach. Once, when he had been on military maneuvers in the mountains around Guadalajara, the ambulance he was riding in lost its brakes. He'd been so frightened he'd emptied his bladder into his khaki pants. In all likelihood, he would not survive the mission Juan described. *Why did I become involved with these people in the first place?* He thought, *I can't turn down Juan Diaz, not if I want to live. I am screwed one way or the other.*

His mouth was so dry, Roberto wasn't sure he could speak. Swallowing hard, he said, "If Pepe has a high fever and a lung abscess, I'm not sure he can be moved safely. The purulent material may have to be drained. He'll need a CT of the lung and many things we do not have available in our hospital and certainly not here at your hacienda. I'm not sure this can be done safely, Juan."

Juan could feel fear radiating from the man across from him. It disgusted him and made him angry. Placing his elbows on the desk, he said in an even voice, "You'll have everything you need to look after my brother. Once we're across the border, if Pepe needs something you're not capable of, we'll put him in a Learjet and take him to Mexico City. Do I make myself clear?"

There was no question of clarity. Roberto understood quite well what Juan was telling him. Either he went with them on their raid across the border, or his wife and daughters would never see him again. He sighed and said, "How much time do I have to get my supplies together?"

Juan smiled. He was used to having men submit to his will. He hadn't wanted to threaten his friend, but the man's cowardice made it necessary.

He extinguished his cigar in the silver tray, glanced at his watch, and said, "We'll lift off at 1800 hours tomorrow, so you have plenty of time to get together whatever you need."

Roberto's mind was racing. Pepe probably had an IV and a chest tube, but what if he was on a respirator as well? "Do you think it would be possible to talk to the orderly?" he asked. "He could tell if Pepe is connected to a chest tube, a respirator, and things like that."

"Manuel will have a call at 0800 hours tomorrow. You can talk to the man then."

"How much can I bring and how should I pack it?"

"Take only what you absolutely need. I'll have one of my men supply you with some military containers."

Roberto relaxed. Perhaps with a small amount of luck, he could pull it off. "If you don't need me further, Juan, I'll try to get a good night's sleep. I want to be as fresh as possible to take care of Pepe."

"Tell your wife you have to go out of town for a few hours. A wealthy man in Monterrey wishes a consultation from you. Bring all your supplies here by 1700 hours at the latest. Wear your military fatigues once you've left your hospital. You'll be supplied a sidearm when we're under way."

Roberto extended his hand and said, "I'm happy to be of service to you, my friend, and rest assured I'll do everything in my power to bring your brother back alive."

Juan said, "I know you will. 1700 hours. Don't be late."

Juan spent the next three hours perfecting every detail of his clandestine raid. When he finally fell asleep in the king-sized bed in the adjacent bedroom, he didn't move a muscle until nine o'clock the following morning. He awakened relaxed and ready for his journey. After one of Maria's famous breakfasts of ham, scrambled eggs with onions, salsa, and tortillas, he went for a walk in his garden to relax his mind.

JUAN HAD AN AIRPLANE MECHANIC'S LICENSE as well as his pilot's license. He spent the afternoon changing the oil in the transmission of the helicopter and fueling it. He'd recently given the machine its scheduled one-hundred-hour service, so he knew everything was in excellent condition.

He'd obtained the surplus Huey helicopter through his military contacts and modified it to suit his needs. Instead of the self-sealing fuel tank, he'd installed two larger ones on either side of the ship to give it a longer range. The pilot and copilot's seats were covered in soft Italian leather like his Jaguar convertible, and the instrument panel was outfitted with the very latest communication and navigational equipment that money could buy. The helicopter's registration number could be changed or taken off completely, depending upon the situation.

The black helicopter was seldom armed. However, Juan never went anywhere without his Colt, and he always had bodyguards with him. For this mission he'd decided on full armament. This meant M-60 machine guns were mounted in the doorway on each side of the helicopter as the U.S. Army had done in Vietnam. In addition, twin M-60 machine guns that were controlled by the pilot had been attached outboard of each door. Juan could point the helicopter at a target and discharge a series of standard 7.6 mm NATO rounds at seven hundred per minute. Juan also carried two shoulder-fired rocket-propelled grenades known as RPGs. These weapons could take out an armored car.

Three men were going with him besides the doctor, all battle-hardened soldiers who'd fought other cartels with him for the past five years. Emilio Gurya hadn't risen to the top of the Chihuahua cartel by being an altar boy or having angelic employees.

Each man had a special talent, making him essential to Juan's plan. Jose Ibanez, while small in stature, was a consummate kick-boxer who could kill a man quickly and quietly without the aid of a weapon. He was in his late twenties, had no family, and had been raised as an orphan by Jesuit priests at the monastery in the west coast village of Los Mochis. He came to Juan Diaz's attention when he killed one of Juan's top bodyguards in a saloon brawl. The captain was so impressed with the young fighter that he had hired him on the spot.

Ricardo Cueva was, for a Mexican, a bull of a man. Five feet eight inches tall, he weighed in at a little over 225 pounds. He had no neck and his biceps measured twenty inches in diameter when flexed. His specialty was brute force. He could lift a small car off its wheels and turn it over. A quiet man, he'd been married to the same woman for more than twenty years and had no children. Before coming to work for Juan Diaz, he'd toiled as a day laborer in a concrete block factory in Monterrey.

Julio Goya, better known as Julio the Romeo, was a ladies' man. When he wasn't enforcing strict discipline among the members of the cartel for his boss, he was changing bed partners like musical chairs. A tall, chisel-faced descendant of the Mayans, he exhibited the characteristic prominent nose that curves back into a sloping forehead. He was by no means handsome. His success with women stemmed from his vast knowledge of South American literature. He could quote Jorge Guillén and Gabriel García Márquez and he had the ability to compose short poems of a romantic nature incorporating a specific lady's name. His value to Juan Diaz lay in his uncanny grasp of things mechanical. An ordnance expert, he could take apart and reassemble all known semiautomatic pistols, automatic assault rifles, and machine guns. He understood the principles of physics and chemistry and could make an explosive device from most household products found in the average kitchen. Dynamite and plastic explosives were his area of greatest expertise. He was also a helicopter pilot.

Roberto Gomez arrived at the hacienda heliport promptly at 1700 hours, as he'd been instructed. Dressed in fatigues, he carried two aluminum suitcases filled with medical supplies. They contained a full surgical kit for minor surgery, a small oxygen bottle, endotracheal tubes, a tracheotomy set, antibiotics, painkillers, and intravenous solutions. A third container, made of plastic, held a small battery-operated respirator. He parked his Mustang convertible and took the suitcases out of the backseat.

As Roberto approached the helicopter, Juan was performing a preflight check, standing on top of the machine, looking at the hub of the rotor blades. Roberto shaded his eyes against the low-lying sun and yelled at his friend, "Be sure the Jesus nut is on tight, Juan. You know I'm afraid of these damn choppers."

Juan laughed and said, "I never take off without checking the hub assembly. You have nothing to worry about." The truth of the matter was that Juan Diaz was a fanatic when it came to the maintenance of his helicopter. The Jesus nut held the entire rotor assembly in place. Should a saboteur want to disable or kill Juan Diaz, all he'd have to do would be to loosen it.

Julio was loading the machine guns as Roberto lifted the medical supplies into the bay of the helicopter. He extended his hand to help the doctor climb aboard and said, "It's always good to have a doctor on a mission. Welcome, my friend."

Roberto knew Julio because he'd treated him for a severe case of gonorrhea two years previously. It seemed that one of Julio's girlfriends had been somewhat less than honest about her past. The infection turned out to be penicillin resistant, leading Roberto to the conclusion that the young woman had been a professional.

At 1745 hours Juan assembled his team to give them their final instructions. His ever-present cigar was clenched unlit between his teeth as he spoke. He'd laid a road map of Texas and one of Mexico on the ground in front of them. He preferred the maps to aeronautical charts because he'd be flying a mere one hundred feet above ground level, or AGL. If necessary, he could follow road signs to Uvalde.

He cleared his throat and said, "We lift off at 1800 hours. I'll fly and Julio will act as copilot. Jose and Ricardo will man the door guns and you, Roberto, will act as a lookout.

"Our flight plan will take us northeast to the border town of Piedras Negras across from Eagle Pass, Texas. Just south of town we have a staging warehouse where Jet A fuel is stored. Once refueled we'll proceed north along our side of the border until we are approximately halfway between Piedras Negras and Ciudad Acuña, at which point we'll cross the Rio Grande and enter Maverick County, Texas. Using our GPS, we'll fly directly to the town of Uvalde. That should put us at the hospital heliport at 2130. Are there any questions?"

Roberto raised his hand and asked, "What happens when we touch down?"

Juan took the gold lighter out of his pocket and lit his cigar even though he'd already chewed it down to a stub. Inhaling deeply, he said, "The plan is quite simple. The orderly tells us that the heliport is adjacent to the emergency room of the hospital. It's used by the University of Texas medical evacuation helicopter out of San Antonio. We're all in fatigues, so when we land, most will assume we are a U.S. Army helicopter delivering or picking up a patient.

"Julio will remain with the ship, keeping the rotors at takeoff rpm. Jose, Ricardo, you, and I will enter the hospital and proceed directly to the surgical intensive care unit as depicted on our floor plan. There's no policeman guarding Pepe. You will examine Pepe and determine how best to move him. Then Ricardo will carry him back to the helicopter. You'll deal with the various tubes that are necessary for Pepe's safety. Jose and I'll make sure no one interferes with our mission. It's not my intention to inflict casualties. In fact, I wish to avoid them.

"Our main goal is to extract Pepe safely. Emilio and I will be carrying silenced MAC-10s in case we have to blast our way out. I have a

Colt .45 for you because I know you're familiar with this weapon. But firepower is to be used only in the case of an emergency.

"Once Pepe is aboard the helicopter and you assure me he's okay, I'll fly us back across the border retracing our previous route. Any more questions?"

Again, Roberto raised his hand and asked, "Isn't there a radar blimp somewhere on the border near Eagle Pass?"

"Yes, a GE aerostat blimp is tethered at ten to fifteen thousand feet. I've arranged for it to be temporarily inactive during both of our passages across the Rio Grande."

It all sounded too simple to Roberto. Perspiration cascaded down his sides, and he felt queasy.

Juan's three henchmen, on the other hand, were excited about the mission. Since the Gurya cartel had taken over the Chihuahua trafficking operation five years previously, there'd been little action requiring their specialized skills. They'd been reduced to accepting minor and unimportant jobs for the cartel. This mission was a dream come true. Not only would there be excitement and danger, but they'd be of service to a man they respected and admired. To save the life of the captain's brother would bring them great honor among their peers.

Roberto said, "I assume you have a plan if we're followed by the police or military."

Juan smiled. "It would be a fight they wouldn't soon forget. It is less than 100 miles to the border. Even with a quick response team, the chances of them scrambling anything into the air in time to stop us are slim. We'll deal with whatever comes up. If there're no more questions, it's time to go."

Juan dropped his cigar to the ground, rubbed it into the dirt with the heel of his boot, and picked up the two maps. The four men took their places, and Juan slipped into the pilot's seat. Methodically, he went through a written pre-ignition checklist and then fired the twin jet turbine engines. Increasing the throttle slowly, he brought the rotor blades to takeoff speed and set the rpm governor on the collective as he pulled up on it. The ship went to a hover about three feet off the ground. He checked all engine instruments to make sure they were in the green and that his GPS and compass were accurate. He lowered the nose of the helicopter and started his takeoff run, quickly passing out of ground effect into transitional lift. He climbed to an altitude of five hundred feet AGL and put the nose of the ship on a course that would take him to Piedras Negras.

CHAPTER 8

Monty had been promising to take Martha Jo to the movies in Uvalde for two months. Of all the towns surrounding Utopia, Uvalde was the only one that had a movie theater. It was a small multiplex with three screens on Highway 90 on the east side of town.

"Are you sure you don't want me to drive? Aren't you still pretty sore?" Martha Jo asked, as Monty slipped behind the wheel.

"No, I'm fine," he said, handing her the small nylon bag containing his portable police radio and his Glock. "Put that on the floor on your side, will you?"

"I'm really worried about Cindy Moffitt," Martha Jo said. "I went by to see her this afternoon because she wasn't at the Circle M. You were right. That man is her ex-husband. He raped and beat her up pretty badly. I tried to get her to swear out a warrant, but she's scared to death and won't do it. I don't believe she'd have told me about him if I hadn't seen what kind of shape she's in."

Monty frowned. "He raped her?"

"That's what she said."

"I'll talk to her tomorrow."

"She'll probably deny the whole thing."

"We'll see." Monty shook his head. "Why do women put up with that stuff?"

"People do crazy things. Love, fear, insecurity, poor self-image. Lots of reasons."

Martha Jo pulled the shoulder strap of her seat belt under her right arm, saying, "Don't fuss at me. I can't stand having that strap across my chest. I feel like I'm in a straightjacket."

"If you see we're going to have a head-on collision, please put it back where it belongs."

Both Monty and Martha Jo rode in silence for several miles. On the other side of Sabinal, Monty glanced at his wife and said, "What movie are we going to?"

"I haven't even looked. Let's just go and see if there's anything we'd like to see."

They got to the theater at seven o'clock and found their choices were *Shiloh*, *Austin Powers: International Man of Mystery*, and *Breakdown*. They chose *Austin Powers* because Monty wanted to see something light. The events of the last couple of days had deeply disturbed him.

The movie ended about nine fifteen. As Monty turned the key in the ignition, Martha Jo asked, "Do you want to go by the hospital and talk to the Mexican? He might be more receptive tonight."

Monty laughed. "There you go, reading my mind again."

CROSSING THE BORDER HAD BEEN EASY, and the GPS guided Juan directly to the Uvalde Memorial Hospital. He identified the heliport and checked the windsock. It indicated a strong wind from the southeast. He set up the approach and slowed the forward speed of the helicopter, then lowered the collective and started his descent. Julio followed each movement lightly on the dual controls.

Juan brought the ship to a hover above the pad and then set the helicopter on its skids. He checked his watch and saw that it was 2115 hours. They'd made good time without incident. Juan motioned for Julio to take the controls and went to collect his men.

Ricardo and Jose were already on the ground, and Roberto was unlashing the smallest of the suitcases containing the medical supplies. Juan led the way, followed by Jose, Roberto, and Ricardo. Juan had memorized the floor plan of the hospital and was impressed by the accuracy of the orderly's drawing. Perhaps there was a place for such a man in the Gurya operation. They entered the hospital through the emergency room and were not challenged. Their weapons were hidden and the fatigues confused the nurses.

It took only three minutes to traverse the emergency room and enter the main floor of the hospital. They bypassed the elevators and ran up the stairs two at a time. On the second floor, Juan guided them to the surgical intensive care unit and Pepe's cubicle. The injured man was asleep, but when Juan touched his shoulder, he awoke with a startled expression.

"God in heaven," he said in a weak voice. "Pepe's prayers have been answered."

"Lay still, brother. Dr. Gomez is going to examine you."

Roberto placed a stethoscope on Pepe's chest. He hoped the collapsed lung had inflated, and when he was satisfied that it had, he checked Pepe's heart rate. Pepe felt warm to the touch. The doctor clamped the chest tube with a hemostat and took out the intravenous line along with the urinary catheter. They could be restarted in the helicopter. The fewer tubes and plastic bags he had to carry, the better.

Pepe was a very sick man, but Roberto believed he'd survive the trip home. The doctor motioned for Ricardo to pick up the injured man. Softly, he said to Juan, "I think he can make it." Jose had been standing guard at the door for the few minutes it took Roberto to make his decision.

Jose, always cool under pressure, didn't flinch when Ethel Navarro, the night charge nurse, turned the corner with a tray of medication. Ethel was a matronly Mexican woman in her mid-fifties who'd been an RN for more than thirty years. She'd seen her share of sick and injured men and wasn't intimidated by blood and gore. She had a sixth sense of impending danger, and when her eyes focused on Jose, she shuddered. Something bad was about to happen. She could feel it. She was also a realist. Nothing she did would make a difference.

Ethel stopped, turned around, and went back to the nurses' station where she hid behind the counter and dialed the hospital security office. The ward clerk returned from the bathroom at that minute, and Ethel motioned for her to get down. She scanned the unit for the nurse's aide, but didn't see her.

Ricardo lifted Pepe, who'd lost weight, as if he were a baby. Again, Juan led the way, followed by Jose, Ricardo, and Pepe. Roberto carried the suitcase in one hand and the chest tube bottle in the other.

At the bottom of the stairs, just as they started down the hallway toward the emergency room, Bob Mosley, a hospital security guard, pulled his 9 mm Beretta out of its holster and shouted, "Stop or I'll shoot!"

Juan spun his silenced MAC-10 out from under his fatigue jacket with a lightning-smooth motion and fired a short burst. The bullets hit their mark dead-on, throwing the guard backward into the wall. Reflexively, his index finger pulled off two or three 9 mm rounds as his body slumped to the floor.

The Mexicans didn't break stride. They entered the emergency room through which they'd come only minutes earlier. Nurses were knocked aside by Juan and Emilio as they sped through the congested hallway. Dr. Baker was walking out of an examining room as the procession passed.

"What the hell's going on?" he shouted before Jose hit him in the abdomen with the butt of his gun, knocking the wind out of him.

The Mexicans cleared the emergency room without further incident and were almost to the door of the helicopter when Monty Kilpatrick came around the corner of the hospital from the visitors' parking lot.

The shots from the security guard's Beretta had alerted him to the fact that something illegal was going down. He'd grabbed his Glock out of the nylon satchel and ran toward the sound of the rotor blades. When he turned the corner of the hospital and saw Juan and his men, he knew what was going on. The bastards had invaded the United States and had most likely killed a security guard. He wondered how many other casualties they might have left behind.

Monty dropped to one knee and, holding his semiautomatic pistol with both hands, aimed for the lead man. He was able to get off one round that hit the fuselage of the helicopter a mere two inches from Juan's head. The captain spun toward the sound of the discharge and released a burst in Monty's general direction. The game warden heard the slugs embedding themselves into the bricks of the hospital wall behind him.

Monty lay flat on the ground to lessen his silhouette. Once again he took a bead on the doorway of the helicopter and fired twice in rapid succession. The first slug again hit the fuselage, but the second struck Ricardo in the right shoulder, causing him to drop Pepe to the ground.

Infuriated, Juan sprayed the area where Monty lay with five or six bursts from his MAC-10. Dirt flew up all around Monty, who threw his arms over his head. Juan and Roberto lifted Pepe into the cabin of the helicopter and Ricardo climbed in after them. Then Jose climbed aboard and grabbed the trigger of the starboard M-60. Juan rushed to the cockpit and slid into the left-hand seat. Julio already had the ship in a hover by that time. When Juan took the controls, all he had to do was drop the nose and start his forward run.

Monty stood and aimed for the tail rotor, firing off five shots. All missed their mark. At the same moment, Jose sprayed the area with the M-60 machine gun. Huge divots of grass and dirt flew up all around Monty, but by good luck the bullets failed to hit him.

Within seconds the Huey was well out of range of his Glock, so he ran back to the parking lot to let Martha Jo know he was okay and to get his handheld radio. She handed it to him when he swung open the driver's door.

"My God, what was that? Are you all right?"

"Bad guys," he said, grabbing the radio out of her hand. He turned to the Uvalde sheriff's frequency and keyed the microphone. "Mayday! Mayday! This is Monty Kilpatrick. I need an emergency patch to the San Antonio DEA!"

"You got it. Go ahead," the Uvalde dispatcher said.

The local police had made previous arrangements with the San Antonio DEA office to make emergency contact. Drug-related crimes had become so commonplace and increasingly violent that there was often a need for immediate response by the federal agency. The DEA, in turn, had agreements with the U.S. Army at Fort Sam Houston for a rapid-response strike force should a military-type assault be made across the United States border by drug traffickers. Apache helicopters were usually based at Fort Hood in Killeen, Texas, but a small contingency had been assigned to Fort Sam Houston for special duty.

"Go ahead, Kilpatrick. What's up?" said the DEA agent on the emergency line.

"There's a Huey loaded to the teeth with armaments and carrying some Mexican nationals back across the border. I think they got into a firefight with a guard at the Uvalde hospital, and they're rescuing a wounded drug suspect. Have you got anything to intercept them with?"

"How's an army Apache strike you?"

"How long will it take to scramble it?"

"Five minutes. Any idea where they crossed the border?"

"I'd guess somewhere between Eagle Pass and Del Rio."

"Cheeky bastards, invading the US of A."

"Keep me posted, will you?"

JUAN WAS AGAIN AT AN ALTITUDE of one hundred feet AGL and therefore burning fuel at a greater rate than he would have at a higher altitude. He was pushing the cruise envelope to the max. The manifold pressure was almost to the redline on both engines. About 30 miles south of Uvalde, just as he was beginning to relax, Juan noticed the fuel gauge for the starboard tank.

"Mother of God," he murmured under his breath. They'd taken a hit in the starboard tank.

He turned the fuel selector to the starboard tank to use all the Jet A in that one so he could save the fuel in the port tank for the final run to the border. His plan was to watch the gauge closely and, just as the tank was about to run dry, switch back to the port supply. Restarting the engines at one hundred feet above ground was a maximum risk, but he felt he had to take it. He needed every drop of Jet A he could squeeze out of the starboard tank. Juan didn't want to make a forced landing on the wrong side of the border.

MONTY AND MARTHA JO REACHED THE sheriff's office at just about the time the Apache from Fort Sam Houston was becoming airborne. Monty wanted to follow what was going on, and the best place to do that was in Boswell's radio room.

The Apache was piloted by Aviation Warrant Officer John Delozier. AWO Sebastian Fisher, the gunner, sat in front and below him. Delozier took their ship to an altitude of one thousand feet AGL and set a course of 260 degrees out of San Antonio, heading in the general direction of the border south of Uvalde.

They'd started with a seventy-mile disadvantage, but at 200 miles per hour there was a good chance they could intercept the renegade Huey just before it crossed the Rio Grande. Both Delozier and Fisher were battle-hardened soldiers who had seen duty in Desert Storm. If they did catch the intruder, it wouldn't be a fair fight. The Apache was faster, more maneuverable, and very heavily armed.

BEADS OF PERSPIRATION HAD POPPED OUT on Juan's forehead like small blisters. He glanced over his shoulder and saw Roberto starting an IV on his brother. Ricardo, whose wound was not serious, manned the port gun, and Jose, the starboard. If the fuel held out, they might make it.

According to the GPS they were only 15 statute miles from their entry point on the Rio Grande when Juan's radio speaker came to life. He kept one of his radios on the international emergency frequency of 121.5 MHz at all times. He'd meant to turn it off for this mission, but had forgotten to.

The voice on the speaker said in English, "Huey helicopter on a 260-degree heading, this is Warrant Officer John Delozier, U.S. Army. I'm above and behind you in a heavily armed Apache. Turn to a heading of 060 and wait for further instructions."

In the radio room, Monty ran to the scanner so he could hear. Turning to the deputy, he said, "Dammit, I wish we could hear what was being said on their intercom. There's no way in hell that Mexican's going to turn around. I sure hope Delozier knows what he's doing. Why doesn't he hit the bastard with a rocket?"

Delozier had no way of knowing if the Huey had radios, let alone whether the pilot had one tuned to the 121.5 MHz frequency. His only alternatives were to approach the Huey from above and physically force it to the ground or to destroy it with a rocket. The other helicopter was reported to be heavily armed, but he couldn't conceive it was any match for his 30 mm machine gun or 70 mm ballistic rockets. He told his gunner to arm the auto-track switch and waited for some response from the Huey.

"How did that bastard find us?" Juan asked Julio, disbelief in his voice. They were running with no lights, and the ship was black with no insignia.

"Most likely he has powerful radar or a heat-sensitive scanner," Julio said.

Juan looked at the starboard fuel gauge and saw that the Jet A was dangerously low. For safety's sake he switched to the port supply. No time to run out of fuel in the middle of a dogfight. He knew he was terribly outgunned, and he had no idea how many Apaches were out there or might be on the way.

He still had a few things in his favor. The army pilot had no idea how he was armed. Plus, the other pilot didn't know whether Juan had heard his instructions on the radio. That meant the U.S. Army man had two choices: he could fire at Juan with a rocket, or he could try to force him physically to the ground. What the man really wanted was for Juan to make a 180-degree turn and head back to San Antonio. There was no chance in hell he'd do that. No gringo jail for Juan Diaz. He would escape or he would die with honor.

The Mexican could feel adrenaline pumping into his bloodstream. His mind was racing and, like a mainframe computer, sorted through possible solutions. The only logical conclusion was to set up a trap for the Apache.

A cloud cover worked in their favor. Had there been a full moon they would have been more exposed. Now, Juan wanted desperately to see the ground. His ploy was to pretend he didn't know the Apache was above him. He decided to land in an area that might look as though he was planning a rendezvous. If the army pilot thought he could catch Juan unaware on the ground, then perhaps he would come alongside to force a surrender.

Juan saw a light ahead in a parking lot adjacent to a narrow paved road. He lowered the collective and slowed the Huey's forward motion to approach speed. At his low altitude he'd touch down very quickly. He was worried about telephone and power lines, but he had no choice but to land in the parking area. As they got closer he saw that there was a large Texaco sign on a pole, indicating some type of gasoline station and convenience store.

He brought the helicopter to a hover and lowered it gently to the ground. Keeping the rotor blades at takeoff rpm, he motioned for Jose and Ricardo to arm the RPGs and waited patiently for the Apache to take his bait.

Deputy Sheriff Gordon Petty had just left the parking lot of the Texaco station as Juan's helicopter came to a hover. Recognizing the classic *thump, thump* of the Huey, he pulled his state truck to the side of the road on a slight rise about a quarter of a mile from the market, got out, and trained his binoculars on the helicopter.

Warrant Officer Delozier observed every move of Juan's helicopter. It appeared that the Huey was going to land. The pilot must not have heard his message and might not even realize he was under surveillance. He decided to bring his ship to a hover out of ground effect so he could ascertain what the Mexican was going to do. Since he was in the air, he had the advantage over the Huey. Perhaps they planned to make contact with someone on the ground.

"What are they doing?" Fisher asked.

"I'm not sure. Maybe he doesn't know we're up here. I'm going to hold back for a few minutes and then go down and signal for them to surrender."

"I'd be damn careful. It could be a trap."

"We've got them outgunned and I don't see any activity on the ground."

"They haven't shut down their engines. The rotors are still going full speed."

"They could be waiting to pick someone up and want to be able to get off the ground quickly."

Delozier was arguing with himself, trying to make a decision. Should he or shouldn't he hit them with a rocket? This was the helicopter they'd been sent to find. It was unmarked and flying without navigational lights. He had every right to take the ship out. It would be easy enough, but something kept eating at him. They were most likely not low-level drug people. There was a chance there might be some big fish on the chopper. With the exception of Manuel Noriega, the Panamanian dictator, the United States had seldom bagged the top associates of any of the cartels. It sure would be nice to turn those guys over to the DEA and FBI in one piece.

Military men are trained to evaluate situations and make decisions. There's no place for indecisiveness in a combat condition. Delozier decided to try for a capture rather than a kill.

He pressed the microphone switch on his cyclic control and asked Fisher, "Do you have your chin gun armed and on servo?"

"Yes."

"And the rockets?"

"Yes."

"I'm going to drop down to a hover in front of the Huey and hand-signal for them to shut off their engines. If anyone exits the ship, hit him with the chin gun."

"You got it, Captain."

Juan had briefed Jose and Ricardo with a number of possible combat situations in which they might find themselves. They'd worked out a set of hand signals that would allow them to cover several possible scenarios. He felt the RPGs were his best chance for defense. If he could get the Apache close enough, he felt quite sure either Jose or Ricardo could score a direct hit. The main problem had to do with the pilot of the Apache. He could evaporate the Huey if he chose to. Juan's hope was that the pilot would try to capture them on the ground.

When Juan saw the helicopter swoop down in front of him, he motioned for Jose and Ricardo to swing out each door on harnesses they'd rigged for just such an event. As the Apache settled into a hover, both grenades were launched simultaneously and hit their mark. The helicopter exploded in a fireball, bits and pieces flying in 360 degrees. A large part of the rotor slammed into the gasoline pumps of the Texaco station, igniting them. Next, the gasoline storage tanks erupted.

Gordon Petty was thrown back against his truck by the blast. Picking himself up, he whispered under his breath, "Jesus Christ."

Juan had a difficult time keeping the Huey under control with all the turbulence caused by the multiple explosions. The second he saw the Apache explode, he yanked hard on the collective and pulled his cyclic control back and to the left. His helicopter spun around and was airborne once again, heading away from the inferno below.

He circled around, set his course to 240 degrees, and ran for the border. The sky behind him was engulfed in flames, and repeated explosions sounded as other flammable solutions were set on fire. Juan Diaz had friends all along the Mexican side of the border. Most of the army units and practically all the police were beholden to him. Once he made it to the other side of the Rio Grande he'd be safe.

Petty jumped in his truck and reached for his microphone as bits and pieces of burning debris dropped around him. He keyed the Uvalde sheriff's office and said in a panic-stricken voice, "Come in, Uvalde! This is Officer Petty."

Monty rushed to the dispatcher's desk and picked up the microphone. "That you, Gordon? This is Monty Kilpatrick. What's up?"

"I just saw a helicopter blown to smithereens."

"Where are you?"

"On FM 1908. There's a Texaco station and convenience store about a quarter of a mile from where I'm standing. Damn pumps just exploded."

"Which helicopter?"

"What?"

"Which helicopter got blown up? There were two."

"It looked like an Apache. The other one was a Huey. It just took off and headed south."

"You're sure it was the Apache that got hit?"

"I'm sure."

"Are you okay?'

"Yeah. What are you doing at the sheriff's office?"

"I'll explain later. Call the fire department."

Monty handed the microphone to the dispatcher, shaking his head in disbelief. Gordon must be mistaken. How had the bastard done that? The Apache had him outgunned a hundred to one. How much firepower did the Huey have? And for God's sake, where did he get it?

CHAPTER 9

J uan's palms were so wet he had difficulty managing the collective and cyclic controls. Perspiration dripped from his forehead and his shirt was soaked. The starboard tank was empty, the port tank was dangerously low, and they were several miles from Piedras Negras. Julio had never seen his boss appear so nervous. Perhaps it was because his brother's life hung in the balance. Truth be told, Julio was a bit nervous himself.

The GPS showed them passing over the Rio Grande, but it was so dark they couldn't see the river. Ricardo's wound, while not life threatening, nonetheless caused him great pain and continued to ooze blood. Roberto, completely occupied with Pepe, had no time to attend to him. Pepe was delirious because his fever had spiked to 105 degrees. At one point, Pepe tried to sit up on the stretcher and in doing so lost his balance and fell to the floor, almost rolling out the open door. Roberto caught him by his hospital gown just as he was about to free-fall a hundred feet to his death.

The doctor's hands shook as he and Ricardo rolled Pepe back on the stretcher. His hands, like Juan's, were wet with perspiration and his mouth was so dry he could barely speak. *If we get Pepe to Juan's hacienda alive it'll be a fucking miracle*, Roberto thought. *Thank God Juan is preoccupied with the helicopter and didn't see that disaster.*

Once over the river, Juan dialed in the coordinates for the warehouse in Piedras Negras. It appeared they were within 10 miles of their destination. He began to breathe more easily. "Take over, Julio. I want to check on Pepe," Juan said.

They'd been using red lenses on flashlights instead of the interior lights of the helicopter. Juan didn't want any visible light emanating from the ship. It was important that they not be seen, even in Mexico.

It was obvious to Juan the minute he saw Pepe that his brother was very ill. Pepe's eyes had a dullness to them that alarmed Juan. "What do you think, Roberto?" he asked.

"Pepe is very sick. His temp is 105 and he's been delirious. It's been very difficult working with the flashlights. When can we get more light?"

"We're almost to the warehouse. Another five minutes."

Juan returned to the cockpit and took the controls from Julio. He flipped on the navigational lights and the landing light and set the Huey up for the approach to the warehouse heliport. He brought the chopper to a hover and settled it gently on its skids. Juan got out of the seat and left Julio to shut the machine down. In the bay of the Huey, he assisted Roberto in getting Pepe off the helicopter.

There was an apartment in the Piedras Negras warehouse similar to the one in Ojinaga. In the bedroom, Juan and Roberto transferred Pepe from the stretcher onto the double bed. The doctor handed the IV bag containing Ringer's lactate to Juan and said, "Hold this until I can figure out a way to attach it to the wall."

"Look in that drawer. I think there's a hammer and box of nails in it. Just stick a nail in the wall," Juan said.

Roberto did as he was told and Juan left the room. The doctor made sure the IV was running correctly and then set the chest bottle on the floor next to the bed. He took the hemostat off the tube, and puss drained into the bottle. *That's not good*, Roberto thought. Next he inserted a Foley catheter.

Pepe opened his eyes as the catheter threaded up his penis. "Roberto, is that you?"

"Yes, Pepe. Lie still. I'm going to give you some aspirin for your fever. Can you swallow?"

Pepe nodded.

At that moment, Ricardo walked into the room. "How is Pepe?" he asked.

"Not well," Roberto said softly, so as not to alarm Pepe. "Come here and let me take a look at your shoulder."

Ricardo sat in a chair next to the bed and Roberto tore his shirt away from the wound. Blood still oozed from the edges. When the doctor pressed around the area, Ricardo winced.

"It looks like a through-and-through wound, Ricardo. I don't think the bullet is lodged in your shoulder. A pressure dressing and some antibiotics should take care of it. Is there much pain?"

Ricardo shook his head. "I can live with it."

Out on the heliport, Juan was assessing the damage to the Huey. The starboard tank was dry and the port almost dry. He knew he had to repair the starboard tank if they were to make it back to Chihuahua. He tried to figure out a quick fix. The bullet hole was small so Juan figured he could plug it with something, but he didn't know what to use. Julio, who stood next to his boss, said, "Perhaps, Captain, we could use Bondo. My cousin has an auto repair shop in Chihuahua and he uses it all the time."

"As soon as it's daylight, take the truck into town and buy some. I'm going to check on Pepe again," Juan said.

Pepe was incoherent and babbling nonsense when Juan walked

into the apartment. Roberto had a worried look on his face that bothered Juan. The doctor was in the process of removing Pepe's hospital gown. "How is he?" Juan asked.

"Delirious. I've given him aspirin, but now I've got to sponge him down with cold water. I've got to break the fever if he's to survive."

"Do what you must. We should be able to head for Chihuahua in four or five hours," Juan said.

At eight o'clock that morning Julio drove into Piedras Negras and bought a can of Bondo at an auto parts store. When he returned to the warehouse he found Juan pacing back and forth in front of the Huey smoking a cigar.

"Did you get it?" Juan asked.

"Yes, Captain. I called my cousin on the mobile phone for instructions. He said we'd have to let it harden for a few hours before filling the tank."

Juan made the repair himself and checked the time on his chronometer so he'd know how long to let it cure. He planned to cut things a little short in order to get back in the air. He wanted to get Pepe back to the hacienda where Roberto would have more equipment.

None of them had eaten since the evening before and Juan's stomach growled. He sent Julio back to town for breakfast tacos. He knew they needed to keep their strength up. He wasn't worried about the police or army because they were in his debt, but he had a lot of territory to cover.

When Juan checked on Pepe after they'd eaten breakfast, his fever had broken and he was lucid. Roberto was pleased and told Juan, "I believe Pepe is doing better. The temperature is down to 100. If I can keep it there he'll be okay. When can we leave?"

"I'm planning to take off at noon. Can you have Pepe ready by then?"

"Yes. I'm pumping antibiotics into his bloodstream as fast as I can, but we need to get back to Chihuahua soon."

As Julio filled the starboard tank, everything looked good at first. But by the time he'd filled the port tank the starboard was leaking a steady stream. Juan shook his head and screamed, "Fucking gringo! Take the damn tank off."

Juan knew they'd have difficulty making the distance with reduced fuel. Flying at altitude would help conserve fuel. If he had to, he'd stop at a filling station and fill up with auto diesel. It was close to Jet A and he thought the jet engines would work on diesel. Julio removed the injured tank and did a preflight on the Huey. At 1:00 p.m. Roberto and Ricardo brought Pepe out on the stretcher and loaded him on the helicopter. Juan brought the ship to a hover, checked the gauges, lowered the nose, and set a course for Chihuahua.

They made it to Juan's ranch, but not the hacienda. The Huey's engines died from fuel starvation and Juan had to auto rotate to a landing. The ship was 5 miles from the casa. Juan keyed his radio to a frequency monitored by his men and when one answered, said, "I'm north of the casa near the water tower. Send two Suburbans immediately."

AFTER THE APACHE EXPLODED, MONTY AND Martha Jo were waiting in the sheriff's office for Deputy Petty to return. Tim Boswell entered the radio room first. "Jesus, how did those Mexicans pull that off?"

"We're waiting for Gordon Petty. He saw the whole thing," Monty said.

"Come into my office and we'll have a cup of coffee while we wait," the sheriff said.

Forty-five minutes later, a visibly shaken Deputy Petty walked into his boss's office. His face had several fresh scratches and his hair was a mess. He'd lost his hat in the aftermath of the firestorm. He methodically explained everything he'd seen in great detail. Monty was fascinated by the whole episode. He'd ridden in a lot of Huey helicopters in Nam and simply couldn't believe the Mexicans had been able to take out an Apache.

On the way back to Utopia in Martha Jo's car, Monty shook his head and said, "I'm so worked up I'll never be able to sleep. I'm going to look for that damned cougar tonight. I'd like to do something constructive for a change."

"I'm going to take a sleeping pill, myself," Martha Jo said.

Monty kissed her good night and went to his truck. The moon was full and the sky was cloudless. An eerie bluish wash covered the landscape. He set out, deciding to look for the Greeley brothers, who had taken some exotic animals off the Triple T Ranch two nights previously. He parked on a slight rise about two hundred feet from the ranch's front gate. He held a pair of high-powered binoculars to his eyes, and he started to scan the front pasture one quadrant at a time.

Suddenly, the cougar walked into his line of vision. The graceful animal was stalking a calf about a hundred feet in front of Monty's truck. Monty felt a gentle breeze on his cheek and realized he was downwind to the creature. Otherwise, the puma wouldn't have come that close to a human. In a panic, the cattle scattered in every direction and Monty reached for his AR-15. At that instant the big cat pounced on the calf and dragged it into a cedar brake.

"Damn," Monty muttered under his breath.

He got out of the truck and walked to the area where he'd spotted the cougar. When he arrived at the spot, all he found was some blood and evidence of the animal being dragged off. There was no use trying to follow the cat's tracks in the dark, full moon or not.

The cougar seemed almost mystical. Like the Greeley brothers, he picked off the wildlife and domestic animals right before Monty's eyes and then he'd just vanish. Monty wasn't the kind of man to feel sorry for himself or to give in to depression, but he had to admit he was feeling pretty low. If he could solve just one of his problems, he knew he'd feel better. He was smitten by a girl half his age for the first time in his marriage, and he couldn't protect her or catch a couple of worthless poachers, or a cougar.

He strolled back to his pickup and climbed behind the wheel. Lighting a cigarette, he looked at his watch and saw that it was five o'clock. He wondered if Cindy was awake yet. He knew she opened the Circle M at seven. Maybe he'd stop by there on his way to the Lost Maples. Buy a lottery ticket or a pack of smokes.

CHAPTER 10

The fact that Bobby Littlejohn had been murdered outside Utopia wasn't lost on Jimmy Rhea, but he wanted Cindy so badly that his muddled mind simply went into denial. He continued to live off Darlene and plot his next move with his ex-wife.

Jimmy Rhea stayed in the apartment drinking beer and watching ESPN on Darlene's old 21-inch Magnavox television. *Surely*, he thought, *the damn Mexicans can't find me holed up in this shit box.*

Meanwhile, Vic was merely biding his time. He saw no reason to play his hand yet. He looked forward to a little cat and mouse with that poor white trash, Jimmy Rhea Moffitt. As he'd told Juan, he knew where his mark was living but didn't want to take him in daylight or when the woman was around. He wanted to pick him up at night like he'd done with Bobby.

For his part, Jimmy Rhea was fucked out. He laughed to himself just thinking about it. He'd never known a woman who loved to screw as much as Darlene did. Wanting a reprieve from his duties as her stud, he suggested they take in a movie in San Antonio. She jumped at the invitation and suggested they have dinner before the movie. There was an Olive Garden restaurant near a multiplex theater on IH-410 South where Darlene went occasionally.

Jimmy Rhea drove Darlene's old Dodge Dart because he was afraid one of the Mexicans would recognize his truck. They arrived at the restaurant at six o'clock. The place was almost full, despite the early hour. Jimmy Rhea ordered spaghetti and Darlene asked for lasagna. They both had Budweiser drafts.

Vic entered the establishment moments after Jimmy Rhea and Darlene took their seats. He asked the hostess to seat him directly across from their table. Sipping a Jack Daniel's on the rocks, he ordered a small Caesar salad and watched them with bemused detachment. The world would be a better place without the likes of Jimmy Rhea Moffitt, Vic was certain. And he wondered what that good-looking woman saw in such a loser.

Darlene paid their bill and the two of them left the restaurant with Vic close behind. The movie theater was across the parking lot from the Olive Garden so they walked. Darlene bought them tickets to *Breakdown*. Vic did the same.

Halfway through the movie, Jimmy Rhea whispered to Darlene that he had to pee. He walked up the aisle to the lobby of the theater. Vic, who had taken a seat behind Jimmy Rhea and Darlene, followed.

Jimmy Rhea was at the urinal when Vic walked into the restroom. Standing next to him, Vic glanced at Jimmy Rhea and said, "I hate to pee in the middle of a good movie."

Jimmy Rhea looked at the man and said, "You could always wet your pants." Then he laughed. There was something about the man that seemed familiar to Jimmy Rhea but he couldn't place him.

Vic grinned and thought, *You'll wet your pants tonight, asshole.*

After the movie, Jimmy Rhea and Darlene walked back toward her car. As Darlene stopped for a moment to look in a store window, Vic walked up beside Jimmy Rhea and stuck his .22 automatic in Jimmy Rhea's back. "Keep moving, asshole, and don't look around."

"Oh, shit," Jimmy Rhea whispered. It puzzled him that the man wasn't a Mexican. Maybe this was just a stickup. He did as he was told.

Darlene turned to leave the store window just as Vic forced Jimmy Rhea into his car. All she saw was the back of Vic's head. Confused, she ran after them, but as she reached the rental car, it pulled out of the parking space. Her Dodge was ten spaces away. She ran to it and slid behind the wheel.

Jimmy Rhea drove Vic's car with his abductor sitting in the passenger seat. Vic had his pistol leveled at Jimmy Rhea's heart.

"I ain't got no money, fellow. You're wasting your time. Hell, I just got out of jail," Jimmy Rhea said.

"It's not your money I'm after, Jimmy Rhea."

Jimmy Rhea's mouth went dry, and his heart pounded. He held on to the steering wheel with white knuckles. "Oh, shit," he said. "Where're we headed?"

"I thought we'd take a little trip up to Utopia. You seem to like that area. Soon you'll be joining your old buddy, Bobby. You remember Bobby, don't you?"

"It was Bobby's idea to steal that shit. Hell, I tried to talk him out of it. I ain't got no problem with those Mexicans. Look, I'll pay them back. I'll work for them or something."

Vic laughed. "It's a little late for that, partner. You don't piss off a man like Juan Diaz. You're history. Face it like a man. You've been a jerk all your life."

"What do you know about my life?" Jimmy Rhea asked.

"Just watching you for the last few days tells me all I need to know. You're a scumbag."

"And you're a fucking saint? What kind of man goes around killing people?"

"In my case, a rich one."

"How much you getting to kill me?"

"Ten big ones. Same as for Bobby."

The fellow still seemed familiar to Jimmy Rhea. Then it dawned on him. This was the man who'd come into Cindy's store the first day Jimmy Rhea had gone to see her. No wonder he'd felt a chill. He couldn't believe he was actually talking to the bastard about his own murder.

They were passing through Hondo and Jimmy Rhea fell silent. He didn't want to talk anymore. All he wanted was out of that damned car. When they got to Sabinal, Vic said, "Turn right at the next street."

"Why you taking me all the way to Utopia? Hell, you could kill me in Hondo."

"I think it's poetic to meet your maker in Utopia, don't you?"

"Fuck you."

Vic laughed. "Think of it this way. You've had some of the best fucking in your miserable life these past few days. I might try Darlene myself after I do you. She'll be a sorrowful and lonely girl after losing her dear boyfriend."

Jimmy Rhea clamped his jaws together and tried to think of a way to get the upper hand on Vic. *He and the hit man were about the same size. Maybe he could knock the gun out of Vic's hand. Get a choke hold on the bastard.* His mind was racing, his pulse galloping. *What should I do?*

"Just before you get to Utopia, there's a gravel road off to the right. That's it," Vic said.

They drove along the rutted road with yellow dust billowing behind them. At the ford on Little Creek the rental car splashed through, and water sprayed the windshield.

"Slow down, asshole," Vic said. "I don't aim to get myself killed in a fucking car wreck."

Jimmy Rhea pressed the accelerator to the floorboard and the car leaped ahead. At the first curve, they slid off the road into a ditch and Vic was thrown against the door, his head hitting the window glass with a thud. Jimmy Rhea was thrown against the steering wheel and had the air knocked out of his lungs when the airbag exploded.

Gasping for breath, he grabbed the door handle and yanked it open. At that moment, Vic lunged at Jimmy Rhea and hit him over the head with the butt of his pistol.

"Okay, scumbag. Get out of the fucking car!" Vic yelled.

Vic threw Jimmy Rhea against the hood and pulled his arms behind him. Then he cuffed him with two large cable ties. "I'll drive the rest of the way," he said. "Get in the passenger seat."

It took five minutes of rocking the car back and forth by going from drive to reverse to get it out of the ditch. Jimmy Rhea's head hurt and a trickle of blood made its way slowly down his right cheek.

Vic set his jaw and glared through the windshield. They came around a curve and a buck followed by two does jumped in front of the car. Vic slammed on the brakes and the deer scampered over a fence and disappeared into the darkness.

Five miles out of Utopia, Vic turned right and passed over a cattle guard and into the front pasture of the Triple Bar Ranch. He followed the gravel road for one mile and then parked under a large oak tree, leaving the engine running and the headlights on. Turning to a still dazed Jimmy Rhea, he said, "Get out, scumbag. This is the end of the line."

"My damn hands are cuffed behind my back. I can't open the door."

Vic climbed out of the car and walked around to open the door for Jimmy Rhea. "Get out," he said.

Jimmy Rhea swung his feet out of the car and stood, momentarily staggering. Vic grabbed his shirt collar and pulled him in front of the car.

"I've got some money stashed," Jimmy Rhea said. "I'll pay you twice what the Mexicans are offering."

Vic laughed. "Don't give me that shit. You haven't got two nickels to rub together. Besides, when I take a contract, I honor it. If I didn't, I couldn't stay in business."

The hit man kept pushing Jimmy Rhea in front of him. About twenty yards from the car he abruptly stopped. He spun his mark around and said, "You want it in the back of the head or in the fore-head like your buddy Bobby?"

Jimmy Rhea closed his eyes and shook his head. "Please don't do this," he said in a weak voice.

At that moment, the rental car leaped forward, accelerating rapidly, with gravel flying from its rear wheels. It was headed directly for Vic, who spun around, aimed for the windshield, and squeezed off four silent rounds from his pistol. The car hit Vic, throwing him violently over the hood, onto the windshield, and finally over the top. He landed on the gravel with a sickening thud, his neck broken.

The car slid to a stop, the door opened, and Darlene stepped out. She rushed to Jimmy Rhea and threw her arms around his neck. Still dazed, he looked at her with disbelief in his eyes. "Where did you come from?" he asked.

"I followed you and that man after you left the parking lot. I didn't know what was going on, but I knew it couldn't be good. When you turned onto the gravel road, I cut my lights off so he wouldn't know I was behind him. Come on, we need to get out of here."

Jimmy Rhea shook his head. "You've got to wipe his car clean. Otherwise the cops will lift both our prints."

"Good thinking. Give me your handkerchief."

Darlene climbed back into the car and ran the handkerchief over the steering wheel, the gearshift, and all door handles. When she'd finished, she said, "Come on."

They ran back to Darlene's car that she'd left some twenty yards behind Vic's. She opened the door for Jimmy Rhea and said, "I'll cut those cuffs off when we get back to the apartment."

A visibly shaken Jimmy Rhea got into the passenger seat of Darlene's car. His head pounded along with his heart. He'd never come that close to death and he hoped he never would again anytime soon.

Darlene drove fast along the gravel road, trying desperately to stay in the middle. Jimmy Rhea said, "Careful, girl, watch those curves. We need to get these damn cuffs off me so I can drive."

"There won't be anything open in Utopia but there's a filling station in Sabinal where I might be able to buy a knife or a pair of scissors," Darlene said.

"Shit. Where's my fucking brain? I've got a pocketknife in my trousers. Stop the car," Jimmy Rhea said.

Darlene stepped on the brake and brought the old Dodge to a stop. She got out of the car, walked over to Jimmy Rhea's side, and opened the door. "Get out, honey, so I can get my hand in your pocket."

Jimmy Rhea scrambled out of the car and stood next to Darlene. She slipped her hand into his pocket and curled her fingers around the handle of a small knife. On the way out of his pocket, she pushed her hand against his penis and scrotum.

"Don't even think about it till we get home," Jimmy Rhea said.

Darlene opened the knife and sawed one plastic cuff in two, leaving the other intact. "We'll get the other one off at home," she said.

Jimmy Rhea rubbed his wrists and ran to the driver's side of the Dodge. He slid behind the wheel, then he gunned the car and they fishtailed down the middle of the gravel road until he got it under control. Once they reached the asphalt, he headed for Sabinal and floored the accelerator. Darlene glanced at the speedometer and shuddered. They were barreling down the highway at 90 miles an hour.

They were between Sabinal and D'Hanis on Highway 90 when Jimmy Rhea looked in the rearview mirror and saw red and blue flashing lights closing in on him. "Shit." He was seized with indecision. As far as he knew, he wasn't wanted by the police. Yet he never liked dealing with the fuzz. He was afraid they'd arrest him just for the hell of it. Should he pull over or make a run for it?

Jimmy Rhea took his foot off the accelerator and the car coasted to a stop on the shoulder of the road. He fished around in his hip pocket, feeling for his wallet. He pulled it out and extracted his license. Then he rolled the window down.

A tall highway patrolman walked up to the car with his hand on his weapon and shined a flashlight into Darlene's car. When he saw

Jimmy Rhea had his license out he asked, "Where's the fire, buddy? I clocked you at ninety."

Handing the policeman his license, Jimmy Rhea said, "I'm sorry, officer, I just wasn't paying attention."

"I need your insurance card, too," the officer said. Examining the card, he lowered his head and asked Darlene, "Is this your car, ma'am?"

"Yes, sir, it is. It's up to date, isn't it?"

"Looks like it. I'll be back in a minute."

Jimmy Rhea hoped he wouldn't have to step out of the car. The plastic cuff was still around his left wrist. The patrolman walked back to his car to check out the documentation. Moments later he handed both the license and card to Jimmy Rhea.

"I should take you in for driving so fast, but it's late and there's not much traffic. I'm going to let you off with a ticket. If I ever catch you doing this again, you're headed for jail."

"Thanks for cutting me some slack, officer, I really appreciate it," Jimmy Rhea said with a smile. No need in bringing the damn highway patrol down on him.

"Slow down and go home," the patrolman said as he headed back to his car.

"I almost wet my pants when I saw those lights," Darlene said. "You handled that just right, honey. Let's get home. I'm a nervous wreck."

TWO DAYS LATER, TIM BOSWELL CALLED Monty Kilpatrick on his cell. When the game warden answered, Tim said, "The foreman at the Triple Bar just found a body in their front pasture, plus a rental car. I'm on my way out there now if you want to join me."

"I'm only a few miles from there," Monty said. "See you in a few minutes."

Monty arrived first. The foreman was sitting on a stump smoking a cigarette. The rental car, its windshield broken, sat in the middle of the gravel road. Vic's body lay sprawled some ten feet behind the car; his silenced pistol was still gripped tightly in his right hand. The heat had bloated the skin and fire ants had been at the man's eyes.

Shaking a Camel out of its pack, Monty slipped it into his mouth and lit it. He walked around the car and checked the front. The grille was dented and one headlight was smashed. It was evident what had taken place.

Moments later Sheriff Boswell and Dr. Baker drove up in a patrol car. Boswell went to where the foreman sat and asked, "What time did you find the body?"

"About an hour ago. I called your office immediately."

"Did you touch anything?"

"Come on Sheriff. I watch TV like everyone else."

Tim Boswell laughed. "I guess that Hollywood craziness may have some positive effect after all." Turning to Monty, he said, "What do you think?"

"He was obviously hit by the car. Front end is damaged along with the windshield. The fact that he has a silenced .22 in his hand makes me think this is the guy who killed Littlejohn. Someone turned the tables on him."

Dr. Baker went directly to the body, slipped on some latex gloves, and rolled Vic onto his side. "This one's been here a couple of days," he said. "Rigor mortis and livor mortis have both set in."

"If this guy killed Bobby Littlejohn, I wonder who he was after this time?" the sheriff said.

"There's an ex-con who's been hanging around Cindy Moffitt. She works at the Circle M in Utopia. Her ex-husband. He looks like the kind of guy who could have a contract out on him. But I don't think he's smart enough to kill a hit man. And he's definitely too lazy to walk out of here," Monty said.

"Ballistics may match the gun to the bullet that killed Littlejohn. That would answer that question. The mark must have had someone come to his rescue. I'm going to have my guys dust the car for prints."

"My guess is it's been wiped clean."

"We'll see."

"The EMS ambulance should be here in a few minutes," Dr. Baker said as he stood. "The coroner in San Antonio is going to think we're in the middle of a gang war."

"We may be," Monty said. "Something unusual is going on, that's for sure."

CHAPTER 11

Jimmy Rhea Moffitt rolled onto his stomach and moved his hand across the bed until he found the curve of Darlene's buttock. He cupped it and gave a gentle squeeze. "Darlin', you're the best lay I've ever had, so help me God. Besides that, you saved my life. Hell, I think I'm in love."

Darlene put her arms around his neck, pulled him to her, and opened her lips, ramming her tongue into his mouth. Afterward, in a breathy voice, she said, "I love it in the morning most of all. You're the best, Jimmy Rhea, and I love you with all my heart. I'd do anything for you, baby."

Jimmy Rhea had actually thought of getting a job in Sabinal or Hondo the night he left Cindy's trailer. But why bust his balls working as a day laborer when he could sponge off Darlene and get a little pussy on the side? It was a perfect setup. He could hump Darlene while he tried to win Cindy back.

He'd screwed up bad with Cindy, and he knew it. Sometimes he felt sorry for the way he treated Cindy and the others. He could blame it on booze some of the time but not always. He just lost it every once in a while and beat the shit out of his current squeeze. He didn't know why, because he loved Cindy. Why else would he have married her? His dick could find a home anytime it wanted, but not with the likes of Cindy.

Jimmy Rhea had never felt about any woman as he had for his ex-wife. Somehow he had to win her back. He'd apologize, beg her forgiveness one more time, and make himself behave. Jimmy Rhea Moffitt would turn over a new leaf. Yes, he could do it. He knew he could. Now he had a goal. He'd never had a goal in his life, but he was determined to reach this one.

Cindy, on the other hand, had made a solemn promise to herself. She'd be free of Jimmy Rhea Moffitt if it was the last thing she did on this earth. The when and how were up for grabs, but as God was her witness, it would happen. And she'd do it herself. The law had failed her too many times.

Her eye was still swollen when she went back to work, but her lip had returned to normal. She had full, sensuous lips. Men had always mentioned them when making love to her. Once, Cindy had watched a Brigitte Bardot movie made in the mid-1950s. She'd seen the famous pouting lips and decided that hers were just as beautiful. For weeks she'd practiced sexy smiles in the medicine cabinet mirror of her small bathroom.

WHEN MONTY KILPATRICK WALKED INTO THE Circle M at eight o'clock that morning, Cindy was still sleepy because she'd stayed up until the wee hours watching *An Affair to Remember* on the AMC channel. This particular morning, Monty reminded her of Cary Grant. Perhaps it was the way he smiled at her as he came through the door. It could've been that he was tall, good-looking, and easy in his manner. Or perhaps it was the cleft in his chin. She felt a slight flutter in her chest.

"Morning, Monty," she said.

"Morning, Cindy. You okay?"

"I'm fine."

"Anything you want to tell me?"

"Can't think of anything."

Monty was determined to flush Cindy's plight into the open, but he wasn't quite sure how to do that.

"You know, Cindy," he said, "if you ever need my help, I'm here for you."

Cindy assumed Martha Jo had told her husband about Jimmy Rhea. Why else would he be making such pointed comments? But she wasn't about to involve the police again. She'd deal with Jimmy Rhea in her own time, in her own way.

"I appreciate your offer. The question is, how are *you*? I heard you were in a shoot-out last night."

"I damn near got shot."

"Who were those guys?"

"Drug people. The fellow who cut me up was in the hospital over in Uvalde. Must have been a high up because they came and rescued him. They're a gutsy group, to say the least. Flew across the border, snatched their comrade, and blew the hell out of an army Apache helicopter in the process."

"Do you think they'll ever catch them?"

"Once they made it back across the border they were safe. Those guys have so many people in their debt they can do anything they want. I'm on my way to talk to the FBI. Evidently, the president's really pissed off about the whole deal."

"I hope everything goes okay. Do you want your weekly ticket?"

"Give me a quick pick. I'm sure the state of Texas needs my dollar."

"The politicians always manage to look out for themselves, don't they?"

"You can count on it. By the way, you got a bottle of aspirin?"

"You sore?"

"I just need a little something to take the edge off."

Cindy said, "Come back here, Monty, and I'll get you some Tylenol and a glass of water."

Cindy shook two pills out of a bottle and handed them to Monty. As she filled a small Styrofoam cup with water she said, "How bad's your cut?"

"Long, but the doctor said they heal from side to side, not end to end."

Handing the cup to Monty, Cindy stepped close and said, "Could I see it?"

Monty reddened.

"I won't bite," Cindy said with a grin.

"Okay," Monty said as he unbuttoned the top three buttons of his shirt.

The incision still had the sutures in place and was fiery red. Cindy moved closer and traced the line of the incision with her finger.

"How far down does that go?"

Monty could feel his heart pound, and he felt the stirrings of sexual excitement. He'd not felt like this since he was a high school kid. He swallowed hard and said, "Below my belt."

Cindy said, "Don't worry. I won't make you take your pants down." Then she stood on the tips of her toes and kissed Monty softly on the lips as she whispered, "Just yet."

Monty placed his hands on Cindy's shoulders and tried to decide whether to kiss her or push her away. He held her by her shoulders at arm's length for a moment and then pulled her to him as he kissed her on the forehead. Releasing her and shaking his head, he said, "Cindy, I can't."

Cindy's face flushed. She turned away and said, "I'm sorry, Monty. I shouldn't have done that."

"Let me help you, Cindy."

Cindy wiped the tears from her eyes. "Nobody can. Just forget about me," she said as she headed back toward the front of the store.

Monty followed. As they reached the glass counter, Webb Foster, the postmaster, walked through the front door.

"Morning, Monty, Cindy."

Cindy smiled. "Hi, Webb. What can I get you?"

"Copenhagen."

"I thought Margaret got you to quit."

"When I'm by myself, I still indulge."

Monty was glad to have a distraction in the appearance of Webb Foster. He glanced at Cindy and said, "Remember, if you need me, just call. If you can't get me, try Martha Jo."

"I will, I promise." Cindy knew she wouldn't call. She was afraid to, and besides, she'd just made a disastrous pass at Monty.

Monty hoped nothing serious would happen to Cindy or her daughter while she was making up her mind. He now realized he had feelings for Cindy that were more than fatherly. His pulse quickened as he thought of her fingertips on his incision and the touch of her full lips on his. Once in the truck, Monty dialed Martha Jo.

"I'm on my way to Uvalde. You need anything?"

"Stop by Walmart and get me a sack of potting soil. Will you be home for dinner?"

"Unless something comes up, I should be home about seven. I just left Cindy Moffitt. I don't believe she's going to press charges. I don't understand. It's driving me nuts."

"Maybe I should try again, but I don't think it'll do any good. The poor child is scared to death."

MONTY ARRIVED IN UVALDE AT ELEVEN o'clock and parked beside Sheriff Boswell's patrol car. He suspected the DEA agent would be there as well as the FBI. His friend Boswell would at least be a friendly face.

A deputy ushered Monty into Boswell's office. Seated there were the sheriff and a man Monty had never seen before. A third man stood next to the only window, looking out at the street. Sheriff Boswell motioned to the man at the window and said, "Monty Kilpatrick, Drew Lloyd, FBI." Turning to the seated man, he said, "This is John Pepper, DEA."

Monty said, "Good to meet you." After shaking hands with Pepper, he asked, "Where's Freeman?"

"We think he's skipped the country. Seems he's been siphoning a few thousand bucks off his busts. Our best guess is that he's got about five million in a Cayman Island account. We didn't tumble onto him for a long time because he was smarter than that Ames fellow. He lived frugally on his DEA salary and evidently planned an early retirement."

Monty smiled and, glancing at Boswell, said, "Just what we were talking about the other day."

Monty realized the FBI man was sizing him up, trying to get a fix on him. But there were no hidden agendas with Monty Kilpatrick. *Stay on your toes, Monty*, he told himself. *These guys are always looking for scapegoats.*

Lloyd's first impression of the game warden was off base. He mistakenly took Monty for a country hick out of his element in the big league of law enforcement.

"Do you get involved much in drug work? Isn't that a little out of your line?" Lloyd asked.

"Certainly wasn't my intention," Monty said. "I was just acting on a hunch. I've done some undercover work from time to time for the DEA, and sometimes I make a bust on my own. But I'd rather deal with poachers any day."

Lloyd was a veteran agent posted in the San Antonio regional office and an honest cop. His greatest flaw was his sense of elitism. He was a physical fitness nut, and his physique belied the fact that he was fifty-five years old. He looked ten years younger and carried himself with pride. His disdain for locals, as he called policemen, sheriffs, and such, was legendary. Tim Boswell had felt the sting of his ridicule on more than one occasion.

The FBI agent picked up a folder and flipped through a few pages. Glancing at Monty, he said, "It seems these guys knew exactly where to go in the hospital to find their man. They couldn't have been on the ground more than ten minutes. Any thoughts about that?"

Monty shrugged and said, "My guess would be that they had someone on the inside. An orderly, a janitor, possibly a nurse."

"How could they do that?"

"I'm positive there were two cars traveling together when I stopped the Mexican on Highway 90. My suspicion would be that after dropping off his shipment, the second driver doubled back to check on his friend. It'd be easy to bribe someone in the hospital to look in on the injured man and report back to the people in Mexico. It's amazing how much cash the guys carry around in their pockets."

Addressing John Pepper, Monty asked, "Do you still think this has to do with the Chihuahua cartel?"

"Our sources across the border tell us they're definitely with the Emilio Gurya cartel. In the last few years, the Cali gangsters have evidently shifted more and more of their drug trafficking activities to the Mexican border rats. They transport drugs like they did whiskey in the days of Prohibition. Juan Diaz, security chief of the Chihuahua cartel, led the raid."

Monty raised his eyebrows. "Isn't it a little unusual for a top man to get involved so personally in such dangerous business?"

"The reason has to do with the identity of the injured man. Our people think he's Pepe Diaz, Juan's younger brother."

"But why would he be driving a cocaine delivery across the border? That's a job for low-level, dispensable mules," Monty said.

Lloyd said, "That has us puzzled as well. We can't figure out why a man in his position would take such a risk."

"Do you think I could get some information on this Juan Diaz?" Monty asked.

Pepper said, "Our San Antonio office has a whole profile on everyone of importance in the Gurya cartel. I'll call my boss and see if he'll let you look through our files.

"There's got to be a reason why this Pepe took such a chance," Pepper added. We just don't know what prompted him to do it in the first place. I guess I can understand Juan trying to rescue his younger brother, for security reasons if nothing else."

Monty could certainly understand a big brother trying to save his younger sibling. He carried deep guilt about his own son. Monty still awoke sometimes at night reliving that day.

Lloyd put the folder back on the sheriff's desk and said, "Do you have any thoughts, Kilpatrick? You had the first contact with him."

Monty shrugged. "Not really. The man attacked me without warning or provocation. Under most circumstances these mules give up without resistance. Most probably they've been instructed to do so by their superiors."

The FBI man said, "Perhaps this Pepe Diaz had gotten involved by mistake. I'm not sure how, but let's say he found himself about to get caught and decided he couldn't make a run for it. He's the brother of a big shot in the drug business, so if he got busted, it would really look bad for the cartel. Maybe he thought he could kill you and get away with it."

Monty said, "I doubt the man relished the thought of wasting away in a gringo jail for the rest of his life."

"Didn't you interview this Pepe in the hospital?" Pepper asked.

"I tried, but the man wouldn't say a word. I even spoke to him in Spanish, didn't do a bit of good."

"I guess it's a moot point," Lloyd said. "I doubt we'll ever get to the bottom of this."

Turning back to Monty, he continued, "How is it that you were at the hospital last night?"

"I took my wife to the movies. When we got out, I decided to have another run at the Mexican. See if I could get him to talk to me."

"It says in this report that you wounded one of the men as they were getting back into the helicopter. Tell me about that."

"I came on the guys making a break for it and opened fire on them.

I hit a big fellow in the right shoulder. He was carrying the Pepe guy. When he got hit, he dropped the injured man to the ground."

"How did you know what was coming down?"

"I heard shots and recognized the sound of a Huey. When I rounded the corner of the hospital, I was able to put two and two together. Wasn't any question what was going on."

"You certainly have a knack for being in the right place at the right time," Lloyd said. "I'm impressed with your grasp of this situation, Kilpatrick. I'd like you to keep me posted."

Tim Boswell couldn't help but chuckle. It was the closest thing to a compliment Drew Lloyd had ever paid a local.

Monty stayed in the sheriff's office after the two federal agents left. "I'm ready for that cup of coffee you offered me the other day," Monty said.

"Come on back to the kitchen. We always have a pot brewing."

Monty followed his friend and poured himself a cupful of black coffee. He took a sip and said, "I've got a situation in Utopia I'm really concerned about. Remember when I mentioned that Moffitt fellow? Well, he raped his ex-wife but she won't press charges. It's obvious he's scared the devil out of her. My wife and I've both tried to reason with her but she just won't listen. Any suggestions?"

Boswell shook his head. "As peace officers we don't do a good job protecting victims of domestic violence. No one understands all the psychological reasons women stay with abusive husbands and boy-friends. Insecurity, fear, poor self-worth, the list is as long as your arm."

"That's almost exactly what Martha Jo said. I've just never run into it before. Poachers I can deal with. This I can't."

"Even when a protective order is issued by a judge, it doesn't ensure the woman will be safe," Boswell said.

"Texas has a concealed handgun license available to those who want one. Maybe we should just issue the women a license and let them shoot the bastards."

Boswell laughed. "That's a little radical, Monty. It'll be interesting to see how it works."

CHAPTER 12

Pepe Diaz's bloodshot eyes scanned the room. The helicopter ride had been frightening and painful, even though Dr. Roberto Gomez had stayed by his side throughout the trip, giving him painkillers and moral support.

The doctor had turned one of the hacienda's bedrooms into an infirmary complete with a hospital bed and twenty-four-hour nursing care. He continued Pepe's powerful intravenous antibiotics and monitored his white blood count and temperature. For the first time since his surgery, Pepe's temperature had returned to normal, and Dr. Gomez was convinced his patient would survive.

Roberto had not slept since they'd left the hacienda the evening before, and he was exhausted. Never had he come so close to death, and the experience had shaken him to the core. He wanted to go home to his wife and children but knew Juan would insist that he stay with Pepe until he was further along in his recovery. Roberto had been given a comfortable room with a private bath and he'd decided he had no choice but to make the best of the situation.

On their arrival at the hacienda, Juan Diaz had gone directly to his quarters, where he took a long, hot shower. He shaved, combed his hair, and put on slacks, boots, and his customary guayabera shirt. Then he started his routine workday by planning the arrival of a new shipment of cocaine from Colombia. He took a light lunch at his desk and worked until two o'clock when he rang Maria and told her he was going to take his siesta. She knew to awaken him promptly at four.

When Juan opened his eyes, he saw Emilio Gurya standing over him. His boss was a handsome man who had been schooled in Europe and had adopted many of the European customs. In the coolness of the old hacienda he wore a light sweater thrown over his shoulders like a Spanish patrician. The wine cellar in his massive mansion was filled with the best and most expensive French wines. Emilio Gurya was a man of style and grace. His appearance belied the fact that he was a ruthless and dangerous crime boss.

Juan looked past Emilio at his ever-present bodyguards, three feet behind their boss. They appeared calm and their hands were visible. He began to relax a bit but still touched the cocked .45 Colt automatic pistol he kept under the light blanket he covered himself with when taking a siesta.

Emilio spoke first. "Maria assured me it was time to end the siesta, my friend, or we wouldn't have disturbed you. A man needs his rest, particularly when he's been working all night. I myself enjoy the siesta from four to six, so today I will be an irritable man."

Juan swung his feet to the floor and sat up. He kept his pistol covered but at his side. He smiled wearily at his employer and said, "It would sadden me greatly, Emilio, if I thought I was responsible for you missing your siesta. I know you are a man of regularity."

"How long have we been friends, Juan? How long have you worked for me?"

Juan pulled on his boots slowly, wanting to portray a man at ease. He stood and faced his boss. "We've been friends, Emilio, since we were children on your father's ranch. We played together, you the boss's son and me the foreman's. You went to college in Europe and I went to the army. In this business, I have worked faithfully for you for ten years. Why do you ask me things you already know?"

"Because I wondered if you had forgotten, my friend."

"Why would I forget? You're like a brother to me."

Emilio motioned for his bodyguards to leave, and then he sat on the couch. He propped his feet on the coffee table and patted the cushion next to him. "Come sit with me, Juan. We need to discuss what's happened in the last few days. I have only bits and pieces of information and I need more. I must understand the circumstances of your most unusual activities."

Juan felt quite safe in the room alone with Emilio. The man knew nothing of guns or knives, and while he was in good physical condition, he'd be no match for Juan. Leaving his pistol under the cover, Juan walked across the room and sat on the couch sideways facing his boss. He smiled and said, "I know the one thing in this world that makes you the angriest is being uninformed, caught off guard. I am sorry not to have kept you posted throughout this ordeal. My only excuse lies in my deep love and concern for the safety of my younger, somewhat irresponsible brother."

Emilio placed his hand on Juan's knee and said, "I know these feelings, my friend. Could you not trust me, your oldest comrade, with your problem?"

"It was my intention to free you of worry and concern. The events unraveled quickly and without warning. I simply didn't want to bother you with the details until it was over. I have already started a detailed report. If I have offended my oldest and dearest friend, I will never forgive myself."

Emilio smiled for the first time. He'd heard what he came for, a sincere apology. The business with Juan's brother had been poor judgment on his friend's part. It could have jeopardized their whole operation and ruined their relationship with the Cali cartel. But Juan had pulled it off and everything was under control. That, for Emilio, was the bottom line.

"I fully understand these things, Juan, and I accept your apology. The fact remains, you must keep Pepe under control. He's a loose cannon, and in our business that presents a dangerous situation. Already our friends in the government are under tremendous pressure from the Yankees. We've been told to keep a low profile for a while. This will cause all of us to lose money. Perhaps the Colombians will seek other partners in the meantime. These things take on proportions of their own. Sometimes events spin out of control. It's a precarious position your brother has placed us in."

Juan swallowed hard because he realized every word his friend spoke was true. He himself was furious with Pepe. He said, "I understand fully, Emilio. Pepe lies near death as we speak. If he survives, he will never place you in a compromising position again. You have my word on this, sealed with my life."

Emilio nodded and said, "I always take you at your word, my friend. We do have another problem we should discuss. It seems Vic failed his last assignment. He was unable to take care of Mr. Moffitt."

"I just learned of Vic's demise this morning. I've already contacted Wallace."

"Good. We can't allow people to interfere with our business. We must never appear weak."

"I understand fully, my friend. What I don't understand is how Mr. Moffitt got the upper hand. Vic was an experienced and vicious killer."

"We may never know the answer to that one. Be sure Wallace understands that this Moffitt fellow may not be as dumb as we think."

"Perhaps I should have used Wallace in the first place."

MONTY KILPATRICK PARKED HIS TRUCK AT a meter on St. Mary's Street in San Antonio and entered the NationsBank Plaza building. The DEA office was on the ninth floor, where the receptionist introduced Monty to Maxwell Mangum, the district supervisor.

"My man John Pepper tells me you want to look at our files on the Gurya cartel," Mangum said, extending his hand.

"Yes, sir, I have a personal interest in this one. I'm sure you don't approve of personal vendettas, but Pepe Diaz almost killed me."

"I have no problem with personal vendettas when it comes to drug dealers," Mangum said, as he led the way into a large room filled with filing cabinets. He selected one and retrieved a thick manila file. Handing it to Monty, he said, "Everything we have on these bastards is in here. You can sit at that table over there and look through it. Take your time."

"I really appreciate this, Mr. Mangum. Do you hunt?"

"Dove. Sometimes quail."

"Call me around the first of September and I'll take you on one hell of a dove hunt."

"If you need anything, let me know."

Monty opened the file. He was transfixed by what he read.

> Juan Diaz is the chief of security for the cartel and was a captain in the Mexican army. He lives on a twenty-thousand-acre ranch west of Chihuahua where he raises fighting bulls. Known as a strict disciplinarian, he has a reputation as being tough but fair in his dealings with his men. His relationship with his younger brother, Pepe, is often strained. One analyst has stated that it has to do with Spanish heritage, an older brother taking responsibility for a younger sibling. Not much is known about Pepe other than he is the antithesis of his brother. He is thought to be reckless, undependable, a womanizer, and a borderline alcoholic.

While Juan has no formal education past high school, he worked his way up in the army from enlisted man to captain. He is thought to be widely read and has educated himself in literature and the arts.

The one aspect of his personality that is mentioned in every interview is his sense of loyalty. His word is considered his bond. Anyone threatening the cartel, friend or foe, is sentenced to death. He is not married, has no female companions, and devotes his considerable energies solely to his work.

There was a photo of Juan in the folder. Monty picked it up and looked at it carefully. Diaz appeared to be about five feet six inches tall with a slim but muscular build and a thin mustache. He was wearing army fatigues and standing in front of a black Huey helicopter.

The one profile other than Juan's that interested Monty was that of Emilio Gurya, the head of the Chihuahua cartel.

The youngest son of a rich Mexican cattle rancher, Emilio Gurya was educated in France. Most of his mannerisms and his taste for fine wines and expensive clothes reflect his European education. His ruthlessness is thought to be a natural, inborn trait. He is believed to be responsible for ordering the deaths of more than twenty men in order to ascend to the head of the Chihuahua cartel. His bodyguards carry silenced MAC-10 machine pistols and have instructions to shoot first and ask questions later.

Monty found a second photo taken at what appeared to be a birthday party. Several small children in paper hats, eating ice cream, surrounded a tall, handsome man. His long black hair was swept straight back from his forehead, and he wore a tailored guayabera shirt and white slacks with expensive-looking loafers.

Monty whistled under his breath and said softly, "These are two tough hombres."

There was nothing else in the file that interested Monty, just some pictures and short bios of lower-echelon members of the cartel. It was Juan Diaz who fascinated Monty. Monty hated to admit it, but he felt some admiration for the Mexican. It had taken guts and a certain recklessness to pull off the rescue of his brother.

Monty got back in his truck and drove to a gun shop on San Pedro Avenue, not far from the North Star Mall. With an idiot like Jimmy Rhea Moffitt on the loose and possible retaliation by the Mexicans, Monty wanted Martha Jo to have some protection. He purchased a small Beretta .32 caliber Tomcat semiautomatic along with two boxes of shells. For a brief moment, he considered buying a second one for Cindy.

When they'd first married, Monty spent hours instructing Martha Jo in the handling of various guns. With his tutoring, she'd become an excellent shot. She remained cool under pressure and he knew she could protect herself in an emergency if she owned a firearm. But he didn't have the time to train Cindy and didn't know her well enough to anticipate how she'd react in a confrontation with her ex-husband.

On the drive back to Utopia, Monty tried to analyze all the things that had occurred in the past week. Since becoming a peace officer his life had never been dull, but the recent events had been over the top. He knew he loved Martha Jo even if he did take her for granted. Their sex life of late hadn't been great, and he wondered if that contributed to his feelings for Cindy. For the first time in his life, Monty was beginning to question his motivations. And he felt ineffective in his job. The Greeley brothers continued to evade him, and he felt helpless to defend a young woman obviously in mortal danger. The Mexicans were an unknown and he had no idea where his entanglement with them would lead.

CHAPTER 13

Late that night Monty sat on the hood of his pickup, cradling his AR-15 and smoking a cigarette. He was parked at the Triple Bar Ranch, ruminating. *Why would Pepe Diaz take such a chance of being caught?* Maybe Pepe had a reason for driving that car, but Monty just couldn't think of one.

A full moon hung in the pristine sky and the Milky Way was unusually brilliant. With no surface light to interfere, the sky was ablaze. There was always a gentle southeasterly breeze at this time of year. On this evening the aroma of freshly cut hay drifted over the landscape.

Monty had picked this particular spot because the cougar had been more active on the Triple Bar spread than any other. And there was a large herd of cattle sleeping on the ground in front of him. He'd placed himself downwind of the animals so his scent would be swept away from them in case the cat showed up. He checked his watch's glowing dial and saw that it was 2:00 a.m.

He noticed movement out of the corner of his eye and looked to his right. He saw the mountain lion moving stealthily toward the herd in what appeared to be a crouch, almost like a house cat slipping up on a field mouse.

Monty raised the AR-15 and flipped on the nightscope. He sighted through the lens and could see the puma clearly. He placed the crosshairs on the cat's shoulder and squeezed the trigger. The cougar went down momentarily but sprang up and limped away. The bullet had not hit a vital organ. Monty cursed under his breath. He didn't want an injured puma roaming around the countryside. It might even attack a human. His only choice was to track the animal and deliver a lethal shot.

He took out his powerful flashlight and walked over to where he'd seen the cat. The herd had panicked at the loud report of the rifle and cattle were scattering in all directions. There was a trail of blood that Monty felt he could follow without much trouble. There was a possibility that the animal would die of blood loss, but there was also the chance that the cat would turn on Monty. He knew he had to keep his wits about him.

For the next thirty minutes Monty felt he was walking in circles. Finally, he saw where the bloody trail entered a thick cedar brake. Indecision gripped him. Should he walk in or make noise in hopes of flushing the big cat out of hiding? He'd just decided on the second choice when he heard a deep growl and the branches of the closest cedar tree parted. The mountain lion rushed Monty and forced him to the ground, knocking the AR-15 out of his hands. The big animal began to maul Monty, crushing him under 250 pounds of muscle.

Monty had his left arm over his face trying to protect himself from the cougar's teeth. At the same time he tried to pull his Glock out of its holster. The safety strap wouldn't give. Monty thought he was a dead man. As he tried to fend off the huge animal and at the same time free his weapon, the gun finally slipped into his hand and he brought it to the mountain lion's chest, firing off five rounds. The cat dropped dead right on top of Monty, knocking the air from him. The animal was so heavy Monty couldn't breathe. With all his strength, he rolled the puma off and lay beside his kill gasping for breath. He'd never had such a close call with an animal in his entire career. The whole thing had happened in seconds.

When he regained his breath, Monty examined the cat with his flashlight. The first thing he did was look at the right rear paw. There was the broken toe Monty had first seen in his plaster cast. Convinced that this was indeed the animal that had been causing so much trouble, Monty sat on the hard ground and pulled a cigarette out with a palsied hand. He didn't like coming that close to death.

Monty had a hoist in the bed of the pickup. He walked back to the truck and got behind the wheel. He winched the cougar up and into the bed of the pickup. *Now*, he thought, *if I can just bag those damned Greeley brothers.*

He spent the remainder of the night driving the county roads looking for poachers. At daylight, he headed for the Lost Maples. When he walked into the restaurant, Arthur Jepson was sitting in their usual booth. When he saw Monty, he motioned for the game warden to join him.

Monty shook his head and said, "Come out and see what I've got in the bed of my pickup."

When Arthur saw the mountain lion, he whistled and said, "That's the biggest damn cougar I've ever seen. How did you get him?"

"He damned near got me. I wounded him and tracked his blood trail. Then he rushed me. I had to kill him with my Glock."

"I noticed the scratches, but thought maybe Martha Jo had been on your case."

"Don't be ridiculous. I'm a little concerned about my marksmanship, though. I'm going to the range for some target practice. I missed the damn Greeley brothers' tires when I fired at them, and I didn't hit but one of those Mexicans."

"Hell, shooting is like everything else," Arthur said. "You've got to practice to stay in shape."

"I'm going to practice a lot. I don't think we've heard the last from those Mexicans," Monty said.

CINDY MOFFITT OPENED HER CONTACT CASE, removed one blue lens, and then inserted it in her eye with her index finger. After repeating the process for the other eye, she stood and looked at herself in the bathroom mirror. She'd been wearing the contacts for well over a year and their tint seemed natural to her, more so even than her own hazel color. What had started out as a disguise had somehow become a part of her persona, like her bleached hair. She was comfortable now with being a blonde, and the bleaching process had given her limp, mousey-brown hair more body. She felt more attractive as a blue-eyed blonde, but now that Jimmy Rhea had found her, was it really necessary to hide her true identity?

Jimmy Rhea hadn't been around since the night he'd raped her. She had no idea where he was or what he was doing. Perhaps he was afraid she had talked to the sheriff. But she had no doubt he'd be back. He always came back, like a recurring nightmare. She shuddered at the thought and took a deep breath.

She ran her fingers through her hair and wondered what the people of Utopia would think if she let her hair grow out and stopped wearing the contacts. While she liked being a blonde, the whole masquerade made her uncomfortable. It wasn't in her nature to live a lie, even a small one. Now that her ex-husband had found her, she might go back to being her old self. She now knew more about hair color and cosmetics than she once had. She was confident she could make herself attractive. Her gut feeling was telling her to be herself.

In her small kitchen, Cindy poured a bowl of Raisin Bran for herself and placed a box of Cheerios on the table for Jody. Her daughter had been upset by the visit from her father. She'd built an image of her absent father in her mind that was simply not true. She'd been terrified of him by the time he left their trailer that night. Since his visit she'd been quiet and withdrawn.

Cindy was concerned about her daughter and wished there was someone she could talk to. Jimmy Rhea had taken what small savings she had accumulated out of her Circle M salary, so she had no reserves. Missing a few days of work because of the swollen eye had put her in a critical financial situation. There was no way she could afford health insurance or a therapist for her daughter. She prayed that neither of them got sick.

The only people she really knew in Utopia were Monty and Martha Jo Kilpatrick. She needed desperately to talk to someone. She picked up the wall phone and dialed Martha Jo's number, but she replaced the receiver after two rings. After making a pass at Monty, she couldn't call Martha Jo. And if she said anything to Monty, he'd arrest Jimmy Rhea. When he got out of jail, he'd come looking for her again. It'd be the same old thing. There was no solution for her problem. She'd just have to deal with it. Except for Jody, she was alone, with no one to depend on but herself.

Cindy finished her Raisin Bran and went back to Jody's bedroom. The child was in the bathroom, trying to brush her hair. When she saw her mother, she said, "I'm a big girl."

Cindy took the brush from Jody and said, "Let me finish brushing your hair, honey. You've got a big tangle here."

"I can do it."

"Maybe I should tie it back in a ponytail at night. Keeps mine from doing this."

Cindy had let Jody's hair grow almost to her waist. It was a light honey blonde color, like Cindy's had been at that age. Her own hair hadn't turned dark until she was a teenager. Both Cindy and her daughter had limited wardrobes, but Cindy kept everything clean and freshly ironed. Jody had one Sunday dress. The rest of the time she wore jeans, like her mother.

Cindy was a coffee fiend and drank ten to twelve cups a day at the Circle M. She'd been letting Jody drink small amounts since she was about two years old. She poured a mug half full of coffee, added milk to the top and a teaspoon of sugar, and set it on the table next to Jody's cereal bowl. She sat across from her daughter and watched her eat. She loved to watch Jody do anything: eat, sleep, play, and laugh. As much as she hated Jimmy Rhea Moffitt, she would always be thankful for Jody. She loved the child so much it frightened her. She lay awake at night staring at the ceiling, worrying about Jody. Life without Jody was unthinkable.

She dropped her daughter off with Mrs. Warton, the babysitter, at ten minutes to seven. The temperature was already climbing toward the predicted 95 degrees and the humidity was unusually high. A few scattered clouds dotted the sky, and Cindy wondered if it was going to rain. That wonderful southeasterly breeze felt marvelous on her face, and she looked forward to the day ahead.

Cindy drove the four blocks to the Circle M and opened the store promptly at seven o'clock. She took two quarters out of her purse and bought a *San Antonio Express-News* from the stand in front of the store, made a pot of coffee, and had her second cup of the day while she read the paper. The front page was full of stories about the Latino gangs and the latest shootings in Laredo. The new chief of police in Nuevo Laredo had been murdered the evening before.

The door opened and Cindy looked up to see Monty cross the threshold. Her pulse quickened. He looked tired, more so than usual, and his limp was more pronounced.

"Morning, Cindy. What's the lottery up to?" he asked.

"Thirty million. I might buy a ticket myself."

"I'll take one. Cash option," Monty said, smiling.

"I hope you win so I can get my million."

"I did promise you that, didn't I? Well, don't let me forget."

Cindy loved Monty's visits. They were the high point of her day. She just wished he'd stay longer. "Believe me, I won't let you forget," she said.

"I still want you to deal with your ex-husband. Why won't you sign a protective warrant?"

"It sure is a pretty day. I notice your limp is bothering you. Is it going to rain?"

"That's not funny, Cindy. This is a serious matter. You've got to take it seriously."

"Oh, Monty. I do take it seriously, believe me. There's just nothing you or anyone else can do," she said tears filling her eyes.

Cindy pulled the handle on the big lottery machine and handed Monty his ticket. Then she picked up his dollar and placed it in the cash register. He stood silently shaking his head. She wanted desperately to believe he could protect her. Finally, he smiled and said, "You know how to reach me. Don't wait too long." He walked out the door with a heavy heart.

Monty got back in his pickup and drove up the street to the Lost Maples. Arthur wasn't in their usual booth. Monty took a seat and Gertrude poured his first cup of black coffee. "Have you seen Arthur this morning?" he asked.

"No, haven't seen that rascal since yesterday. Maybe he has a new girlfriend."

The thought of Arthur having a girlfriend made Monty chuckle. Of all the men Monty knew, Arthur was the most confirmed bachelor, possibly in the whole state of Texas.

Moments later Arthur walked in and took a seat opposite Monty. "Where've you been?" Monty asked.

His friend's eyes were bloodshot and he looked hungover and unusually tired.

Arthur glanced at his watch, but didn't say anything. He motioned to Gertrude for his coffee and continued to ignore Monty.

"Cat got your tongue?" Monty asked.

"I was detained."

"You want to explain that statement?"

"No."

Monty laughed. Maybe Gertrude was right. "If you ask me, you look pussy whipped."

"Mind your own damned business for a change."

AFTER MONTY LEFT, CINDY BUSIED HERSELF filling the glass cabinet with packs of cigarettes. At seven thirty the labor force started through town. Carpenters, electricians, plumbers, and day laborers drifted in to buy coffee, soft drinks, cigarettes, chewing tobacco, and foodstuff for lunch. Some got ice for their coolers and all flirted with Cindy. Most of it was good-natured.

About eight the traffic died down until the next big push at noon. In between, ranchers and townspeople stopped to buy gasoline, pick up milk and bread, get a paper, buy a lottery ticket, or return a rental movie. The steady stream kept Cindy on her feet constantly and gave her little time to rest. By one o'clock things finally settled into a more leisurely pace.

Cindy had just poured her eighth cup of coffee when the door opened and Jimmy Rhea walked in with a big smile on his face. He was clean shaven and his hair was cut conservatively. He wore a clean white shirt with heavy starch, ironed blue jeans, and highly polished cowboy boots.

Cindy's stomach churned, and she felt light-headed. She'd known it was just a matter of time until Jimmy Rhea showed up.

"My God, you look beautiful, girl. Damn if I don't like you as a blonde."

Cindy mustered all the courage she could and said, "Why did you come back, Jimmy Rhea? Why don't you just leave us alone?"

Jimmy Rhea ambled up to the counter and rubbed the back of his hand along Cindy's cheek. The smile never left his face. "I love you, darlin', and I've missed you something terrible. I just can't stay away from you."

"Please, Jimmy Rhea, please stay away from us. I'm not your wife anymore."

"I know, darlin'. I've been bad to you and I'm sorry. I really am. I don't know what come over me that night. I guess I just wanted you so bad I lost all sense of right and wrong."

Cindy couldn't believe Jimmy Rhea was apologizing to her. He'd never done that before and it took her by surprise. For a split second she wanted to believe him, but her better judgment kicked in and she said matter-of-factly, "I don't believe you, Jimmy Rhea. Nothing in the past would lead me to think you're telling the truth."

Jimmy Rhea pulled a small box from his hip pocket. It was elongated and wrapped in white tissue paper with a red bow. He handed it to Cindy and said, "I've turned over a new leaf, honey. Honest. I got a job over in Hondo at the lumberyard. I ain't had a drink in a month, neither."

Cindy shook her head in disbelief.

"Open your present, darlin'. I spent my whole last paycheck on it."

In truth, he'd stolen a small gold bracelet from Darlene, box and all. He'd taken it from her pitiful little jewelry collection while she slept. When she couldn't find the bracelet, he somehow convinced her she'd lost it on their last date when they'd been dancing.

Cindy took the box and placed it on the counter. "I can't accept this, Jimmy Rhea. It wouldn't be right. I don't want to be with you. Please leave me alone," she said.

Jimmy Rhea picked up the box and began to slowly unwrap it, never once taking his eyes off Cindy or losing his smile. He untied the red ribbon and pulled loose the tissue paper. He opened the box and took out the bracelet, which he unfastened and placed around Cindy's thin wrist. "It looks great on you, darlin'. It was worth every penny I paid for it." His smile widened to produce two charming dimples in his cheeks.

She didn't want it, but she was afraid not to take it. He might get mad and hit her if she refused.

In a weak voice, she said, "Thank you, Jimmy Rhea, but this doesn't change anything. I still want you to leave."

Then Jimmy Rhea did something that shocked Cindy. He said, "I'm glad you like it, darlin'. I'm leaving now, 'cause I know you're upset. I do want to come calling, though, to show you how I've changed. I want to prove to you I'm a new man and you can trust me. I want you back, darlin', with all my heart." With that statement, Jimmy Rhea walked to the door. Just as he stepped through the threshold he turned, smiled broadly once again, and blew his ex-wife a kiss.

Confusion sapped Cindy's breath. She'd never seen Jimmy Rhea act like that, even when they were first dating. Could he be serious? Even if he was, the chances of him changing his basic personality were awfully slim. He'd need some kind of therapy for that.

Jimmy Rhea was sure he'd made an impression on Cindy. She had to like the bracelet. It was Darlene's favorite. That shit about him having a job must have thrown her for a loop. The thought of him working in a lumberyard broke him up. Darlene had taken him to Walmart and bought him the new shirt and jeans. He'd polished the boots himself.

His plan was to keep Cindy off guard, convince her that he was a changed man. He thought he'd made a good start. Now all he had to do was keep Darlene from finding out his plan. He had the distinct impression she would be a vindictive bitch if she found out he was two-timing her.

CHAPTER 14

P epe Diaz lit a cigarette in the flower garden at his brother's hacienda. Dr. Gomez had told Pepe to give up smoking because of his severe pneumonia, but Pepe, having learned little from his recent illness, ignored the doctor's warnings. The two and a half months since his rescue from the Uvalde Memorial Hospital had been difficult for him. Accustomed to a life of whores and wild parties, his forced seclusion had been boring. He longed for a drink, which Juan forbade, and wanted a woman to ease his sexual tension. Pepe considered cigarettes to be his only vice, so he cherished each one he smoked.

All in all, it was a miserable time for Pepe. Not only was he consumed with the fear of death, but his day-to-day existence was uncomfortable and painful. During the hours, days, weeks, and months of his illness, Pepe had kept one thought in his mind: he would kill the man who had caused him all this suffering. If it took him ten years, he'd have his revenge. That one pledge to himself brought him through the difficult days of his recovery. If it was the last thing he ever did, Pepe Diaz would kill Monty Kilpatrick.

"So you continue to smoke despite Dr. Gomez's instructions. Do you think this is wise, Pepe?" Juan had just walked into the garden and was lighting his trademark cigar.

"You smoke, Juan. Why shouldn't Pepe?"

"I haven't had pneumonia, a tracheotomy, and all manner of illness in the last two months. It's a bad habit and one day I'll quit, but you, my brother, have a real incentive. Roberto told you if you don't stop, you'll die."

"Everyone dies one way or the other. Pepe prefers to enjoy himself while he can. Facing death changes a man, Juan. It makes him take stock of his life."

"I've faced death many times, brother. You can enjoy life with caution, like me, or you can throw caution to the wind, like you, and live only for the moment."

Pepe thought about what his older brother had just said. "Yes, Pepe has always lived freely, but Pepe never properly appreciated the joys he experienced. Now Pepe will savor each moment."

Juan laughed. "It's true, from tragedy comes the meaning of life. Roberto tells me you are almost fully recovered, so we must discuss your future."

"Pepe's future?"

"Your place in our organization. Your decision to disobey my direct order not to cross the border resulted in disastrous consequences, not the least of which was your near-fatal encounter with the gringo policeman. This must never happen again. In fact, I've given my word, on my life, that it won't happen again. You must not fail me, Pepe. When I give you an order concerning business, it is to be obeyed without question. Do I make myself clear?"

"Yes, Juan, perfectly clear."

"On another subject, you're very lucky to be alive. Do not, under any circumstances, consider seeking revenge for what's happened to you. It's not in the organization's best interest or yours. Do you understand?"

Pepe let a gentle smile cross his face as he went to Juan. He placed his arms around his brother and said with all the sincerity he could muster, "But of course, Juan, the thought never crossed Pepe's mind."

"I have received a report from our attorneys in Dallas on the gringo policeman. He is more than he appears on the surface. His name is Dr. Montgomery Kilpatrick, a veterinarian. He's a game warden, but his duties aren't limited to wildlife management. He has the same powers of any law officer. He's a worthy adversary. He received the Purple Heart in Vietnam and has been a policeman for twenty years. He's killed three men in the line of duty and is responsible for the seizure of ten million dollars' worth of our own cocaine. This is not a man to trifle with."

Pepe had no intention of telling his brother of his plans to kill the gringo. He'd make a supreme effort to please Juan. He'd follow orders and do his best. He'd even refrain from alcohol during business transactions, but he'd not give up his pledge to kill Monty Kilpatrick. He'd make his plans slowly and carefully, and when he was ready, he'd dispatch his adversary quickly.

In fact, Pepe had laid out a campaign to improve his health and strengthen his body. He'd need all the strength he could muster to deal with the policeman. And he must keep his wits about him. He had to keep his plans secret from Juan and his henchmen. Like Jimmy Rhea Moffitt, Pepe Diaz for the first time in his life had a goal.

BACK IN HIS OFFICE, JUAN CALLED Maria in the kitchen on the intercom and said, "Bring Wallace to my office, please."

Moments later, the door opened and a small bald man with a white fringe of hair over his ears walked into the room. He was at least 20 pounds overweight, and a small gut hung over his wide belt. Juan had always suspected Wallace's success as a hit man was due to his non-threatening appearance. He was the opposite of Vic, but just as lethal, possibly more so.

"Have a seat, my friend. Would you like a cigar?" Juan said.

Wallace shook his head and said, "Heavens, no. They make me terribly dizzy."

"I need your services once again. The fee is the same as always. A certain Mr. Moffitt has caused our organization some minor difficulty, but as you well know, we must never appear weak in the eyes of our enemies. You will find him in and around a small town in Texas. He lives with a woman in a place called Castroville."

"Does he go armed?" Wallace asked.

"I don't know."

"Has someone else tried the hit?"

Juan was reluctant to admit that he'd hired someone else first, but he knew he had to be honest with this man. As effeminate as he appeared, he was nonetheless a vicious killer. "I sent a well-qualified man after Moffitt, but somehow Moffitt managed to run my man down with his own automobile. So be careful. He may appear stupid, but he's lucky."

Placing his hand over his heart, Wallace said, "Juan, I'm crushed that you'd give a job like this to someone besides me. Particularly when you know I'm the best."

Juan smiled. "We all make poor choices from time to time. Please accept my sincere apologies."

Wallace nodded. "Done. Unlike others, I do require half the fee up front."

"I trust you so much, my friend, I'm going to give you the entire fee now," Juan said as he removed a wad of hundred-dollar bills from his desk drawer. He tossed them to the hit man, who caught them with his right hand.

"What was it this unfortunate fellow did to raise your ire?" Wallace asked as he slipped the bills into an expensive-looking briefcase.

"He and a buddy ripped us off. Lifted a kilo of powder and $50,000 in cash."

"The rascal. Of course he must pay for such a dastardly deed," Wallace said with a wicked smile.

Juan often wondered about Wallace's sense of humor. It was macabre, to say the least. No wonder he was such an efficient killing machine.

CHAPTER 15

Jimmy Rhea Moffitt lay naked on the sweat-soaked bed and stared up at the slowly rotating ceiling fan. Driblets of perspiration slid down the sides of his rib cage and pooled in the small of his back. An unfiltered Camel cigarette dangled from his mouth. It was in the early hours of the morning and the temperature was in the low nineties. The last of July in southwest Texas was as close to hell as most people ever wanted to get. Darlene's window unit had finally given up the ghost, its Freon dripping onto the hard ground outside her bedroom like blood from a severed artery. The fan worked, but all that accomplished was to force hot air into the room.

Darlene, also naked, lay on her stomach beside Jimmy Rhea. She slept soundly, emanating small gurgling sounds as she exhaled. A neon sign at the Mexican restaurant next door created a reddish glow on her buttocks each time it flashed. She mumbled in her sleep and ground her teeth. The gnashing sound grated on Jimmy Rhea's nerves. Almost everything Darlene did annoyed Jimmy Rhea.

He'd used her shamelessly for the past months, living off her meager earnings at the Exxon Gas 'n' Go. She'd clothed and fed him and bought his cigarettes and beer and filled the tank of his Toyota with 87-octane Exxon gasoline. She'd even saved his miserable life, but he'd grown tired of her. The sight of her naked body still aroused him, but it was too hot to fuck. Without sex to hold him, Darlene was drifting out of Jimmy Rhea's sphere of interest. She'd served her purpose. She was disposable, like a used rubber.

Jimmy Rhea sucked his cigarette, inhaled deeply, and let the smoke drift out his nostrils so he could enjoy the rush of nicotine. He closed his eyes and thought of Cindy, undressing her in his mind. He ran his tongue over his lips at the thought of her pink nipples and ample bosom. He imagined running his tongue down her flat stomach to her navel and sucking gently on it.

Hot ash fell to his sweat-soaked chest and sizzled as it burned his skin. He was so enthralled in his fantasy, the pain only intensified his arousal. He wanted to devour Cindy's body, to make love to her until she was exhausted from pleasure and begging for more.

Jimmy Rhea had found that having a goal and reaching it are sometimes poles apart. He was proud of his effort. He'd laid out a campaign of deceit the devil himself would have been proud of. Over a four-week period he'd made several trips to Utopia to visit his ex-wife. On each occasion he'd acted with great restraint and suppressed his desire to physically possess her. He'd used his considerable charm to convince her he'd changed his ways. He'd lied about having a job and abstaining from alcohol. He'd been polite and thoughtful and always left after talking to her for only a few short minutes. It was his impression that she was softening toward him just a little, and a little was all he needed. He had a foot in the door.

He was ready to dump Darlene and pursue Cindy full time. Unfortunately, that might require a temporary bout of gainful employment. Jobs were scarce in rural areas, and Utopia was no exception. The last time he'd been there he'd noticed a sign in the Circle M window advertising for a Bobcat operator. Some enterprising fellow from Medina had started a brush-control business with two of the little machines and needed a helper.

Jimmy Rhea looked at the clock radio and saw that it was 4:00 a.m. If he left now, Darlene wouldn't know until she awoke at six to go to work. He'd be long gone by then. He stubbed his cigarette in the ashtray on the bedside table and swung his legs over the side of the bed.

Darlene moaned and rolled over on her back. Jimmy Rhea was fascinated by the bushiness of her pubic hair. It formed a huge inverted triangle that went all the way up to her navel. He had never seen anything like it, and after weeks of sexual encounters he still found himself staring at the mound of curly hair as he stepped out of bed. He would miss fucking Darlene. Of course, if he wanted to, he could always drop by from time to time for a little roll in the hay. She'd be unable to resist the temptation. After all, Darlene had told Jimmy Rhea he was the best lover she'd ever had.

He stumbled around the room in the semidarkness looking for his clothes. The neon light from next door cast its eerie red glow on all the objects in the room. His jeans were on the floor next to the bed and his underwear was on top of them. He pulled them on and started looking for his boots and socks. Jimmy Rhea's habit was to wear underwear and socks until they were either too stiff or too smelly to put back on. Darlene had at least coaxed him into using three pairs a week.

His socks were in the bathroom next to the commode. He remembered taking them off when he took his crap the night before. He couldn't find his T-shirt. After bumping into the dresser three times he remembered he'd stuck it under his pillow.

Once dressed, Jimmy Rhea threw some cold water on his face, brushed his teeth and hair, and threw his shaving articles into the canvas sack he used to store them. Back in the bedroom he quietly opened the dresser and took out all his underwear, socks, and T-shirts. Then he went to the closet and took his extra jeans off the hangers and threw all his clothes into a small duffel bag. He carried his boots and walked quietly on his toes to the kitchen, where he opened the refrigerator and pulled out a bottle of Budweiser. After twisting off the top he took a long swig while he looked for the carton of Camels Darlene had bought him the day before. He found the cigarettes in the cabinet over the refrigerator and threw them in the duffel bag with his clothes and shaving gear.

Turning to the kitchen door, he noticed a grocery list lying on the table. He turned it over and scribbled out a message for Darlene and left it on the refrigerator door.

Darlene

Hey, guess what? I got me a job out of town and will be gone for a few weeks. Keep that pussy warm, darlin, cause I'm coming back to fill it with my love. I'm gonna miss you something terrible, baby.

Your loving Jimmy Rhea

Once out the kitchen door, Jimmy Rhea pulled on his boots. As luck would have it, he'd filled the Toyota's gas tank the night before. The little engine roared to life, and Jimmy Rhea was on Highway 90 a few minutes past four thirty. He stopped at the Texaco Mart on the outskirts of Hondo and bought a cup of coffee and a pecan roll.

On the edge of town he turned toward Bandera. With the back window of the little pickup open, there was a fair flow of air through the cab, even if it was hot. He took out a Camel and lit it with the dashboard lighter.

Jimmy Rhea had no idea how he'd find the Bobcat man once he got to Medina, some 50 miles north of Hondo. It was such a small place he figured he'd just ask around. He passed through Bandera at about five fifteen. The streets were still empty. He turned onto Highway 16 and drove out of town heading north. He passed the Bandera Electric Co-op building and the turnoff to Tarpley. He figured to be in Medina by six o'clock and with any luck to have landed the Bobcat job by six thirty or seven.

He'd gone about 10 miles when the front driver's side tire began to make a flapping sound. Pulling onto the shoulder, he turned off the engine and got out of the truck. The tire was flat as a pancake. He kicked it with his boot and said, "Shit."

Jimmy Rhea was not high on preventive maintenance and had no idea if he had a spare or whether it contained air. He wasn't even sure where the spare was on the truck. He walked to the back, knelt on the gravel, and looked under the bed of the Toyota. To his surprise, the tire actually looked to hold the correct amount of air. Now if he could just find the jack. After rummaging through the vehicle he found it under the hood.

He jacked the truck up and removed the flat. As he turned to pick up the spare, he accidentally hit the jack and the truck fell onto the bare brake rim. Disheartened, he sat on the spare and lit a cigarette.

After fifteen minutes of cursing, he managed to get the jack out from under the truck. By the time he'd changed the tire it was eight o'clock. He figured the Bobcat man would have already gone to work clipping cedar trees. He'd have to get with the man later in the day. He drove back to Bandera because he was closer to it than Medina, and he knew he could get a tire at the Texaco station he'd passed earlier in the morning.

He decided on a retread because it cost about a third of what a new tire would. While the filling station attendant put the tire on his wheel, Jimmy Rhea sat on a stack of new tires and lit another Camel. He was tired and hungry. By the time he was ready to go it was almost ten thirty. He paid for the tire with Darlene's credit card, got in the Toyota, and drove to the center of town.

Darlene had brought him dancing at least once a week to the Silver

Dollar Saloon, so he knew his way around Bandera. He figured on stopping for a hamburger and a beer before he headed to Medina later that afternoon.

He parked the pickup in front of the Silver Dollar and walked down the stairs. The place was dark as usual, and George Strait's "Ocean Front Property" played on the jukebox. Five or six couples were eating an early lunch, and a skinny kid of about nineteen was playing the pinball machine.

Jimmy Rhea sat at a table next to the young man and ordered a hamburger, fries, and a Budweiser. While he sipped on his beer he watched the boy out of the corner of his eye. The youngster was impatient, and about halfway through each game he tilted the machine and lost his money.

Standing up and walking casually to the machine, Jimmy Rhea said, "You got to treat them things like a woman, boy. With gentle hands. You're too rough. I could teach you a thing or two if you like."

The young man looked at Jimmy Rhea with an irritated expression. "Think you could teach me a thing or two, huh?"

"If you're interested."

"How much money you got, partner?" the boy asked with a grin.

Jimmy Rhea felt a light go on somewhere in his feeble brain, but he ignored it.

"Enough to clean your whistle, smart-ass," Jimmy Rhea said in a rush of bravado.

"Five dollars a game. Whoever has the highest score takes the bill. Can you handle that, big spender?" the boy asked with a shit-eating grin on his face.

Jimmy Rhea did some mental arithmetic and realized that after buying the retread he had a scant twenty dollars to his name. What the hell? If he couldn't clean this kid's whistle, he deserved to be broke. He hadn't spent the better part of his youth in pool halls for nothing. He damn well knew how to win at pinball.

To Jimmy Rhea's amazement, the two were evenly matched. He had ten years' experience on the boy, and yet the young fellow was staying right with him. And he wasn't tilting the machine, either. It finally dawned on him that the fellow had done that as a ploy to draw Jimmy Rhea into a series of games.

After twenty games and about five beers each, neither of the hustlers had won a dime from the other. Jimmy Rhea was tired and figured if he didn't quit soon, he'd get careless and lose all his money. He let the boy finish his last game and then said, "You're pretty good, buddy, I'll give you that. What's your name, anyway?"

"Casey Jones. I know all about that train shit. My old man was a brakeman for the CSX railroad. What can I say?"

"Well, Casey, I was just thinking," Jimmy Rhea said as he lit a Camel, "we're pretty well matched. Ain't neither of us going to make a killing. Why don't we just have a few beers?"

Casey took a swig of his Miller Lite, belched, and said, "Okay, partner, suits the hell out of me. I'd just as soon listen to George Strait and get drunk anyway."

The two men left the pinball machine and sat in a corner booth. Jimmy Rhea fed two dollars' worth of quarters into the jukebox and pressed all the George Strait buttons.

Over the next three hours Casey Jones and Jimmy Rhea Moffitt each drank another six bottles of beer. Casey could hold his beer better than Jimmy Rhea.

"You got a hollow leg, Casey?" Jimmy Rhea asked.

"What?"

"I got to piss six times to your one."

Casey laughed and said, "I trained my bladder to stretch. When I first started drinking beer, me and my buddies would chugalug a mug of beer and see how long we could go without going. We'd bet five bucks and the guy who went first paid up."

"Well, I'll be. I ain't never heard of such a thing. Damn if I don't learn something new every day."

"I got to go, buddy. I got a hot date tonight. Aim to get me some pussy," Casey said, weaving as he stood.

Not to be outdone, Jimmy Rhea rose and, holding on to the table to steady himself, said, "I got one too, with my ex-wife. She's begging me to come back to her. If she plays her cards right and gives me some tonight, I might even consider it."

"Well, ain't she the lucky one? See you around, Jimmy Rhea. You ain't a bad sort," Casey said as he staggered toward the stairs.

Jimmy Rhea made one last stop at the urinal on his way to the stairs. He held on to the handrail and pulled himself up one step at a time. "That Casey is one hell of a fellow. Imagine stretching your damn bladder for a lousy five bucks," Jimmy Rhea said under his breath.

Jimmy Rhea staggered up the stairs and got into the truck. It wasn't the first time Jimmy Rhea had driven his Toyota drunk. Luckily, both for Jimmy Rhea and for the people he met on the highway, he managed to keep the truck under reasonable control. In some ways he managed better drunk than sober because he drove much slower. He only made it as far as the outskirts of Bandera when he was suddenly overcome with sleepiness. He pulled the truck onto the side of the road, flopped over on the bench seat, and fell soundly asleep.

CHAPTER 16

Jimmy Rhea awoke around four o'clock that afternoon with a splitting headache and a foul taste in his mouth, not to mention a terrible crick in his neck. He started the engine and headed out Highway 16 with the idea of cutting across to Tarpley and then driving to Vanderpool. He'd heard there was a boarding house there, and he was thinking of taking a room. He turned the radio to a country station and turned the volume up until the cab of the little truck vibrated. All the way to Tarpley he kept hearing Casey Jones say, "I aim to get me some pussy."

"Hell, I wasn't kidding either. I'm going to see Cindy. She's got to be aching for my body by now. I've played her real cool long enough. Time to fish or cut bait," Jimmy Rhea said out loud.

When he got to Utopia, he couldn't remember where Cindy's trailer was. "Damn place ain't that big," he said to himself. "I'll just drive around until I see the sucker."

After passing the trailer three times, Jimmy Rhea parked the

Toyota behind Cindy's Pinto and staggered up to the front door. It was about five o'clock, and Cindy had just unloaded the dishwasher. She was placing the dishes in the kitchen cabinet over the sink when Jimmy Rhea pounded on the door.

No one ever knocked on her door in the afternoon. She knew in her heart it had to be Jimmy Rhea. Desperately, she looked in the drawer for her butcher knife. It wasn't there. Her heart racing, she tried to remember what she'd done with it. She'd used it to cut some carrots, so she knew it had to be in the kitchen. The pounding got louder and Jimmy Rhea shouted, "Open up, darlin'! It's me, Jimmy Rhea!"

Calm settled over Cindy, something like the calm before a twister comes through town, throwing the roofs off houses and upturning trailers. Cindy looked in the dishwasher and found the knife. It was long and sharp and, she hoped, deadly. She picked it up and held it behind her back in her right hand.

She looked into the living room and saw Jody staring at the front door, a terrified look on her face. Cindy motioned for Jody to go to her bedroom. She didn't think Jimmy Rhea would hurt the child, but if he was drunk, there was no telling what he might do.

As soon as Jody had left the room, Cindy walked over to the door and slipped the chain in place. She cursed herself for not having done so the minute she'd gotten home.

"Open up, darlin'! I need you, baby!" Jimmy Rhea shouted.

"Go away, Jimmy Rhea. How many times do I have to tell you to leave us alone?"

Jimmy Rhea was becoming angrier by the minute. Who did Cindy think she was? Hell, she'd be plenty happy to see him after he'd made love to her. He used to drive her crazy in bed. He could still do it. He knew he could.

He put his shoulder to the door and hit it with all his might. The lock burst open, but the chain held. Cindy screamed and stepped back from the door. Jimmy Rhea hit the door a second time and the chain popped loose, sending the small screws from the doorjamb flying across the room.

Jimmy Rhea stepped up into the trailer and stood looking at Cindy. She had on a pair of cutoff jeans and a tight tank top with no bra. He thought about his lips on those pink nipples and staggered toward her.

Cindy held her ground. "Jimmy Rhea, I'm telling you one more time. Go away before it's too late. If you lay a hand on me, I'll kill you."

Startled, Jimmy Rhea stopped in his tracks. He'd never heard Cindy say such a thing. She was just testing him, testing his love. She wanted him. It was as clear as the nose on her face. If not, why had she dressed in his favorite outfit? Hell, she was just joshing him. Besides, he didn't see a gun. Cindy kill him? What a joke!

"Come here, baby. I want you. I want to cover your body with kisses like I used to. Remember? You used to love it," Jimmy Rhea said with a drunken smile on his face.

"Jimmy Rhea, don't do this. Please."

He put his arms around Cindy and lifted her off her feet. Holding her tight against his chest, he started walking backward toward the couch, his beer breath making her retch.

Cindy swung the butcher knife around with all her strength and buried it to the hilt in Jimmy Rhea's back. The blade, deflected by his shoulder bone, slid under the muscle and just missed piercing his lung. Jimmy Rhea screamed in pain and pushed Cindy away with an astonished look on his face. When he realized what had happened, he brought the back of his right hand across her face, cutting her lip.

He reached behind his back with his right hand and pulled out the knife. Seeing his own blood, he began to heave and vomited a stomach full of stale beer onto the carpet.

By then Cindy had locked herself in her bedroom and was fumbling for the phone. She dialed 911 and screamed at the operator that she was being murdered. Jimmy Rhea kicked the door down and walked into the room with the bloody knife in his hand. He was breathing heavily and looked like a wild man. His hair was tousled, and he hadn't shaved for two days. His eyes were fiery red, and Cindy was convinced his soul had been possessed by the devil.

He lunged across the bed and grabbed her by the hair. Throwing her on the bed, he began to unbutton her jeans. Every time she tried to get loose he hit her with the back of his hand, until both her eyes were almost swollen shut and her lip was bleeding. He ripped off her tank top and squeezed her bare breast.

Cindy felt for the knife she knew had to be lying on the bed next to Jimmy Rhea. She could barely see out of her right eye, but she knew he was unbuttoning his pants. While he was distracted she grabbed the knife from beside his left knee and in one motion swept it toward her ex-husband's throat. The blade missed its mark and Jimmy Rhea grabbed the knife from her hand and plunged the twelve-inch blade through his ex-wife's heart.

Realizing what he'd done, Jimmy Rhea sobered up quickly. He couldn't believe he'd killed the only woman he'd ever loved. Gasping for breath, he staggered from the room. He threw the knife into the sink and ran out the front door.

He slipped behind the wheel and with a trembling hand turned the key. Then he floored the accelerator and the Toyota's back wheels threw gravel as he headed for the pavement. His heart raced and he took shallow, rapid breaths. He whispered to himself, "Cindy, darlin', I'm so sorry. Oh, Jesus, what have I done?" Once on the asphalt, he headed south for Sabinal. He wanted to be across the border into Mexico as quickly as his little truck could carry him.

MONTY KILPATRICK WAS THE FIRST POLICE officer to receive the emergency call placed by the 911 operator in Uvalde. The sheriff's office had issued an alert to any law enforcement officer within ten minutes of Utopia. From the scant description the operator had received from Cindy, Monty was certain the call had come from her. He was about 2 miles out of Utopia on the road to Garner State Park when his radio speaker came to life with the message. He flipped on his emergency lights and siren and jammed the accelerator to the floorboard. The pickup leaped ahead, and he was in front of Cindy's trailer in less than five minutes of receiving the message.

He slammed on the brakes, the pickup sliding to a stop in a cloud of dust, and he jumped out. He pulled his Glock from its holster as he approached the front door. Monty saw that the door had been forced open and the living room was empty. Holding his pistol with both hands in front of him and at arm's length, he stepped into the trailer. Once inside, he could hear Jody screaming.

Monty advanced toward the child's voice. He stepped over several broken dishes and two pots that had been knocked to the floor in the little kitchen as Cindy and Jimmy Rhea struggled.

Stepping into the bedroom, Monty gasped. Cindy's bare chest was covered in a pool of blood. Monty knew she was dead. He dropped to his knees beside the bed and took Cindy's hand in his.

"Mommy okay?" Jody said in a small voice from the doorway. Monty had forgotten about the child. He stood and pulled the blanket that lay on the foot of the bed over the little girl's mother. Then he took her in his arms, holding her wet face against his and patting her gently on the back. "It's okay, honey. Let's go back to your room. Mommy's . . ." He didn't know what to say. Would the child understand death? She was only three years old.

Jody's little arms were clamped around Monty's neck so tightly he could barely breathe, and she sobbed hoarsely as she clung to him.

Just then Monty heard a second siren and a vehicle coming to an abrupt stop in front of the trailer. A door slammed shut, and in a few seconds he heard Arthur Jepson call out, "Monty, you okay?"

"Come in, Arthur. Everything's under control."

When Arthur walked into the room, his face went white. He said, "Oh, my God, what happened?"

Monty asked Arthur, "You still carry that Polaroid camera in your truck?"

"Sure."

"Get it and make some pictures of this mess."

"I'll be right back."

Holding Jody's head against his neck so she couldn't see her mother, Monty pulled the blanket covering Cindy back momentarily and wondered why people did such terrible things. *It was no wonder domestic violence took so many lives. People simply couldn't control their emotions. How was a child, a baby really, supposed to deal with the emotional trauma of such a ghastly ordeal?* He wondered.

A flash of light brought Monty out of his thoughts as Arthur began to take photos of the murder scene. When Monty was satisfied that the pictures were adequate, he said, "Call the sheriff's office in Uvalde, would you? Tell them to send an ambulance for the body. The medical examiner can check things out at the Bexar County Forensic Center in San Antonio tomorrow. There's no question as to the cause of death or when it happened. The body's still warm, for Christ's sake."

"Are you taking the daughter home with you?"

"Yes."

Monty helped Jody into the backseat of the pickup cab and snapped her seat belt. As they turned onto the main drag through town, Monty picked up his mobile phone and pressed the number one button.

When Martha Jo answered, he said, "Honey, I'm bringing some company home for a few days."

CHAPTER 17

Martha Jo said, "My God, Monty, what happened? Are you all right? Where's Cindy?"

"Take the child. She's seen and heard too much as it is. Cindy's been murdered. I'll tell you about it later."

"That's awful. I can't believe it. Let me have Jody and I'll take her to the bathroom and clean her up."

Monty handed the little girl to Martha Jo, and the child wrapped her arms around his wife's neck and buried her head in Martha Jo's bosom.

Heading for the door, Monty looked over his shoulder and said, "I'm going after Cindy's ex-husband. I'm sure he did this. Look for me when you see me."

He ran out the front door and climbed into his truck. He had no idea which direction the idiot had taken. Monty's best guess was that Moffitt was headed for the border, either Eagle Pass or Del Rio. He didn't think the felon was stupid enough to head north. He had to be trying for Mexico because every cop in the state of Texas would be looking for him.

WALLACE HAD BEEN FOLLOWING JIMMY RHEA all day. He even watched as the bastard had changed the tire on his truck. And he'd sat next to Jimmy Rhea in the saloon. Wallace's plan was to follow his mark until dark and then take him. By the time Jimmy Rhea arrived at Cindy's trailer, Wallace was fed up and wanted to end things quickly. He'd been just about to enter the trailer when Jimmy Rhea ran out the front door.

As the Toyota pulled onto the street, Wallace climbed back into his rental car and fell in behind Jimmy Rhea. He didn't know what had transpired in the trailer, but Jimmy Rhea had left in an awfully big hurry. Wallace stayed a good five car lengths behind the Toyota as it headed toward Sabinal.

Jimmy Rhea's back hurt like hell. Each time he leaned back in his seat he got a sharp pain between his shoulder blades that took his breath. He still couldn't believe he'd killed his ex-wife. He kept wiping perspiration from his forehead with the back of his hand. Tears filled his eyes and he had difficulty seeing the highway. Should he pick up Darlene on his way to Mexico or leave her? He'd never felt so confused.

Jimmy Rhea had kept a cheap Saturday night special in the glove compartment of his truck for years, despite the fact he'd go to jail if the police found it. Since his run-in with Vic, he'd kept the snub-nosed .32 in his hip pocket. To reassure himself, he reached around with his right hand to feel its bulge.

His mouth was so dry he couldn't swallow. Each time he loosened his grip on the steering wheel, his hands shook uncontrollably, and he'd grab the wheel again to steady himself. He couldn't remember which was closer, Del Rio or Eagle Pass. He sped through Sabinal and headed for Uvalde, so intent on escape that he never noticed the car behind him. His one desire was to cross the border, to get away from the police.

Wallace had already figured out Jimmy Rhea's plan. The idiot was obviously headed for Mexico. The hit man smiled. The whole episode was playing right into his hands. Depending on Jimmy Rhea's route out of Uvalde, Wallace would know exactly where to take him.

MONTY HAD NO IDEA WHAT TYPE of vehicle Jimmy Rhea drove. The one time he'd met the jerk, Monty hadn't noticed an unfamiliar car or truck in front of the Circle M. He knew the bastard couldn't be too far ahead of him but Jimmy Rhea had at least a thirty-minute lead.

As his state pickup barreled down 187 toward Sabinal, Monty glanced at the speedometer and saw the needle pegged at 110 miles an hour. He picked up his microphone and quickly dialed the Uvalde sheriff's frequency. When the dispatcher answered, Monty said, "This is Monty Kilpatrick. Where's the sheriff?"

"I think he's at home."

"Patch me through, please."

Monty heard three rings before the sheriff said, "Boswell."

"Tim, Monty. A woman's been murdered in Utopia. I feel sure it was her ex-husband. His name's Moffitt. I suspect he's headed for the border. Can you set up a series of roadblocks in and around Uvalde?"

"Sure. It'll take a few minutes. I'll have to call some deputies in. What's he driving?"

"I don't know. He's a tall, skinny guy with red hair. I met him once. He's an ex-con. I don't know if he's armed or not."

"Where are you, Monty?"

"Just coming into Sabinal. Would you call the Border Patrol and alert them as well?"

"Sure. I'll get back to you in a few minutes."

The line went dead and Monty replaced the microphone. He felt like he was looking for a needle in a haystack. As he approached Sabinal, he switched on his blue and red lights and hit the siren as he ran the stop light on Highway 90. Barreling toward Uvalde, he shook his head and whispered, "I let you down, Cindy. I'm so sorry."

AS HE APPROACHED UVALDE, JIMMY RHEA slowed to 30 miles an hour. He didn't want to be stopped by the police; every cop in Texas was probably looking for him. He glanced at his gasoline gauge and his heart raced. It was sitting close to empty. He wanted to get through Uvalde before stopping for gas.

Wallace always kept his tank full when possible. He couldn't afford to run out of gasoline when he was stalking a mark. When a sheriff's patrol car drove past Jimmy Rhea without pulling him over, Wallace realized the police didn't know what the felon was driving. That was valuable knowledge.

Jimmy Rhea's heart almost stopped when he glanced in his rearview mirror and saw the sheriff's cruiser coming up behind him. Momentarily he shut his eyes. When the policeman passed him, Jimmy Rhea let out a long sigh. Maybe his luck would hold. He might actually make it to Mexico. What he'd do when he got there, he had no idea. As usual, his pockets were empty. But he did have Darlene's MasterCard.

He made it through Uvalde and took the farm-to-market road to Eagle Pass. Every time he spotted a patrol car he held his breath. Just as he passed the last intersection on his way out of town, he saw two police cars form a roadblock. He couldn't believe he'd made it through before they'd set it up. What would happen when he got to the border? What if the Border Patrol was looking for him? Maybe he'd have to wade across the damned river.

His gasoline gauge was dangerously low. He knew he'd have to stop at the first station he sighted. As luck would have it, he passed a Shell station about 5 miles south of Uvalde. He made a quick U-turn and almost sideswiped a Ford sedan driven by a bald guy who'd been a few car lengths behind him. The man had to swerve to miss Jimmy Rhea's truck.

Jimmy Rhea used the MasterCard to fill his tank. The Ford pulled up to another pump and the bald man stepped out to fill his tank. Jimmy Rhea tried to avoid looking at the fellow.

"Pretty quick on that U-turn, buddy. You almost clipped me," Wallace said with a grin.

"Sorry."

"Where're you headed?" Wallace asked.

"Down the road apiece," Jimmy Rhea said, slipping behind the wheel of the Toyota.

He floored the accelerator as he peeled out of the station's parking lot. There was something about that man; maybe it was his strange eyes that gave Jimmy Rhea the willies.

MONTY SLOWED WHEN HE REACHED UVALDE. He had no idea which direction to go. He'd have to take a farm-to-market road to Eagle Pass or Highway 90 to Del Rio. He tried to think what could be going through Jimmy Rhea's addled mind. The shortest route would make sense. Also, a less-traveled road would help. Using that logic, Eagle Pass seemed the best destination.

When he turned onto FM 481, he came upon the sheriff's road-block on the outskirts of Uvalde.

He stopped and rolled down his window. "How long have you fellows been here?"

"About fifteen minutes, Monty. I sure wish we knew what kind of vehicle that guy's driving."

"Me too. He's a tall, skinny redhead, that's all I can tell you. I'm going to Eagle Pass. Tell Tim Boswell I think he should head for Del Rio."

Monty's gasoline gauge showed half a tank. At the Shell station he pulled in for a fill-up. While the pump ran, he walked into the store and asked the woman behind the counter, "Have any cars or pickups stopped for gas in the last ten or fifteen minutes?"

"You ain't supposed to leave your truck running when the pump's on," she said with a frown on her face.

"Answer my question. Forget the damn pump."

The woman blanched. "Well, I swear. There was a Toyota pickup, one of those little ones, and a Ford sedan."

"What did the drivers look like?"

"Toyota was a redhead. Ford an old bald guy."

"What color was the truck?"

"Faded red."

"How long have they been gone?"

"Ten minutes or so. What'd they do?"

Monty ran back to his truck and pulled the hose out. Back on the highway, he pinned the accelerator to the floorboard. A farmer on a New Holland tractor pulled onto the highway about fifty yards in front of Monty. He flipped on his siren and the farmer froze, stalling the tractor in the middle of the road. Monty swerved onto the gravel shoulder and spun out, almost flipping the truck. Cursing under his breath, he hit the gas and straightened the truck, just missing the tractor. Back on the straightaway, he floored the accelerator.

JIMMY RHEA LEANED FORWARD IN HIS seat to take pressure off his back. His head throbbed and he felt light-headed. He glanced at the speedometer and saw that he was pushing 85. He needed to go faster but that was all the little truck could muster. His eyes wandered to the temperature gauge and he groaned. "Jesus, the fucking engine's heating up. Holy shit."

Just when he thought things couldn't get worse, the new retread tire lost its rubber and the front end of the truck began to wobble. He fought the wheel to keep the pickup on the road. He pulled onto the shoulder, shut the engine down, and climbed out of the truck to inspect the damage. The tire was destroyed.

He went around to the back of the truck and looked at the spare. Dropping it to the ground, he kicked it. It was flat.

Jimmy Rhea began to cry. He felt completely defeated. He even considered placing the Saturday night special in his mouth and pulling the trigger.

While he was deciding what his next move was, the Ford pulled alongside and the passenger window slid silently into the door. Jimmy Rhea looked at the driver and wondered what the bald man wanted.

"What's the problem?" Wallace asked.

"What's not the fucking problem?"

"Where're you headed? I'm on my way to Eagle Pass. Can I give you a ride?"

Jimmy Rhea hesitated. He didn't trust this man. But he was stranded on the side of the fucking road in the middle of nowhere. He sure as hell couldn't walk to Eagle Pass. And he had his .32. If push came to shove, he'd just kill the bastard.

"That's mighty neighborly of you, mister. I'd really appreciate a ride. I can come back for my truck later."

Jimmy Rhea climbed into the passenger seat and gave a deep sigh. "How far you reckon it is to the border?" he asked the driver.

"An hour or so," the bald man said. "You going into Mexico?"

"Thinking about it. I need a piece of pussy. Them Mexican whores know how to satisfy a fellow."

"I prefer the guys, if you know what I mean," Wallace said with a grin.

"You a queer?"

"I like young boys. That bother you?"

"Hell, every man to his own vices."

They drove in silence for several miles. Jimmy Rhea kept feeling his right hip pocket. He figured he could pull the little pistol out in about three seconds if he needed to. The queer sure didn't seem threatening, and he wondered why he'd been frightened in the first place. In fact, the farther down the highway they traveled, the more relaxed Jimmy Rhea became. Hell, he could take this guy in a heartbeat. Fucking queers made his skin crawl.

"MONTY, PICK UP!"

Monty reached for his microphone. "That you, Tim?"

"Yeah. Where are you?"

"Headed for Eagle Pass on 481."

"I've asked the sheriff over in Del Rio to set up roadblocks and alert the Border Patrol. Any other suggestions?"

"I'm on the bastard's trail. He's headed for Eagle Pass. Call the border station and alert them. He's in a small Toyota truck, faded red. He's only a few minutes ahead of me."

"Will do. Be careful, Monty. The jerk may be armed."

"I hope he is."

"Don't be a fucking hero. Take the bastard alive."

Monty didn't answer.

"You hear me?"

Silence.

"Take him alive, Monty."

Monty turned off the radio.

WALLACE AND JIMMY RHEA RODE IN silence. Jimmy Rhea was so stressed and tired, he laid his head against the door frame and drifted off to sleep. Wallace smiled and looked for a place to turn off the highway.

Five miles farther along the two-lane blacktop, Wallace spotted a gravel road entering a mesquite thicket. It looked like it would give good cover. The idiot's body wouldn't be found for days. By then Wallace would be safely at home in Houston.

MONTY SPOTTED THE TOYOTA PICKUP ON the side of the road and pulled in behind it. He couldn't see anyone and wondered what was going on. Then he noticed the shredded front tire and flat spare. He'd already taken his Glock out of its holster, so he returned it. His mind raced as he tried to put the pieces together. The lazy bastard surely hadn't decided to walk. He must have flagged someone down. Could it be the Ford? With nothing else to go on, Monty jumped back in his truck, gunned the accelerator, and headed for the border.

THE FORD HIT A RUT IN the gravel road, jarring Jimmy Rhea awake. He glanced at Wallace and asked, "What're you doing?"

"I've got to pee, won't take but a second."

Wallace glanced in the rearview mirror. It looked as if they were far enough off the highway not to be noticed, so he stopped the car and opened the door. Stepping out, he walked to Jimmy Rhea's side and opened the door. Then he pointed the silenced pistol at Jimmy Rhea's head and said, "Get out."

Jimmy Rhea felt his crotch flood with urine. How had this guy found him? Who was he? He didn't look like a killer. "Oh, shit," he whispered.

He wasn't sure his legs would work. He thought he might be paralyzed. Jimmy Rhea just stared at the little bald man through dilated pupils, unable to move.

"Get out. Now!" Wallace shouted as he grabbed Jimmy Rhea's

shirt collar and pulled him out of the car. Jimmy Rhea stumbled out and immediately fell to the ground, covering his head with his hands.

Wallace lifted Jimmy Rhea up and shoved him away from the car. Then he leveled the pistol at Jimmy Rhea's head.

MONTY WORRIED THAT JIMMY RHEA MIGHT panic and kill the person who'd offered him a ride, but he simply couldn't get any more speed out of his pickup. The speedometer was still pegged at 110. Luckily the highway was fairly straight. Up ahead, Monty thought he saw a car turn off the road. He wasn't sure if it was a Ford or not. Indecision gripped him as he tried to decide what to do. If Jimmy Rhea was in that car, the driver could be in danger. "Shit," he said under his breath.

He took his foot off the accelerator and eased on the brake. He didn't want to make any sound as he approached. He figured he'd only lose a few minutes by checking on the car.

Monty turned onto the gravel road and swerved to miss the rut that had awakened Jimmy Rhea. What he saw when he reached the clearing where the Ford was parked confused the hell out of him.

A short bald man had a silenced pistol aimed at Jimmy Rhea's head. Monty slammed on the brakes just as the man turned and fired a series of shots at his pickup. The windshield exploded as the truck slid to a stop. Monty rolled out and onto the ground with his Glock firmly in his right hand. He came up into a kneeling position, firing a series of short bursts at the bald man, who was knocked backward off his feet.

Jimmy Rhea took that opportunity to reach for his Saturday night special. He had no intention of letting that damn game warden take him to jail.

Monty turned to face Jimmy Rhea just as the felon aimed his pistol at Monty. Before Jimmy Rhea could fire the .32, a slug from Monty's

Glock hit him squarely between his eyes, throwing him into a mesquite tree.

Exhaling, Monty surveyed the scene with a racing pulse. He hadn't had to kill anyone in years, and his hand trembled as he slipped the Glock into its holster. He wandered over to the bald man and studied his body. The fellow sure didn't fit the description of a hired killer. Maybe that was how he got away with it.

Back in his pickup, Monty dialed the sheriff's frequency and said, "Uvalde, Monty here. Tell Sheriff Boswell I've killed the felon and another fellow. I think the other guy was a hit man. I'll wait here until he arrives."

"You okay, Monty?"

"Just a little shaky. Tell Tim to hurry. I'm on a side road off 481. I'll place a flare on the highway so he'll know where I am."

CHAPTER 18

Fifteen minutes later, Monty heard several sirens headed his way.
He was on his third cigarette and his hands still shook. The Ford
was running. He knew not to touch anything until the forensics
people got there. He also knew he'd be put on administrative
leave until an inquiry had cleared him. He wasn't concerned about
that. He'd acted in self-defense. Jimmy Rhea was a felon and the bald
guy probably was as well.

Tim Boswell's patrol car slid to a stop behind Monty's state pickup.
He stepped out and walked to Monty's open window. Looking at the
two bodies, he said, "Jesus, Monty, what happened?"

Monty filled him in as three other sheriff's cars arrived. Deputies
swarmed over the scene until they realized there was no further danger.

Boswell said, "I've called a forensic team in San Antonio. They'll be
here in about two hours. I'll post a couple of my men until they arrive.
You'll need to call your supervisor and report in. I don't anticipate any
problems there."

"I don't either," Monty said, lighting another Camel.

"I guess that guy was a second hit man sent to take care of Moffitt. The idiot must have really pissed off some Mexican drug guys."

"Be my guess," Monty said. "I can't imagine how Moffitt got the upper hand on the first one. I don't think Jimmy Rhea was the sharpest tack in the box. He must have had help."

"This drug business has gotten totally out of hand. There's so much corruption in Mexico it's almost impossible to deal with."

Monty shook his head. "You know my feelings on the subject. If it weren't for the dopeheads in this country, there wouldn't be any cartels. Well, Europe is full of dopeheads too."

"I don't know the answer. You and I aren't going to change things. We'll just have to keep cleaning up the mess they create. Go home and get some rest. I'll take care of everything here," Boswell said.

"Thanks, Tim. I'm a little shaky. Haven't had to pull a trigger on anybody in a long time."

IT WAS DARK WHEN MONTY PULLED into his driveway. Lights were on all over the house and he wondered why. He walked through the kitchen looking for Martha Jo. It was quiet; not even the television was on. Lighting a cigarette, he walked down the long hallway to their bedroom.

"Martha Jo, where are you?" he called out.

He found her in Monty Jr.'s old bedroom rummaging around in the top of his closet, looking for a box of her son's old clothes. She had saved his things for years in hopes of having them for her grandchildren. When her son had been killed, she'd known she'd never have grandchildren, but she'd kept the clothes anyway. Most of his things had been worn to shreds, but she'd managed to save a few from each age range. When Monty walked in, she'd just found a box labeled "Two-Three."

"Thank God, I knew they were here somewhere," she said.

"What're you doing, honey?" Monty asked.

"I've been looking for something Jody can wear. I think this box has some jeans Monty Jr. had when he was about her age."

"Where is she?" Monty asked, looking around the room.

"There on the bed. Poor dear's exhausted."

Monty had completely missed the child. She lay sleeping in the middle of his son's double bed. Martha Jo had placed a small hand-made quilt over her frail little body. Her right thumb was jammed in her mouth and her wet hair was plastered across her forehead. Her breathing was fast and shallow.

"Aren't these just adorable?" Martha Jo said, holding up a small pair of blue jeans. "It's hard to believe our son ever fit into these. When she wakes up, I'll give her a bath and wash her hair. Tell me what happened to Cindy."

"My guess is her ex-husband tried to rape her again and she wasn't able to fight him off. He drove a butcher knife through her heart. She must have tried to use it to defend herself."

"I can't believe Cindy's dead. Oh, sweet Jesus, this poor child. We've got to look after her. The poor dear is exhausted and scared to death."

"We'll talk about that later. I killed Cindy's ex-husband about an hour ago. I asked Arthur to look for some family to take the child."

"You killed her ex-husband?"

"He pulled a gun on me."

"Are you all right? Are you hurt?"

The phone rang. Monty picked up the receiver.

"Monty, it's Arthur. How's the kid?"

"Exhausted and scared. She's asleep now."

"Monty, there's something strange here. I've started a search for next of kin and so far I can't turn up a soul except for her worthless father. Could be this kid hasn't got any other relatives."

"I just killed her father. Guess I'd better call the juvenile judge over in Uvalde. They'll have to figure out what to do with her," Monty said.

"You killed him?"

"About an hour ago."

"Good for you. I'll see you at breakfast."

Monty replaced the receiver and muttered under his breath, "Damn."

"What was that about?" Martha Jo asked.

"Arthur's having trouble finding any relatives to take Jody. I've got to call the juvenile judge in Uvalde and have her made a ward of the court."

"What's going to happen to her? Who'll look after her?"

"I guess she'll be placed in a foster home," Monty said.

"How are we going to explain all this to her? Isn't there anything we can do?"

"Like what?"

"I don't know, try to find her a good family, be her foster parents for a while. I haven't had time to think it through. Could you handle a three-year-old in the house again?"

"Jesus, Martha Jo, you don't want to raise another child, do you?"

"This house seems awfully empty since Monty Jr. . . ." Her voice trailed off to silence.

Monty stared at his wife in bewilderment. He liked children, had loved his son, and harbored fond memories of the boy's early childhood. They'd been great friends and Monty had enjoyed teaching Monty Jr. the fine points of hunting and fishing. He'd served as a coach for his son's Little League baseball team and been a Cub Scout leader for his troop. But could he deal with a girl? He enjoyed the fact that just he and Martha Jo were at home now. He liked having his wife to himself. He didn't want to share her with anyone, let alone a three-year-old child he barely knew. Besides, he worked weird hours.

"Can we talk about this? I mean, let's not jump into something we'll regret later," Monty said, lighting another cigarette.

"Please put that out, Monty. I know you don't want to raise another child, take on all that responsibility. I'm not sure I do either. I'm just worried about Jody. She's such a cutie and we probably owe it to Cindy. Let's take her in just for now, at least until she gets over the loss of her mother. Why don't we think about it?"

"I'll think about it, but I can tell you, I don't think it's a good idea," Monty said, throwing the cigarette into the toilet in his son's bathroom.

"Where's Mama?" Jody asked in a faint voice.

Monty and Martha Jo turned to see Jody standing next to the bed, a bewildered expression on her face.

Martha Jo walked slowly to the child, knelt, and pulled the girl to her bosom. "Your mama isn't here, darling. She's gone away. I'm going to take care of you, so don't be afraid. Come, let's give you a bath and wash your hair. Then I'll make you some cookies."

"I want Mama."

"I know, dear. We'll talk about it later, okay?"

Jody stared at Monty as if she was trying to figure out where she'd seen him before. Martha Jo took her hand and led her into the bathroom. She turned back to her husband and said, "Why don't you go to the trailer and bring back some of her clothes? I'll put her in Monty's little jeans for the time being."

"I can't enter the trailer without permission from the court. In the morning, we'll drive over to Uvalde and buy her a dress and some shoes and socks. Then we can talk to the juvenile judge."

"Thanks, Monty."

Monty watched the two of them walk down the hall hand in hand and shook his head.

THE JUDGE WAS QUICK TO GRANT Martha Jo's request once he heard the story of how Jody's mother had been murdered. He made the child a ward of the court and assigned Martha Jo and Monty as foster parents on a temporary basis pending an investigation into the child's family situation.

Jody turned out to be an exceptionally sweet and good-natured child, and Monty tried to adjust to having her around the house. It was difficult because of his schedule, and many times when he tried to sleep in the morning after working all night, she'd unintentionally keep him awake with her noisy playing. And the child captured much of Martha Jo's time that before had gone to Monty.

On the third morning of her stay, Monty came in exhausted from a rigorous night of dealing with some poachers from Shreveport, Louisiana. They'd slaughtered five big bucks on the Triple Bar Ranch. Martha Jo was pouring milk over a bowl of Raisin Bran for Jody.

Monty hung his Stetson on the hook next to the back door. He'd told Arthur he was too tired to have breakfast with him at the Lost Maples. He looked at his wife and said, "Any chance of getting some scrambled eggs before I go to bed?"

"I just need to get Jody fed and dressed and then I'll fix you some eggs. Have you had a bad night?"

"How long will it take?"

Martha Jo sensed an edge to her husband's voice that she didn't like. Monty was often cross with her when he was tired, but this morning it flew all over her. She set the milk on the table and said, "I'll do it as quickly as I can. I've got other responsibilities now besides waiting on you hand and foot."

"You don't wait on me hand and foot. Hell, you barely have time to talk to me anymore. It's Jody this and Jody that. Jesus, I thought I was through being a daddy."

"Monty Kilpatrick, listen to you. I can't believe we're having this conversation. I've never known you to be so selfish or self-centered. You should be ashamed of yourself. This poor child has only been an orphan for four days, and you're ready to throw her out of the house," Martha Jo said, tears welling in her eyes.

"That's right, cry. When all else fails, cry. Jesus, women!" Monty stormed from the kitchen.

THREE DAYS LATER MONTY CAME HOME after spending the day in court. When he walked into the kitchen, Martha Jo sat at the table with tears streaming down her cheeks. They hadn't spoken since their last argument about Jody, and Monty was still upset. He hated to see his wife crying, even if he was mad at her. He sat down and said, "What's wrong?"

"I'm not sure I can do this."

"Do what?"

"Raise another child. I thought I could, but I'm not sure anymore."

"What happened?"

"Jody got into my dresser and flushed two of my panties down the toilet and it overflowed. I thought I'd never get it unstopped."

"Where is she now?"

"Asleep."

"Well, I don't think either one of us is ready to deal with a three-year-old. I'm sorry, but that's what I've said all along."

"I know. I just feel bad for the child and I've got terrible guilt about Cindy."

"I do too. But I still think it's a bad idea."

Monty was tired of the whole affair and wanted to end their argument as quickly as possible. Martha Jo placed her hand on his knee and said, "Just give it a little time so we can get used to the idea. I think we should try to become involved in the child's life."

"But don't you understand?" Monty said. "The longer she stays with us, the harder it'll be for us to give her up."

"I know, but I think we should take our time to work through this."

"It's not that I don't like Jody. It's just that I don't think I'd be a good daddy to a girl. I know it's selfish, but it's the truth, even if I hate to admit it."

Martha Jo said softly, "Monty Jr. didn't come between us and neither would Jody."

Monty sighed and said, "I'll try. I'll hang in for a while, but I won't make any promises."

MONTY WAS CLEARED OF ANY WRONGDOING in the deaths of Jimmy Rhea Moffitt and Wallace. It turned out that the hit man didn't have a rap sheet. Monty knew that most of the time, those people weren't on anyone's radar screen. They just seem to pop up, do a job, and disappear into the woodwork.

Over the next few weeks, Monty became more self-sufficient at home. He helped with the dishes and began to take Jody around with him in his pickup when he was off duty. Martha Jo had bought Jody a car seat, and he buckled her securely in the back each time they left the house.

Monty had arranged for Cindy's funeral and burial, paying all the expenses out of his own pocket. Jimmy Rhea's body had been turned over to the county. Monty was distraught over his inability to protect Cindy. In addition to the guilt, he was angry for having allowed himself to become physically attracted to Cindy. In all his years of marriage he'd never been tempted to stray until Cindy had suggested she was available. In the weeks since she'd kissed him, Monty had visited Cindy more frequently and stayed longer to talk with her than he'd ever done in the past. He could feel his resolve weakening, and he'd been close to giving in.

And now the poor girl was dead and he was raising her child. How did these things happen? Cindy would be happy that Martha Jo and Monty had Jody. Maybe, in some small way, it would make up for the fact that he hadn't been able to save her life.

After the first week in the Kilpatrick home, Jody had ostensibly adopted Martha Jo as her mother. Even after the third and fourth weeks, she remained standoffish toward Monty, sensing, as children do, his detachment. But as he began to take her for rides in the truck, she slowly warmed to him. He took her by the Circle M to buy popsicles. She especially liked the grape-flavored ones, and when they got home, her lips and tongue were usually blue.

Jody referred to Martha Jo as Ma and later, when she came to better terms with Monty, called him Pa. The three of them gradually fell into an easy alliance. There was seldom a morning when Jody didn't climb up in Monty's lap and, placing her arms around his neck, plant a wet kiss on his cheek.

Martha Jo had been riding Monty so hard about his smoking around Jody that he was actually trying to quit. It was harder than he'd expected. He chewed nicotine gum and got hooked on that. The whole thing was driving him nuts. But he continued to try. Even Arthur, who'd tried to get Monty to give up cigarettes for years, was impressed.

For her part, there was a sparkle in Martha Jo's eyes that Monty hadn't seen in years. She spent the first weeks shopping at the Uvalde Walmart. Monty Jr.'s old room underwent a transformation. New lace-edged curtains replaced the drapes. Colorful striped sheets and a new bedspread were put on the double bed, and the closet was filled with dresses, blue jeans, tennis shoes, and a pair of dainty black patent leather shoes for Sunday.

Several weeks later, during dinner one evening, Martha Jo asked, "Why haven't we heard from the judge?"

"These things take time. Besides, you have to be prepared for the fact that some relative may step forward to claim Jody. We'll just have to wait and see," Monty said.

Martha Jo refused to accept the possibility that Jody could be taken from her. Denial, after all, is one of the strongest human traits. There was little question in Monty's mind that Martha Jo had decided she wanted to keep Jody. Monty had a more reasonable perspective on the whole affair, but he, too, was being drawn to Jody. And despite all his worries about the child coming between him and Martha Jo, he was beginning to see that his wife was happier than she'd been in years.

A happy wife is ever so much easier to deal with than an unhappy one. Monty couldn't remember who'd told him that, but it must have been one of his older friends, a well-adjusted one. Monty glanced across the table at Jody sitting on her booster chair and thought how beautiful she was. He smiled and thought, *I hope she stays with us.*

He guessed he loved her after all.

CHAPTER 19

One evening at the dinner table Monty held Jody in his lap, letting her eat off his plate. She dropped a piece of corn bread on the floor and said, "Sorry, Pa."

"Don't worry, sweetie. I'll pick it up after dinner."

"I swear, Monty. You spoil that child to death. How am I ever going to teach her proper manners?" Martha Jo said.

"You'll manage somehow. You always do."

"I'm really getting nervous about our situation with J-O-D-Y," she said.

"I'll call the judge in the morning," Monty said.

Jody looked first at Monty and then to Martha Jo as if she knew very well who they were discussing.

INSTEAD OF CALLING, MONTY DROVE TO Uvalde the next morning and visited Judge William Smothers to find out the status of their petition to adopt Jody. When Monty entered the judge's office he found His Honor sitting at his desk with several file folders in front of him. The older man looked up and said, "Morning, Mr. Kilpatrick. Have a seat."

Monty did as he was told and asked, "Any word on Jody?"

"Human Services has located a sister of Mrs. Moffitt, a woman by the name of Jackie Willowy. She lives in Houston. I was going to call you this morning."

Monty felt as if he'd been shot through the heart with an AR-15. A sensation of dizziness swept over him and his heart pounded against his sternum. Taking a deep breath, he asked, "Does that mean she automatically gets custody?"

"She is the next of kin. I talked briefly with her yesterday. She seems like a mature individual. I've invited her to come discuss the situation with me. She'll arrive day after tomorrow."

"You know, Judge, Martha Jo and I've become very attached to the child. I believe we can provide a stable and loving home for her."

Judge Smothers smiled. "I know that. But if the child has a relative who wants her, there's nothing I or anyone else can do. Unless, of course, that individual is unfit for some reason to accept responsibility for Jody."

Monty couldn't believe his ears. After all the times he'd told Martha Jo to be prepared to lose Jody, he hadn't done so himself. How could he face his wife? How could he accept the fact that this sister of Cindy's could tear up his new family? What a disaster.

Monty asked, "Would it be possible for Martha Jo and me to meet with this woman?"

"I want to interview her first to determine her interest in her niece. Depending on her response, I have no problem with the three of you having a conference."

Standing, Monty handed the judge his business card and said, "Thank you, Judge. Could you call me on my mobile when you know more?"

The drive to Utopia was one of the longest and most difficult Monty had ever made. He dreaded telling his wife the sad news. His stomach churned and he felt bile enter his throat. As he drove into town, he stopped at the Circle M for some Tums. The new daytime manager was a woman by the name of Marsha Johnson. Plump and matronly, she was the opposite of Cindy in looks but just as accommodating and friendly.

When Monty entered the store, Marsha said, "Morning, Monty. What can I get you?"

"Tums. My stomach is killing me."

She plucked a roll from the shelf behind her and handed them to Monty. "Sorry. Anything I can do?"

He shook his head. "I wish. How much?"

"Seventy-five cents."

Monty paid her and left. Then he turned back and bought a pack of Camels. He tore the package open and took out a cigarette. He lit it with the truck's lighter and inhaled deeply. The nicotine rush did little to improve his mood.

When he got home Martha Jo and Jody were just getting into her car. Monty asked, "Where're you headed?"

"Walmart."

"Come back in the house. We need to talk."

A stricken expression crossed Martha Jo's face. "Is this about Jody?"

He nodded and she said, "Come on, Jody, sweetie, we need to go back in the house."

Husband and wife sat at the kitchen table and Monty filled Martha Jo in on his conversation with Judge Smothers. Martha Jo listened with disbelief. She had dreaded this moment ever since Jody had come into her life. She didn't think she could deal with the loss of two children. It was too much for one person to bear.

Jody had gone to her room at Martha Jo's suggestion and was playing quietly with a doll Monty had bought her the previous week. In the kitchen her foster parents agonized over their next move.

"What options do we have?" Martha Jo asked.

"I don't know. The judge said unless this woman is unfit to raise a child, she has every right to Jody."

"Oh, Monty, this kills me. I don't think I can give her up."

He placed his hand over hers and gave it a gentle squeeze. "I don't believe we have much to say about the situation."

TWO DAYS LATER, MONTY'S MOBILE RANG. It was Judge Smother's secretary. "Mr. Kilpatrick, the judge would like to speak to you."

After a brief hold, the judge came on the line. "I've met with Mrs. Willowy and she appears to be a suitable candidate to adopt her niece," he told Monty. "I'd like to have a hearing in chambers tomorrow to make a decision in the child's best interest. Are you and your wife available at ten in the morning?"

Monty's mouth was so dry he wasn't sure he could answer. "Yes, sir. Should we bring Jody?"

"Not at this time. I assume you can find someone to look after her."

"Yes, sir. That's not a problem. Do we need an attorney?"

"You should be represented if you wish to adopt the child."

As soon as he hit the off button, Monty called Martha Jo. "The judge wants us in chambers tomorrow at ten. Can you find someone to watch Jody?"

Martha Jo had been expecting the call, but when her husband uttered those words she gasped. "Yes, of course. What did he say?"

"That Mrs. Willowy was a suitable candidate to adopt her niece. And that we should get an attorney."

PROMPTLY AT TEN O'CLOCK THE FOLLOWING morning, Monty and Martha Jo entered the courtroom at the Uvalde County Courthouse. Judge Smothers was already seated and Mrs. Willowy and her attorney, a man Monty had never seen before, sat at a table facing the judge. Jackie Willowy didn't resemble Cindy in the least. She was older and had dark brown hair. She wore a tailored pantsuit and high-heeled pumps.

Monty, Martha Jo, and Jackson Walker, their attorney, took the other table. Monty wanted a cigarette so badly he thought he'd scream. Martha Jo was devastated and couldn't look at Mrs. Willowy.

Judge Smothers said, "If everyone is ready, I'd like to begin. We're here to determine the adoption of Jody Moffitt. The child's mother was murdered and I've appointed Mr. and Mrs. Kilpatrick as foster parents pending the identification of a next of kin. Mrs. Willowy, sister of the child's mother, has agreed to take custody of the child. The Kilpatricks have requested custody and we are here to determine what is best for the child. Mr. Walker, would you start the proceedings."

Standing, the attorney said, "Your Honor, I represent the interest of Mr. and Mrs. Kilpatrick. They have been caring for the child since her mother's untimely death. During this time they've provided a safe and loving home for Jody. The child has accepted them as her parents and appears to love them both very much. We feel the trauma of removing her from this loving family would not be in the child's best interest, particularly since she underwent unspeakable trauma with the murder of her mother. Mr. Kilpatrick is a well-respected game warden for the state of Texas and has the financial capability to give the child a comfortable home. We feel it is in the best interest of Jody Moffitt that she stays with her foster parents until they can officially adopt her."

Judge Smothers looked at the Willowy attorney and asked, "Mr. Utter, would you please present Mrs. Willowy's argument?"

"Yes, Your Honor. First let me say that Mrs. Willowy appreciates what Mr. and Mrs. Kilpatrick have done for her niece these past few months. She understands that the Kilpatricks tried to help her sister before she was murdered and she is appreciative of their friendship with her sister. She also realizes that everyone must wonder why she didn't know of her sister's death and didn't step forward immediately. Unfortunately, Cindy Moffitt was on the run from an abusive ex-husband who eventually killed her. Cindy Moffitt refused to tell Mrs. Willowy her hiding place in order to protect her sister from Jimmy Rhea Moffitt. When Human Services located Mrs. Willowy, she immediately contacted the authorities here in Uvalde. She and her husband are childless and have the financial means to provide Jody with a good home. Mrs. Willowy feels she will be a good mother for Jody."

Monty took his wife's hand and gave it a squeeze. He'd never felt so defeated. He was sure Martha Jo felt the same way. The choice seemed straightforward. Monty had little doubt the judge would award Jody to Jackie Willowy.

Judge Smothers said, "I believe, under the circumstances, that Jody Moffitt should be rendered into the custody of her aunt until she can be officially adopted." Turning to the Kilpatrick table, he continued. "The state of Texas appreciates the care Mr. and Mrs. Kilpatrick have given the child as her foster parents. I know this is a difficult decision for you and I'm sorry. Mrs. Willowy requests that you have Jody ready to leave with her this afternoon at three. Is that convenient?"

Monty nodded and said in a hoarse voice, "Yes, Your Honor."

Martha Jo and Monty left the courtroom in a daze. Neither spoke until they were on the steps. Then Monty said, "Thanks, Jackson. The cards were stacked against us from the very beginning."

Husband and wife were silent on the drove home. Martha Jo couldn't believe she was going to lose her daughter to another woman. She tried to assure herself that Cindy's sister would do a good job. She just didn't think anyone would do as good a job as herself. And poor Monty, he'd become as fond of Jody as she had. *This must be breaking his heart as well*, she thought.

IT WAS TEN MINUTES AFTER THREE o'clock that afternoon when Jackie Willowy pulled into the Kilpatrick's driveway. She was alone and driving an old Ford Explorer. She stepped out of the SUV, then walked to the front door and rang the bell. Martha Jo and Monty had spent their time at home collecting Jody's clothes, toys, and her favorite pillow. Martha Jo had dressed the child in her Sunday dress and patent leather shoes. Sitting on the sofa watching the child play with her doll, Martha Jo jumped at the sound of the bell.

Monty and his wife had tried to explain the situation to Jody, but she was obviously bewildered by it all. They'd finally decided they would just have to turn her over to Cindy's sister and hope for the best.

Opening the door, Monty said, "Come in, Mrs. Willowy. Jody's ready to go."

"I know this must be hard for you both. You've done a wonderful job and I really appreciate it. And I know Cindy would as well. I'll try to be a good mother, and please know that you can visit Jody in Houston anytime you'd like. I'm going to leave my address and phone number with you."

Martha Jo said, "If you need anything, just let us know. And if you have any questions about Jody, I'm usually here at the house."

"Thank you. Shall we load up all these toys?" Jackie Willowy said with a smile.

The three adults took Jody's little suitcase and her toys to the SUV. When everything had been loaded, Martha Jo knelt before Jody and said, "This nice lady is your aunt Jackie. She's your mother's sister. You're going to live with her now. She's going to treat you real nicely and you'll learn to love her. Be a brave girl now and get in the car."

Monty felt a hole boring through his stomach and he knew the same sensation was eating at his wife. He flexed his jaw muscles, trying to calm himself.

Jackie took Jody's hand and the child pulled away immediately and ran from the living room to the kitchen. When the three adults went to get her she was sitting under the dinette. Martha Jo said, "Sweetie, come out. Your aunt Jackie needs to get on the road. It's a long way to Houston."

Jody refused to budge, so Monty gently pulled her out from under the table and carried her back through the living room to the front door. She clung to his neck like a leech, burrowing her face in his neck. He placed her in her car seat in the back of the Explorer. She looked at him with pupils dilated. Then she began to scream, tears flooding her eyes.

Monty stroked her face with the back of his fingers and said, "Jody, honey, don't cry. Be a brave girl." Then he turned away with tears sliding down both cheeks. Jody's screams pierced his heart like a well-placed arrow. Martha Jo buried her face in her hands and wept. Jackie Willowy had a stricken expression on her face as she slipped behind the steering wheel.

The Explorer eased out of the driveway and turned onto the street. Monty and Martha Jo could still hear Jody's screams as they walked back to the house, holding hands. The rest of the afternoon was a blur for both of them. Martha Jo went to bed with a headache and Monty got into his pickup and drove up and down county roads in a daze. Had anyone asked him where he'd been he wouldn't have been able to tell them. It was as bad as the day his son had drowned.

CHAPTER 20

August in southwest Texas was always a killer, but Monty drove with the windows down and the air conditioner off so he could hear the night sounds. At 3:00 a.m. he was on County Road 111 passing in front of the Lucky 7 Farm, where the thoroughbred breeders of the 1940s had produced several Kentucky Derby winners. The new owner had no love of horses and was more interested in breeding champion Charolais bulls, so the tile-roofed horse barns were empty and the racetrack had been planted in oats.

Monty loved a full moon because it made it easier for him to travel on the country roads. Sometimes he drove with his headlights off. He knew the countryside better than most, and he'd covered almost every mile of it over the past twenty-five years. Monty wished he wasn't away from home so much and that he'd had more time to spend with Jody. And he was getting a little tired of dealing with poachers and common criminals.

But he'd made a vow to catch the Greeley brothers, and he intended to keep it. At the junction of CR 111 and CR 354 there was a cattle gap. Just as Monty rolled over the metal grid he noted a flash of light to his left.

He decided to walk the rest of the way toward the light. He pulled his Glock out of its holster and wandered through the underbrush, careful not to make any noise. Monty just hoped he didn't step on a rattler. A quarter mile from the road he came upon a clearing in the middle of a thick cedar brake. The Greeley brothers were kneeling beside the carcass of a buck, gutting it. It was a large whitetail, and Monty figured that explained why both brothers had come over the fence to dress him. Their usual modus operandi called for one of them to stay on the road as a lookout.

Monty maneuvered himself between the clearing and CR 354 so the brothers would have to come toward him if they made a break for it. The full moon made it easy for the brothers to see what they were doing.

In an even voice, Monty said, "Lie facedown on the ground with your hands behind your back."

"Oh, shit." Mack threw himself to the ground, followed by his brother. The two men knew they had no chance of escape. It was obvious to both that the voice belonged to Monty Kilpatrick and that he meant what he said.

"I told you to stay on the road, you idiot," Mack said.

"Don't call me an idiot. You're the idiot. I told you it was too soon to come back to this part of the county. Know-it-all, see what you've gotten us into now," Jerry said.

"Shut up. He ain't even read us our rights yet, you fool. Keep your damn mouth shut," Mack said.

While the two brothers argued, Monty took two sets of plastic handcuffs out of his pocket and placed them around the men's wrists. Once they were immobilized, he said, "You have a right to remain silent and have an attorney present when you're questioned. Understand?"

Both brothers nodded their heads and said in unison, "Yeah."

"Okay, stand and start walking toward the road," Monty ordered.

"I can't see where I'm going," Jerry whined.

"You saw how to get in here. You can damn well see to get out."

"What if I step on a rattler?"

"He'll probably give you professional courtesy," Monty said.

"Dammit, Mack, this is your fault," Jerry said.

"Shut up, Jerry, before I stick my foot in your damn mouth."

"Try it, asshole, and see what happens."

"Look, I've had enough of you two. Keep your lips buttoned," Monty said.

When they got back to the road, he had the brothers walk in front of him until they reached his pickup. He lowered the tailgate and said, "Sit on the tailgate and scoot up into the bed."

"I ain't riding in the back of no damn pickup. Not on no damn gravel road. Hell, we'll choke to death," Mack protested.

"Get your ass up in that truck," Monty said as he heaved the man off his feet and onto the tailgate of the pickup.

"Take your hands off me, you SOB. I'll get in the damn truck. I'm going to complain to your superior about cruel and unusual treatment. Your ass is going to be in trouble, buddy. We ain't no goddamn murderers. You can't treat us like this," Mack said as he scooted across the truck bed.

"That's telling him, Mack," Jerry said as he sat down on the tailgate.

"Just get in the truck and shut up. I'm sick of listening to you," Monty said.

"I want to ride in the cab," Mack said.

"Me too," Jerry said.

Monty slammed the tailgate closed and walked around to the cab of the pickup. He reached behind his seat and took out a length of rope and a roll of duct tape. He climbed into the truck bed and turned the brothers so they were sitting back-to-back. Then he wrapped the rope around them so they couldn't move. Pulling a strip of tape off the roll, he placed it across Mack's mouth before the man knew what was happening.

"Hey, you can't do that," Jerry screamed just as Monty stuck another piece across his mouth.

The two brothers were squirming and cursing behind the tape. Monty stood back and surveyed his handiwork. "There," he said, "that ought to keep you two quiet for a while."

On the trip to Utopia Monty hit every pothole he could find on CR 354 and slid the truck through each curve, stirring up as much yellow dust as possible. When he parked in front of Arthur Jepson's house, it was about four in the morning and the justice of the peace was sound asleep. Monty lay on the doorbell until a drowsy and rumpled Arthur presented himself at the door.

"What the hell?" Arthur barked as he swung the screen door out.

"I've got a little surprise for you in the back of my truck," Monty said. "Put your boots on and come out here."

"For Christ's sake, Monty, couldn't this wait until a decent hour?"

"When you see what I've got, you'll understand."

Arthur disappeared into the house and reappeared a few minutes later, still in his nightshirt but with his boots on. He carried a big flashlight and shined it on the porch floor as he walked through the door. "This better be good, Monty Kilpatrick, or your ass has had it," he mumbled, striding ahead of his friend toward the truck.

Arthur aimed the flashlight on the truck bed and began laughing so hard tears came to his eyes. The Greeley brothers had been tossed into a corner by the rough ride and were lying upside down. They were covered from head to toe with yellow dust, their eyes shining through the clay like small bits of coal. The brothers were still attempting to right themselves when the game warden and the JP walked up. They were cursing through the duct tape gags, but their words were mumbled and indistinguishable.

"I'm going to pretend I didn't see the shape these two are in,"

Arthur said. "I don't blame you a bit, but the damn ACLU lawyers would be all over your case."

"I got tired of listening to the bastards, plain and simple. I figured you could arraign them and then I'll take them down to Sabinal and get George Acree to lock their sorry asses up," Monty said.

"Okay, buddy, but if I were you, I'd dust them off outside of town and take the tape off."

At that moment a beautiful young woman with raven hair in a see-through nightgown walked out onto the porch. She had voluptuous, upturned breasts that hung over a tiny waist. She called, "What's going on, honey?"

"You old rascal, you are pussy whipped," Monty said with a grin.

"Say a word about this and I'll cut your balls off," Arthur said.

"Who is she?"

"None of your damned business. Get the hell out of here."

"You've got to book these two assholes first."

"Wait here. I'll be right back."

"Aren't you going to take them in the house? You usually do. Besides, I want to meet your squeeze," Monty said with a grin.

Arthur turned and went back into his house, only to return moments later carrying a ledger. He took care of the paperwork and handed Monty a receipt. "Take these jerks to Sabinal," he said.

By the time Monty made the 22-mile trip to Sabinal and George Acree had taken the Greeley brothers into custody, it was six o'clock. He didn't make it to the Lost Maples until seven. To his surprise, Arthur was waiting in their regular booth.

"Get those bastards deposited in the Sabinal jail?" Arthur asked.

"Yeah. I cleaned them up a little like you suggested. They complained to George but he blew them off."

Gertrude filled Monty's cup and refilled Arthur's and went to the kitchen for Monty's breakfast.

"So, you going to level with me about your girlfriend?"

"She's a schoolteacher over in Uvalde. She just filed for divorce, so technically she's still married. That kind of complicates things."

Monty laughed. "I'd have to agree. Be careful, old buddy. I'd sure hate to see you get your balls shot off."

After breakfast, Monty drove home and when he walked into the kitchen, Martha Jo asked, "Want some coffee?"

"Sure."

"How was your night? Anything exciting happen?"

"Caught a couple of poachers I've been after for a while," Monty said as he placed his hat on the rack. Sitting down, he raised the cup to his lips and sipped on the hot coffee.

Martha Jo sat across from him and did the same. They both enjoyed this quiet time in the morning when Monty had just come in from a night's work. They were silent for a few minutes, then Martha Jo said, "I wonder how Jody's doing. I've been tempted to call Jackie, but I don't want to be a pest."

"I miss that child so much it's killing me," Monty said. "I want to get in my pickup and drive to Houston, but I know that wouldn't be good for Jody. We've got to let her go."

"I can't sleep and I mope around this house like a zombie. It's killing me, too," Martha Jo said with tears filling her eyes.

Monty placed his hand over hers and said, "We just have to take each day one at a time like we did when we lost Monty Jr."

PEPE DIAZ AND A BEAUTIFUL PROSTITUTE named Lolita had been partying for several hours. The evening started with dinner around ten o'clock at the Tail of the Cock restaurant in the center of Chihuahua. It was a fashionable eatery frequented by the wealthy citizens, a number of whom were drug-trade personalities. Fine restaurants in Mexico were somewhat of an oxymoron because much of the food was prepared well but served poorly. At the Tail of the Cock, the food and service were both excellent.

Pepe ate there often, many times accompanied by a high-priced call girl. He'd always frequented the brothels, but since his illness, his taste had become more sophisticated and his desires required both beauty and technical excellence. His ability to perform sexually had been impaired, and to become aroused, he now required younger and more beautiful women.

The first time he failed to sustain an erection he blamed it on too much tequila. The second and third episodes could not be explained away so easily, for he'd been cold sober. He was convinced that the indwelling catheter he'd worn so long after his surgery was responsible for his dilemma. If that was so, he reasoned, Monty Kilpatrick was the culprit who had destroyed his sex life. Each time he failed to perform in bed he blamed the game warden and swore to have his revenge. In Pepe's mind, to cure his affliction, a more comely and sexy woman would make it easier for him to become aroused. On occasion, the plan worked, but with increasing frequency, no matter how beautiful the woman, he could not obtain or sustain an erection.

Dr. Roberto Gomez was convinced that Pepe's impotency was psychological, and he tried to explain this to Pepe without offending him. Pepe would have no part of it, preferring to blame the catheter and Monty Kilpatrick.

As Lolita slowly removed her dress and brief undergarments, Pepe lay propped in bed, watching every sensual move she made. He had to admit she was the most appealing woman he had ever been with. Her milky-white skin hinted of Castilian blood. She had a full bosom, a tiny waist, and small hips, which undulated back and forth as she approached the bed.

The past month had been so frustrating for Pepe that the previous night he'd risked his position with his brother and the cartel by sniffing cocaine just before attempting sex. That failed and left him more depressed.

The women, who were well paid, made every attempt to be understanding and supportive. They blamed themselves, saying that they were not beautiful enough or that they lacked the skill to arouse such an important and powerful man. Or they cited the tequila or the cocaine or the lateness of the hour as the source of the difficulty. But Pepe blamed Monty Kilpatrick for every unpleasant occurrence in his life. The desire to kill the game warden had become an obsession. Pepe thought about it every waking hour, planning every detail of his mission with the cunning and ruthlessness of a Mafia hit man.

Though Lolita was skillful in her arousal techniques and Pepe was hungry for her body, the encounter never came to fruition. Once again, the Mexican lay frustrated, angry, drunk, and deeply depressed on the king-sized bed in his luxury apartment. Lolita was discreet. She lay snuggled in his arms until he went to sleep, then quietly dressed and let herself out of the apartment. Twice in the early morning hours Pepe rolled over in bed, his left arm searching for Lolita. Each time he mumbled, "The big gringo has stolen Pepe's manhood."

THREE WEEKS AFTER JODY WENT TO Houston, the phone rang at 3:00 a.m. and Martha Jo fumbled for the receiver, knocking it to the floor. She turned on the bedside lamp and picked it up. "Hello," she said in a sleepy voice.

"Martha Jo, it's Jackie Willowy. I'm sorry to call in the middle of the night but I'm at my wit's end."

Martha Jo could hear Jody screaming in the background. "What's the matter?" she asked.

"Jody hasn't stopped screaming since we left your house. She cries constantly for Ma and Pa. She's breaking my heart. I've taken her to the pediatrician and even a child psychiatrist. Nothing I do helps. I believe, for her sake, you need to take her back. That is, if you still want her."

Martha Jo gasped. "Of course we want her back. We've missed her so much."

"I think she was with y'all long enough to make a strong bond, particularly so soon after losing her mother."

"We'll come get her today if you like," Martha Jo said.

"That would be great. I can't take off any more time from work. You have my address. What time do you think you can be here?"

Martha Jo looked at the illuminated dial on their clock radio and saw that the time was 3:10. She made some quick calculations and said, "I'll call Monty and we'll be there around seven or seven thirty. Will that work?"

"That's perfect. I can still go to work that way. I've missed so much trying to take care of Jody, my boss has threatened to fire me."

Martha Jo's hands trembled as she dialed Monty's mobile. She prayed he'd be in range of the repeating tower. He picked up on the second ring.

"We've got to leave for Houston immediately," she said with tears streaming down her face. "I just received a call from Jackie. She's agreeing to give Jody back to us. I told her we'd be there by seven or seven thirty."

Monty couldn't believe his ears. He said, "You mean we can adopt her?"

"Yes. Come home. I'll be ready to go the second you get here."

They arrived at Jackie Willowy's house at ten after seven. When Monty knocked on the door he could hear Jody screaming and it made his stomach churn. Martha Jo stood beside him, wringing her hands. Moments later, Jackie opened the door and said, "Come in. I've got all her things ready to go. I'll call Judge Smothers from work this morning and explain everything. I do hope you'll let me visit. I do love her."

"We want you to visit as often as you wish. And thank you for allowing us to adopt her," Martha Jo said.

"I'm convinced it's best for Jody. Come back to her room. I know she can't wait to see you both."

When Monty and Martha Jo entered the room, Jody stared at them as if they were ghosts. She stopped crying, but continued staring, taking deep breaths. Then she extended her arms and said, "Ma, Pa."

Martha Jo lifted the child off the bed and held her close. Jody buried her head in Martha Jo's neck and continued to struggle to catch her breath. "There, there, sweetie, it's okay. You're going home with Ma and Pa."

As soon as Monty strapped Jody into her car seat, she dropped off to sleep and didn't wake until Monty pulled into their driveway in Utopia. Martha Jo had slept the entire trip from Houston and she stirred awake at the same moment. She got out of the truck and opened the back door. Lifting the child out, she said, "We're home, Jody."

It took less than twenty-four hours for the Kilpatrick family to return to normal. Jody acted as if nothing had happened to upset her life. Martha Jo and Monty were ecstatic to have her back home.

Judge Smothers responded quickly to Jackie Willowy's request that the Kilpatricks take custody of Jody and proceed with adoption. He set the process in motion immediately.

CHAPTER 21

Pepe Diaz was making the final preparations for his trip across the border. He told Juan he was going on holiday to Acapulco for a week and had even bought a ticket on Mexicana Airlines to conceal his true plans.

Pepe had shared his secret with no one. For weeks he'd been hoarding cash, and he had $200,000 U.S. hidden in the fenders of his Corvette convertible. In a fake spare tire well of the car's trunk, he'd stored a 9 mm Israeli Uzi machine gun and two 9 mm Beretta semiautomatic pistols. Two hundred rounds of ammunition had been carefully inserted into the cushions of the seats.

He'd lost weight during his illness and had kept in excellent physical condition by working out with weights. In the two months preceding his expected departure, he'd given up cigarettes and alcohol. Running 5 miles a day had given him stamina.

Juan had watched his younger brother's physical metamorphosis with interest and suspected it might have something to do with the gringo policeman. But Pepe had sworn to him that he had put his hatred to rest and that he was not out to seek revenge. Just the same, Juan had kept Pepe under constant surveillance since his recovery.

On the day of his departure, Pepe rose early, showered, shaved, and dressed in an elegant beige linen sport coat and black slacks, Bally loafers, and an Armani shirt. He looked the part of a well-heeled Mexican patrician, someone not to be trifled with. After a light breakfast, he put on his sunglasses, picked up a small overnight bag, and walked to his car.

Pepe drove to the airport and boarded the plane to Acapulco. Just as the flight attendant was closing the door he made an excuse to get off the plane, saying he would take a later one. According to the airline's records, he'd boarded the flight, and there was no indication he'd disembarked.

Once in the terminal, he walked quickly to the parking lot and got back into the convertible. He lowered the top and drove through Chihuahua, headed for Ojinaga and Presidio. At the U.S. border, Pepe showed the customs officials his passport. He was charming as he joked with the officers. His reason for entering the United States, he said, was for a long-deserved holiday in his favorite city, San Antonio.

Pepe had no problem crossing the border. He felt lighthearted and happy as he drove through Presidio. When he reached Highway 90, he turned toward Del Rio and set the cruise control at 70 miles an hour. The radio was turned to a Tejano station in Del Rio, and Pepe kept time to the music by tapping his thumbs on the steering wheel.

In Del Rio he stopped at the Holiday Inn and had dinner. He still wanted a cigarette after each meal, and it was hard for him not to bum one off the waitress. After his mission, he might start smoking again.

On the road again, he went over his plan, pinpointing possible complications and creating solutions he might use to correct them. He pulled into the parking lot of the Uvalde Holiday Inn at nine o'clock. He checked in, took a hot, soaking bath, and watched television until he fell asleep.

The next morning he ate a large breakfast of huevos rancheros and drove to the Uvalde Walmart, where he bought a workingman's outfit. Next he went to a used car lot and purchased a 1994 Ford pickup and had it delivered to the Holiday Inn parking lot.

Texas requires a safety inspection on a yearly basis. The vehicle owner has to show that he or she has liability insurance in order to have a sticker placed on the windshield. To prevent thieves from lifting license plates, the state also requires those renewals to be in the form of a window sticker.

Pepe changed into work boots, khaki pants, and shirt, and he placed a baseball cap that said "CAT" on his head. He went to the parking lot armed with a single-edge Gem razor blade and carefully lifted both a safety sticker and a license off the first unlocked car he found. The stickers were designed to prevent theft, but if the perpetrator was meticulous, it was possible to lift them off intact. Once he had the stickers free, he went to his new truck and placed them on the inside of the windshield on the driver's side. Next, he drove to a quick sign shop and had them paint lettering on both doors of the pickup indicating the truck belonged to the Uvalde Landscaping Company.

The next three days Pepe cruised in and around Utopia casing Monty Kilpatrick's house and obtaining a feel for the community. He made it a point to have lunch at the Lost Maples Café each day so he could acquire some idea of how many policemen might be around at any given time. On the third day Monty Kilpatrick and Arthur Jepson walked right by Pepe's table, but the game warden didn't recognize him. Heartened by this, Pepe began to relax. He'd been very tense each time he'd driven into Utopia. The small size of the community had shocked him. He'd hoped for a large town so he'd be able to blend in more easily. The other thing that bothered him was that there were not many Mexican-Americans. But he figured service people must wander through Utopia on a regular basis.

On the morning of the fourth day he was ready to make his move. He stopped at the Circle M as soon as he drove into Utopia because he was nervous and felt he needed a cigarette. The young woman who'd taken Cindy's job was working the counter when he walked in.

Pepe flashed her a nervous smile as he said, "May Pepe have a pack of Camels, please?"

"Sure." Marsha reached behind her to take a pack off the shelf. She'd noticed the truck from Uvalde for the past few days and wondered who in town was having landscaping done. "You from Uvalde?" she said.

"Sí. Pepe works there."

"You don't live there?"

"Pepe lives there also. How much?" he asked. Even though his English was good he made mistakes when he was nervous. For this reason he'd kept his conversations to a minimum.

"Five dollars and ten cents," Marsha answered. She wondered why the man seemed so tense. Most of the Mexican workmen she knew were very easygoing.

"Gracias," Pepe said as he handed her six dollars.

Marsha rang up the cash register and, handing Pepe his change, said, "Who's having landscaping around here? I usually know most of what goes on, but I can't remember anyone having a big job done."

"North, a rich man's house."

"What's the name?"

"The boss handles the details," Pepe said, making a quick exit.

Once out the door he ripped open the pack of cigarettes and took one out. Perspiration beaded his forehead as the aroma of the tobacco filled his nostrils. He realized he no longer carried his gold lighter and had no matches. He rushed to the truck and pushed in the lighter. The second it popped out, he lit his cigarette and inhaled deeply.

Pepe had learned that Monty had a wife and small child and that he kept fairly routine hours. He worked many nights and came home around eight o'clock in the morning. Pepe had seen Monty leave the house the evening before and was certain his wife and child were still alone. Glancing at his watch, he saw that it was seven fifteen. He had at least thirty to forty-five minutes to subdue the wife before the gringo came in from his nightly duties.

The Mexican left the parking area of the Circle M and drove directly to the Kilpatrick house. Not seeing Monty's state pickup, he pulled into the driveway and parked beside Martha Jo's car.

Reaching behind the seat, he took out a small canvas bag containing the Berettas, the Uzi, a roll of duct tape, and a package of large plastic cable ties used by electricians. He removed one of the Berettas and placed it in his waistband at the small of his back. He then stepped out of the truck holding the bag, walked up the steps, and knocked on the front door.

Several moments went by and Pepe thought of leaving. Finally, the door opened and Martha Jo said, "Yes?"

"Please pardon Pepe, señora. Pepe was told to go to a Mr. Johnson's house on K Street and Pepe cannot find K Street. Could you help?" Pepe said politely as he tried to look past Martha Jo into the house. He wanted to make sure the policeman was not at home.

"There is no K Street in Utopia and the only Mr. Johnson I know lives on the edge of town," Martha Jo answered.

Jody held Martha Jo's leg, scrutinizing the Mexican with wide eyes. "I'm hungry, Ma," she said.

"Just a minute, darling. I'm trying to help the nice man," Martha Jo said. Turning back to Pepe, she continued, "Perhaps if you let me look at your instructions, I can tell what's wrong."

Seizing the opportunity to reach behind him, Pepe lifted the Beretta out of his waistband and brought it in front of him, pointing the barrel directly at Martha Jo's heart. His finger was on the trigger as he said pleasantly, "Please step inside quickly, señora, and you won't be harmed."

Shock left Martha Jo speechless. She obeyed and stepped backward into the living room, pulling Jody with her. Monty had taught her all about guns, and she recognized the Beretta. She was well aware of its clip capacity and knew it had a double-action mechanism. All the Mexican had to do was pull the trigger and Jody would again be without a mother.

Martha Jo had lived in fear of this moment since the day Monty went into police work. He'd downplayed the chance of retaliation by a criminal, but both of them knew the threat was real. She wondered if this was a man Monty had arrested. Her intuition told her she must be very careful in how she dealt with him. Monty had told her not to resist unless she was armed or felt she had a chance to catch her tormentor off guard and overpower him. In this instance, she had no choice but to cooperate.

"What is it you want?" Martha Jo asked.

Closing the door behind him, Pepe stepped into the living room and said, "Follow Pepe's instructions and you and the little girl won't be hurt. Disobey Pepe and you will both die."

Martha Jo knew the threat wasn't a hollow one. She picked up Jody and held her tightly in her arms. Looking directly into Pepe's eyes, she said, "If you want money, I have a small amount in my purse in the kitchen. The only other things of value would be our TV and my mother's silverware. Please take what you want and leave. I won't call the police."

"Pepe has no need for your money, señora, and he wishes you and your daughter no harm. Now please, go to your bedroom," Pepe said with a smile.

Martha Jo was confused. What did he want, and why did he continually refer to himself in the third person? If he didn't want money, why was he standing in her living room with a gun in his hand? And then it hit her. He was there to kill her husband.

A shudder went through her like the aftershock of an earthquake. Her mouth was already so dry she couldn't swallow, and her heart was beating so fast she felt she'd just run a hundred-yard dash. Her palms began to perspire, and she thought for a moment she was going to faint.

Pepe stuck the Beretta into her abdomen and said, "Please, señora, Pepe truly does not want to hurt you, but you must do as Pepe says."

Martha Jo had never been more frightened. She hugged Jody so tightly the child squealed in pain. Walking trancelike, Martha Jo moved through the living room into the hallway and finally to the bedroom she shared with her husband.

Pepe pointed the gun at the bed and said, "Please sit."

Martha Jo said, "You're not going to hurt the baby?"

"No. Now please sit down."

Martha Jo set Jody on the side of the bed and said, "Don't be afraid, darling. Ma must do what the man says."

Pepe handed Martha Jo four cable ties. "Place these around the child's wrists, behind her back. Loop them together like handcuffs. You must make them tight enough that she can't get loose. Then do her ankles the same way."

Martha Jo took the ties and said, "Jody, sweetheart, Ma's going to play a game with you. Put your arms back like this, and I'm going to tie you up and see if you can get loose."

While Martha Jo pulled the cable ties together, Pepe removed the roll of duct tape from the canvas bag and tore off a six-inch piece. He waited until Martha Jo was finished with her task and then handed the tape to her. "Place this over the little girl's mouth," he said.

Martha Jo did as she was told, and Jody began to whimper. It broke Martha Jo's heart. "It's okay, darling, try to be brave. Ma's right here."

"Lay her on her stomach," Pepe said, "and then place this piece of tape securely over your mouth."

Once again Martha Jo followed Pepe's orders. Her mind raced as she tried to outsmart the Mexican. But he was professional in his manner, and she was too anxious to think of a way to get the upper hand.

She took the duct tape and pressed it against her lips. As she did so she let a few drops of saliva slip out of her mouth in hopes it would prevent the tape from sticking firmly. Perhaps she could move her jaw enough to work the tape loose and shout a warning to Monty.

Once the tape was in place, Pepe ran his fingertips over the tape to make sure it was stuck. "Lie on your stomach please, and place your arms behind your back with your wrists together." Martha Jo did as she was told. Once Pepe had secured them, he did the same with her ankles.

She realized she would be useless to Monty when he was forced to confront the Mexican. Something about this man seemed unusual to her. She'd dealt with Mexican-Americans all her life and had found them to be amicable. This Mexican was different. The coldness of his eyes relayed a sense of anger and contempt.

When Martha Jo had been neutralized, Pepe took stock. The woman was in no condition to aid her husband, and the child was harmless.

He whispered, "Lie still and be quiet, and no harm will come to you or the baby. If you disobey, Pepe will kill you both."

Martha Jo had no doubt the man meant what he said. For the first time in her life she didn't know whether she'd live to see the sun set over her beloved Sabinal Canyon. Somehow, she had to warn Monty that he was in danger.

Once satisfied that he had the situation under control, Pepe strode confidently from the room. He went to the kitchen and poured himself a cup of coffee. He took a cigarette out and lit it with a kitchen match. Now that he was so close to success, he'd decided that he liked to smoke too much to give it up. Nor would he continue to abstain from alcohol and whores. Soon he would be enjoying his old life. All that stood between him and happiness was the gringo policeman.

Martha Jo felt a trickle of saliva run down her chin. She'd been able to force her tongue through her closed lips and used saliva to loosen the duct tape. By moving her jaw she could feel the tape give.

Just as she began to have some success, she heard Monty's truck turn into the driveway. The big all-terrain tires made a crunching sound on the gravel. Her pulse raced and her head pounded. Her husband was moments away from death, and there was nothing she could do about it. She buried her face in the bedcovers and began to sob.

CHAPTER 22

Pepe heard the pickup as well and snuffed out his cigarette in the palm of his hand. He removed the second Beretta from the canvas bag and placed it in his waistband at the small of his back. He knew from watching Monty that the game warden always entered the house through the kitchen door. Holding the other Beretta in front of his face, he slipped quietly behind the door.

Monty couldn't imagine what a pickup from the Uvalde Landscaping Company was doing parked in his driveway. Maybe Martha Jo wanted some new rosebushes. But she usually discussed things like that before acting. No. This didn't seem right. He needed to be careful.

He parked the state truck next to his wife's car and walked to the back door. He opened the door and went inside. He expected to see Martha Jo either standing at the sink or sitting at the kitchen table discussing business with someone from Uvalde. When he saw the kitchen was empty, he called out, "Martha Jo, where are you?"

Pepe raised the Beretta and placed the tip of the barrel at the base of Monty's skull. "Do not move. Your wife and child are unharmed. Pepe's business is with you. Put your arms behind your back slowly, and don't turn around."

Pepe carefully switched the Beretta from his right hand to his left. With the right he lifted Monty's Glock out of its holster and threw it to the far side of the room.

Again taking the Beretta in his right hand, Pepe pushed it hard into the nape of Monty's neck.

Monty recognized Pepe's voice the minute he'd spoken. The game warden was furious with himself for letting the man get the drop on him. His thoughts flew to Martha Jo and Jody and wondered where they were. He knew he had a narrow time frame to work in if he was to get control of this situation.

The barrel of the Beretta burned into Monty's neck as his mind sorted through his options. Any move he made, no matter how fast, could cause a reflex pull of the man's finger on the trigger of the double-action automatic. If he tried to spin around, most likely the gun would go off before he could overcome the man.

Pushing the gun harder into Monty's neck, Pepe said, "Sit in that chair." His plan was to immobilize Monty by strapping his hands and legs to the chair with the large cable ties. Then he'd finish the job he'd started on Highway 90. He'd run his knife along the scar on the gringo's chest, but this time it would go deep and he would cut the bastard's heart out. He'd take it back to Mexico in a jar.

At that instant, Monty dropped to the floor as if someone had pulled a rug out from under him. The Beretta fired and a 9 mm bullet parted the scalp on top of Monty's head, showering him with blood.

"Bastard!" Pepe yelled.

At the sound of the gunshot, Martha Jo screamed behind her gag. She fought to free herself from the cable ties, but nothing she did seemed to loosen or weaken them. Jody had cried herself to sleep and was startled by the explosion, her eyes popping open with a look of terror.

Realizing it was too late to shout a warning, Martha Jo was determined to set herself free and save her husband's life. Monty had schooled her in all manner of firearms, and handguns in particular. She was a good shot. She kept the Beretta .32 caliber Tomcat automatic Monty had given her in the gun safe under their desk. If she could get the cable ties off, she'd get it and go after the Mexican.

She kept working her tongue against the tape and was able to rub her face against the bedclothes until it was free of her mouth.

Jody lay wide-eyed at her adopted mother's side. Martha Jo rolled over in the bed and placed her lips against the child's ear. "Jody, darling, Ma needs you to help her."

The little girl stared at Martha Jo without recognition.

"Ssh, sweetheart. Don't cry. Don't say anything. Lie still. Everything's going to be okay. Don't be afraid. Okay? Nod your head if you understand Ma."

Jody blinked her eyes and nodded.

As soon as Monty hit the floor he swept his legs under the Mexican, bringing him down. Pepe lost his grip on the Beretta and it slid across the floor, coming to a stop under the kitchen table.

Monty was on his feet in a second and pulled Pepe up by his shirt. He saw the flash of Pepe's knife as the Mexican swung his switchblade toward Monty's neck. He pulled back, but not before the tip of the blade nicked the skin over his Adam's apple. Blood trickled down the front of his shirt, but the wound wasn't serious.

By this time, Pepe was up, and he approached Monty with the switchblade in front of him, jabbing and dodging like a boxer.

Monty realized the Pepe before him was a different man from the one he'd stopped on Highway 90. The swollen eyelids and beer belly were gone. This Pepe was thin and muscular and dangerous as hell.

Pepe kept advancing, and Monty glanced around the kitchen trying to locate his Glock or the Beretta. He had the small .380 automatic in his ankle holster, but he wasn't sure he could get to it. Blood from his scalp wound ran into his eyes and he had difficulty seeing.

With Pepe's next jab of the knife, Monty caught Pepe's wrist and twisted it. The Mexican lost his grip and the knife fell to the floor. Pepe brought his left fist around and caught Monty on the chin, almost knocking him out. Monty let go of Pepe's arm and stepped back so he could block the next blow.

When Pepe brought up his right fist for a body blow, Monty blocked it and countered with a right karate chop to Pepe's larynx. The Mexican gasped for breath and stumbled backward, landing on the kitchen table and pushing it into the wall. He hit the floor about two feet from the Beretta.

Monty dropped to his right knee and whipped the .380 automatic out of its holster, chambered a round, and aimed it at Pepe, who by this time had retrieved the Beretta and was pointing it at Monty. Pepe sat on the floor, his legs in front of him, holding the automatic in both hands. He wheezed as though he was having an asthma attack.

"Drop the fucking gun," Monty said.

At that instant Monty heard a pop and the sound of breaking glass. A small hole appeared in Pepe's forehead. The Mexican had a look of utter shock on his face as a tiny drop of blood trickled out of the wound. In the next second, Pepe slumped to the floor, dead.

Monty glanced at the window and saw it had shattered. The kitchen door opened, and Juan Diaz stepped into the room holding a silenced Thompson Contender .22 caliber pistol. He was dressed in his army fatigues and had his Colt .45 in a highly polished military holster strapped to his waist. The Mexican walked to where his brother lay dead and looked at Monty.

"It is a terrible thing when a man must kill his brother. It makes me very sad."

Monty was even more confused now. He cleared his throat and said in a hoarse voice, "You must be Juan Diaz."

"At your service, Dr. Kilpatrick. I have no quarrel with you. I came here for my brother. My wish is to give him a proper burial in our family cemetery. I require time to make my escape, so, unfortunately, I must relieve you of your gun and restrain you. I'm sorry, but I have no choice."

Monty still had the .380 auto in his hand. Did Diaz think he would just hand it over?

"You're probably wondering why you should do as I ask," Juan said with a crooked smile. "You see, Dr. Kilpatrick, like yourself, I am a man who must be in control. Obviously, I didn't come here alone. Your life and those of your wife and daughter are at stake, so please do as I say. Lay the gun on the floor."

Monty knew he had no choice. This was a man who didn't make idle threats. He placed the gun on the floor and stood facing the Mexican.

"Just leave my wife and daughter out of this. I'll do as you say."

"Like I said, my quarrel was with my brother, not you. What is in this canvas bag?" Juan said as he bent down to inspect Pepe's tote.

"I don't know. I've never seen it before."

Juan turned the bag over and dropped the contents on the floor. The Uzi hit the tile with a thud, followed by more cable ties and the remainder of the duct tape. Juan picked up the machine gun and said, "Pepe was evidently prepared to fight his way out."

Juan shoved Monty into a kitchen chair and taped his hands behind his back, immobilizing him.

"I guess I should thank you for sparing my life, Mr. Diaz. I'm sorry about your brother."

"I didn't save your life. I simply didn't take it," Juan Diaz said. Then the Mexican raised his right hand and snapped his fingers. Ricardo Cueva entered the room along with Jose Ibanez. Juan motioned for them to pick up Pepe's body and take it outside.

Down the hall, Martha Jo had finally decided on a plan to save her family. "Lay still, sweetheart, and do as Ma says. Ma's going to roll off the bed and I want you to do it too. Okay? It's going to be like falling, but you won't get hurt because the rug will catch you. Okay? Do just like Ma."

Martha Jo rolled to the edge of the bed. She fell to the floor with a thud and panic gripped her.

She'd heard scuffling in the kitchen and the gun hitting the floor earlier and was sure Monty and the Mexican had been fighting. It was quiet now and that terrified her. She knew she had only a matter of minutes to get her situation under control if she was going to save her husband. Martha Jo looked up just as Jody rolled off the bed and fell directly on her.

"That's a good girl. Just lie still. Ma will be back in a minute."

Martha Jo began to roll across the bedroom floor. She'd left her sewing basket in the bathroom because she'd planned to sew a button on one of Jody's dresses. When she got to the basket, she turned it over with her cuffed hands and spilled the contents onto the tile. Feeling blindly with her fingers, she located her scissors. She could work them, but not well enough to cut her own cable ties. Her only hope was to cut Jody's and then coach the child to cut Martha Jo free.

Cradling the scissors in her hand, she began the laborious journey back to where her daughter lay. Martha Jo positioned her back to Jody's and said, "Darling, I want you to lie real still and don't be afraid. Ma's going to cut these plastic things off your wrists. It won't hurt, but you must lie perfectly still. Do you understand?"

Martha Jo slid the blades of the scissors over the plastic tie and prayed that she didn't cut the child's arm. The scissors were sharp, but the tie was tough. The rings of the scissors dug into her fingers, but she was able to slice through the plastic. She freed Jody's hands, but Martha Jo doubted the child would have the strength to sever Martha Jo's restraints.

"That's a good girl. Take the scissors, sweetheart, and cut these white plastic things around my wrist like I did for you. Use both hands if you need to. Okay?"

Jody brought her arms around in front of her and picked up the scissors. She slid the blades over the plastic tie, and as she did, the tip of one pierced Martha Jo's skin, causing a droplet of blood to run down her arm. Martha Jo grimaced but didn't cry out. "Don't worry, sweetheart. Try real hard now to cut the white thing."

Jody's little hands barely managed the big scissors, but she valiantly tried to follow Martha Jo's instructions. What seemed like hours to Martha Jo was only a matter of three or four minutes. Two more times the tips of the scissors pushed through Martha Jo's skin, but she began to feel the plastic give. Jody wasn't able to cut completely through the cable, but she weakened it enough for Martha Jo to snap it with a surge of adrenaline. Once she was free, she sat up and cut through the tie that held her ankles.

Rubbing her wrists, Martha Jo whispered into her daughter's ear, "Ma's proud of her big girl. I want you to crawl under the bed and hide. Okay? Can you do that for me? Pretend we're playing hide-and-seek."

Martha Jo eased the duct tape off Jody's mouth. She put her finger to her lips and said, "Don't cry. Don't say anything. Just lie under the bed."

Martha Jo went to the desk and unlocked the gun safe. She withdrew the small automatic and chambered a round. Tiptoeing to the door, she let herself out into the hall.

"HOW DID YOU KNOW YOUR BROTHER was here?" Monty asked Juan Diaz.

"I've had him under surveillance for months. He was clever enough to throw off one of my men at the Chihuahua city airport, but we soon figured out his plan. I suspected all along he'd seek revenge, even though I'd told him not to. One of my men easily located him here yesterday."

"Did you come by helicopter?"

"Yes. We landed on the outskirts of your community and commandeered a truck from one of your citizens. We'll leave it where we found it. The owner is bound and gagged, but safe."

"Do you think you'll make it back across the border this time?"

"I can assure you this will be my last venture into your country," Juan said with a snarl.

"You don't like this country?" Monty asked.

"Your country is beautiful, and I like it very much. It is your countrymen I don't like."

"Why?"

"They're foolish and morally weak."

"You say this and yet you're a drug trafficker. You and your friends ruin people's lives," Monty said.

"I'm a businessman. Why blame me for the folly of your dope-heads? If there was no demand for our product, we couldn't stay in business. If your citizens decided to stick bananas up their noses, we'd be smuggling them across the border by the truckload."

"But you prey on the weakness of human nature," Monty said.

"Your culture glorifies drugs, from your movies to your popular music."

"We're ready, Captain," Ricardo said, opening the kitchen door.

"Radio Julio we're on our way," Juan said. Turning back to Monty, he said, "I must go now, Doctor. I'd enjoy discussing this issue with you over a bottle of good Spanish port. You're welcome at my hacienda in Chihuahua at any time. Adios." Juan scooped up the Uzi and the canvas bag and was out the back door of Monty's house in a flash.

Monty was in terrible pain. His argument with the drug lord had temporarily distracted him, but he was overwhelmed by the agony of his scalp and neck wounds. He was terrified that Pepe had lied to him and that his wife and daughter lay dead somewhere in the house. For a minute or two he lost consciousness. When he came to, he saw Martha Jo coming through the door.

She looked blurry to Monty. "Are you and Jody okay?"

"Yes. What about you?"

"Okay. Cut this tape, please."

Martha Jo went to one of the kitchen drawers and removed a small steak knife. As she severed the tape to set Monty free, she leaned over and kissed him on the temple. "I wasn't sure I'd ever see you alive again."

Jody walked up and put her arms around Monty's leg. "Jody love Pa," she said.

Monty picked her up and held her against his chest. "Pa loves you too, Jody. Don't be scared. Everything's okay."

"It was Jody who set me free. I thought sure I was going to have to shoot someone," Martha Jo said as she slipped the Beretta into the pocket of her slacks.

Monty recognized the *thump, thump* of the Huey's big rotor blades as Juan's helicopter flew over the house on its way back to Mexico. Martha Jo said, "Are those the Mexicans, the ones who landed at Uvalde?"

"Yes, I'll tell you about it later."

"Should I call the sheriff?"

"Let them go. It's a hopeless situation anyway."

CHAPTER 23

A fter their experiences with Juan and his men, Monty decided the family needed a vacation and got permission from his superiors for a whole week off. Monty and Martha Jo hadn't taken more than a few days off in years. Usually they'd gone to one of the state parks over a long weekend back when Monty Jr. was alive. Since the accident, some ten years previously, they hadn't even taken a long weekend.

Two days before they were to leave, Monty and Martha Jo sat at the kitchen table planning their holiday. Monty had wanted to go to Big Bend National Park in West Texas but Martha Jo thought Jody would enjoy the beach. They compromised by settling on South Padre Island. That afternoon Martha Jo made reservations at a Sheraton hotel.

Monty had bought Martha Jo a new Ford sedan, and on the day of their departure he loaded the trunk with their suitcases and an ice chest. It took the better part of the day to reach the island. It was a boring drive and Jody slept a good part of the way. When awake, all she wanted to know was when they'd get there. They stopped along the way for a McDonald's Happy Meal and bathroom breaks. All in all, Monty thought Jody did exceptionally well.

They arrived at the hotel in late afternoon and checked in. It was a clear day with the temperature hovering in the high eighties. Since it was mid-September, the summer crowds had left and the beach was relatively free of swimmers and sunbathers. Martha Jo thought it best to have an early dinner and let Jody go to bed.

Jody was awake at the crack of dawn the next day and the three of them went to the hotel restaurant for breakfast. Afterward, they walked on the wide beach. Jody stopped at every shell she found and marveled at the waves. "I want to swim," she said, racing for the water. Monty ran after her and said, "You've got to put on a swimsuit first, Jody. You can't go in the water with your clothes on."

She looked at Monty with a scowl. "I'll take my clothes off," she said as she started to unbutton her shirt.

Martha Jo said, "After our walk, I'll buy you a swimsuit and we'll play in the surf. You can't go in there naked."

An hour later, Martha Jo and Monty went into the hotel's gift shop and bought their daughter a bright red one-piece suit and a small life jacket. As they were leaving the store Jody saw a pair of flip-flops and pointing to them, said, "I want those."

"I want, I want. That's all I hear this morning, young lady," Martha Jo said. "You need to be patient."

Back in their hotel room, the three of them dressed for the beach and then headed back out, stepping onto the elevator. "I want to push the button," Jody said, running in front of Monty.

They walked out onto the beach and Monty rented an umbrella and towels. Martha Jo sat in the shade with the ice chest while Monty and Jody went to the water. She wondered if the scene would remind her husband of their son's death. She hoped not.

Jody ran into the first wave. It knocked her down and rolled her back onto the hard-packed sand. She looked up at Monty with a bewildered expression and then started to cry.

He lifted her and said, "I'll walk you in. It's not a good idea to just jump in until you know more about waves."

They walked into the surf and when Monty was waist deep he lowered her into the water. The life jacket supported her and she floated next to him. He grabbed her hand and pulled her through the water as she giggled with glee. They played for about ten minutes and then they walked back up the sand to where Martha Jo sat reading a novel.

"Jody swim good," Jody said.

Looking over the top of her book, Martha Jo said, "I saw. You did really well. Did you have fun?"

Nodding, Jody said, "I like it."

Monty stretched out on the sand and supported his head on a rolled-up towel. Jody sat at his feet and started covering him with sand. He laughed and said, "It's too hot, sweetie. Sit under the umbrella with Ma."

Martha Jo removed a Coke from the ice chest and handed it to Monty. He took it and said, "I've been thinking about resigning, giving up my job. You have a problem with that?"

"What brought this on?"

"Juan Diaz and his brother. I don't want you and Jody ever placed in a situation like that again."

"What would you do?"

"I contacted one of my old professors at Ohio State. I'm going to sign up for a refresher course, reactivate my license, and become a vet again."

Martha Jo placed her book on the towel and looked at her husband. "After all these years, won't that be difficult? Besides, you weren't happy as a vet."

"That's because I tried small animals. I think I'd do better with horses and cows. I want to give it a try."

"I just want you to be sure. I don't want you to be unhappy because of Jody and me."

"I want to spend more time with both of you. And I don't want to deal with criminals anymore."

Martha Jo took Monty's hand and brought it to her lips. Kissing it softly, she said, "I would like for you to spend more time with us. You and I have a lot of catching up to do and Jody needs a full-time father."

Jody walked over to Monty and said, "I want ice cream."

Monty laughed and said, "Your wish is my command, princess."

UTOPIA, TEXAS
2005

Jody Kilpatrick had the sight picture-perfect. As she squeezed the trigger of her 30/30 carbine, she knew she'd bagged her first trophy. The twelve-point buck dropped in his tracks and lay motionless.

"Good job," Monty said. "Clean shot."

They'd been stalking the buck for the better part of an hour on the Triple Bar Ranch. Jody had a moment of doubt when her father threw the big deer on the front of their four-wheeler, and she lost her breakfast later that morning when Monty gutted him.

"It's okay, sweetie," Monty said. "The easy part is pulling the trigger."

Monty tossed the carcass into the bed of his pickup, and they headed for Utopia. Martha Jo had planned Jody's eleventh birthday party for four o'clock that afternoon.

At first, there'd been doubt in Monty's mind about whether he could raise a daughter. Martha Jo had been delighted to have a girl of her own, but dismayed that Monty had made her a tomboy.

On the way home, Monty and Jody stopped at the Utopia grocery store and left the carcass to be butchered.

"What did you get me for my birthday?" Jody asked as they turned into the driveway.

"You'll have to wait and see."

"Give me a hint."

"We won't go hungry."

"Come on, Pa. You can do better than that."

Monty laughed and said, "It's a surprise, for God's sake."

Jody climbed out of the truck the instant Monty killed the engine. She ran to the back door and rushed into the kitchen. Martha Jo was applying the last of the icing to Jody's chocolate cake.

"I want a piece now, Ma," she said.

Martha Jo waved her away. "Go change. You look like a boy in that outfit. Put on a dress for your party."

AT FOUR O'CLOCK, AN ARRAY OF friends including Jackie Willowy descended on the Kilpatrick house. Jody, in a pink dress, met everyone at the front door. Arthur Jepson and his schoolteacher wife were the last to enter. He had a big bouquet of freshly cut flowers in his hand as Jody ushered them in. "You're too old for toys, child."

"Thank you, Uncle Arthur. They're beautiful."

Martha Jo had placed the cake in the middle of the dining room table minutes before. She said, "Come on, everyone. Jody wants to have ice cream and cake before she opens her presents."

Jody closed her eyes, made a wish, and blew the candles out with ease. She cut the cake herself, and Martha Jo placed a scoop of vanilla ice cream on each plate.

"So, what did you wish?" Monty asked.

"That nothing ever happens to you and Ma."

"We're perfectly safe. Open your presents," Martha Jo said.

An assortment of sweaters, skirts, and blouses made up the majority of the gifts. But Jody's favorite was the fly rod and reel Monty had given her. "Thanks, Pa. When're we going fishing?"

"I'm thinking maybe Alaska next summer. In the meantime, we'll start out on the Guadalupe River."

As Jody took her gifts to her room, Monty and Arthur Jepson adjourned to the kitchen table for coffee.

"I talked to a guy from the DEA yesterday," Arthur said. "He said Emilio Gurya was blown to pieces in a car bomb two months ago. Some of the border gangs had been challenging his authority. Juan Diaz hit back hard with a military-type campaign. He's the head of the cartel now and controls the eastern coast and central Mexico."

"Interesting man," Monty said. "The conversation I had with him convinced me the government should legalize drugs."

"It'll never happen, Monty," Arthur said.

Jody walked into the kitchen carrying her rod and reel. "Come outside, Pa, and show me how this thing works."

Monty and Arthur followed her to the front yard, where Monty showed her the basics of casting. As he watched her smooth motions, he realized how fortunate he'd been to have Jody in his life. He couldn't believe how much he loved the child. The tragedy of Cindy's death had haunted him for months, at first. But now, he felt satisfied that she'd be pleased with her daughter's progress.

Monty relished his family and he was at peace with his new life as a large-animal veterinarian. He was happy to let someone else handle the poachers and other criminals.

For the first eight years of his life Michael E. Glasscock III lived on his grandfather's ranch a few miles south of the small community of Utopia, Texas. He has always had a great fondness for the Texas Hill Country and now lives in Austin, Texas.

1. How is the sparse landscape of Texas analogous to Monty's struggle with the cartel? Why does the rural nature of Utopia provide a platform for so many intimately personal stories?

2. The novel portrays families in several different ways. Juan Diaz shares a parasitic relationship with his brother Pepe; Monty struggles with the death of his young son and custody of Jody; Jimmy Rhea forcibly reenters the life of his ex-wife. Do you feel these different groups provide a reasonable examination of family life? Why or why not?

3. This book pits the lone sheriff—in this case a game warden— against a bevy of enemies. What other Western tropes can be found in this book?

4. Several instances of corrupt bureaucracy are found in this book— namely, Monty and Martha Jo's custody battle for Jody, ineffective border search methods, the legal marriage of Cindy and Jimmy Rhea. How far do you think a person should be able to go beyond bureaucratic law if his or her circumstances seem to require it?

5. How do you think the loss of Monty's son affects his fervor for his job? How does it distance him from reality? How does the death inform Monty's custody battle for Jody?

6. Is Juan Diaz's attitude toward trafficking drugs justified?

7. In the penultimate scene, Juan Diaz casually explains that his business of drug trafficking is solely based on the demand he receives from the United States. Do current drug laws in America make it easier for cartels to exist? If laws were changed and drugs were legalized and regulated, how might that affect the economic and criminal landscape of the United States? How would it affect the United States' relationship with Mexico?

8. Do you feel that Juan Diaz is a true villain, or a "business man" as he suggests? If no, who is the true villain in the novel?

9. How has this book shaped your understanding of the Mexican drug cartels? What do you feel are the differences between cartels and other forms of organized crime, such as the Italian Mafia?

AUTHOR Q & A

1. Why did you choose a rural Texas town for the backdrop of Utopia, TX?

I chose Utopia because most Texas game wardens work out of small towns. Hunters by necessity gravitate to rural ranches. The sparse landscape of Texas brings forth the image of the Old West. It helps to solidify the idea of a lone law enforcement officer against a ruthless criminal organization. Utopia provides a platform because it is a small rural community where everyone knows their neighbors and the stories of one another's lives. There is a bond among strangers in small communities that doesn't exist in large cities.

2. How did your background in medicine influence the character designs? Did it also play a larger part in the development of the plot?

Jimmy Rhea Moffitt is a psychopath. Pepe, Juan's younger brother, is an alcoholic, a womanizer, and a slacker. In both characters their illness defines their personality.

3. What works (movies, books, locations, etc.) inspire you to write? Which specific works influenced this book?

I am a great fan of Larry McMurtry and his books about Texas have always inspired me, particularly *Lonesome Dove*.

I read thrillers as well as literature. There are several thriller authors that I enjoy: Lee Chiles, David Baldacci, Daniel Silva, and Tess Gerritsen. Literary writers I enjoy are John Irvin, Mark Twain, Ann Patchett, and Charles Dickens. Utopia, Texas is a thriller, so I tried to incorporate a series of events that would test the protagonist's ability to deal with a variety of vicious criminals.

4. The theme of family is strong in this novel. How has your own family influenced this book?

Families are complicated social entities. In this novel there are different examples of how families function depending on the individuals involved and their relationships with one another. Monty and Martha Jo struggle to keep their marriage together. Cindy Moffitt simply wants Jimmy Rhea Moffitt out of her life. Juan loves his brother but is frustrated by his alcoholism and dysfunctional personality. So this novel represents a microcosm of different families and their dynamic structure.

5. Your novels focus on life outside the big cities, usually where characters can be isolated with their thoughts. Do you feel like storytelling changes outside the hustle and bustle of city life?

Living in rural areas and small towns is vastly different than residing in an urban environment. There are advantages and disadvantages of both. There seems to be a stronger sense of community in small towns and people tend to be more supportive of each other.

6. How do you feel Monty's work as a lone game warden parallels the idea of the Wild West sheriff?

I like to think of Monty as a bit like Gary Cooper in the classic movie, *High Noon*. In that story the lone sheriff must face a group of outlaws with no help from the members of his community. In my novel there are concurrent stories playing out that have a western theme: poachers decimating the wildlife, guns for hire, criminals with vicious methods, and a predator animal attacking a herd of cattle. Monty struggles to defend himself and his family against a group of criminals who want to destroy him.

7. Does Monty face a classic western villain, or is the 'bad guy' more complex?

The two hit men, Jimmy Rhea Moffitt, the Greeley brothers, Juan, and Pepe serve as my villains. So the question is, who is the greatest villain? One could argue that Juan is more businessman than villain. Without a demand for his product he would go out of business. When Colombia was constantly in the news concerning illegal drugs I heard an interview on public radio with a common citizen of Colombia. This individual blamed the American drug addicts for the drug trade, not his country. I tend to agree with him.

8. How do you think the current laws on border security affect the drug cartels? Are they effective?

Our borders both north and south are porous. Drug cartels are relatively new entities. Cartel activity centers on transferring drugs across the border into the United States. The cartels control billions of dollars that can be used to build vast tunnels under our southern border. In addition, they build sophisticated submarines that transport drugs underwater to localities in the United States. And in some areas they can simply walk or float across the Rio Grande. There have been fifty thousand murders in Mexico due to competition between drug cartels. The amount of money available to these gangsters is staggering.

9. Most of your characters struggle with a significant loss at some point in their lives. Do you think this applies to most people in general? How does it help the reader identify with characters?

It is part of the human condition to experience loss. It could be something as simple as the loss of a job that ignites a series of events that quickly send an individual spinning out of control. One of the worst examples of serious loss is the devastation that comes with the death of a child. I wanted to explore that grieving and healing process through Monty.

For Monty, he worked to forget. In his mind if he stayed busy he wouldn't have time to think about the accident that took his young son's life. When presented with the opportunity to bring Jody into his life he hesitated because he didn't think he could raise a girl. He took Monty Jr. hunting and fishing, was scoutmaster of his son's troop, and did the things a father does to educate his son. Monty did not believe any of those accomplishments could be transferred to a girl. Once he realized that he did love Jody, Monty was able to accept her and to give her the attention she needed. It also allowed him to examine his life as a peace officer.

ACKNOWLEDGMENTS

My thanks to all the great people at Greenleaf Book Group LLC and my line editor in White Plains, Tennessee, Dimples Kellogg. To my early manuscript readers who always give me constructive feedback.